When a letter arrives at a small North Carolina newspaper from a man claiming a connection between his missing daughter and the recent murder of another young woman, life gets even more complicated for feature writer Abby Burlew, a recovering drug addict who has bipolar disorder. Since no one else at the paper is available for the assignment, the editor reluctantly sends Abby to a remote barrier island to investigate. What seems like an open-and-shut case quickly turns into a tangle of mysterious goings-on, hidden motives, and unlikely suspects. Abby's problems are compounded when she becomes romantically involved with the island's chief deputy, despite mounting evidence that he's a womanizer and a suspect himself. Her sanity—and ultimately her life—are now at risk as she pursues this increasingly stressful and dangerous assignment.

KUDOS for *Deadly Assignment*

In *Deadly Assignment* by John W. Daniel, Abby Burlew is a feature writer for a small North Carolina newspaper. When the paper's main investigative reporter gets hired by a larger paper, Abby gets her big break—a chance to investigate the disappearance of two young women on an island off the coast of North Carolina. Thrilled at this opportunity, she gleefully heads out to the island, only to discover she's in way over her head, a situation complicated when she becomes romantically involved with the local deputy sheriff. But Abby refuses to give up, getting closer to the truth than she realizes and putting her life in danger. The author has a unique and refreshing voice, a strong plot with plenty of surprises, and realistic and endearing characters. You just can't help rooting for Abby. ~ *Taylor Jones, Reviewer*

Deadly Assignment by John Daniel is the story of a young woman with bipolar disorder. Our heroine, Abby Burlew, is a feature writer for the *Scarboro Gazette*, a small local newspaper in a rural North Carolina town, but when the paper gets a letter from a man who lives on an island off the coast of North Carolina, and the regular investigative reporter can't follow up on it, Abby is given the chance of a lifetime. As she heads off to the island to investigate the disappearance of the daughter of the man who wrote the letter, Abby has no idea what she is getting into. She bumbles her way through the interviews of key people and also stumbles into a romantic relationship with the deputy sheriff on the island. Of course, the fact that the man is the brother of the main suspect deemed responsible for the disappearance of not one, but two, young women complicates Abby's investigation. Will the deputy help her, or will he steer her in the wrong direction to shield his brother? I especially liked the fact that Abby was flawed—in that she suffered from bipolar disorder and was constantly second guessing herself to be sure her decisions were not affected by her disease. I can only imagine how hard that must be. *Deadly Assignment* is a well written mystery with a very touching human side.

ACKNOWLEDGEMENTS

The 1979 edition of *The Insiders' Guide to the Outer Banks of North Carolina* by St. Leger "Monte" Joynes, Kathy and Bill McCarthy, and Dave Poyer was helpful in providing some of the historical data I needed to create Nanticoke, a fictionalized version of the real barrier island Ocracoke.

I'd also like to thank novelist William McCranor Henderson, who read an earlier version of *Deadly Assignment* and offered some helpful suggestions.

DEADLY

ASSIGNMENT

John W. Daniel

A Black Opal Books Publication

GENRE: MYSTERY-DETECTIVE/SUSPENSE/WOMEN'S FICTION

DEADLY ASSIGNMENT
Copyright © 2016 by John W. Daniel
Cover Design by Jackson Cover Designs
All cover art copyright © 2016
All Rights Reserved
Print ISBN: 978-1-626945-45-6

First Publication: OCTOBER 2016

Published by Black Opal Books **http://www.blackopalbooks.com**

DEDICATION

With thanks to my wife Sharon and my son Josh

PROLOGUE

In Lloyd Bostrum's dream, it was pitch black. His daughter Sheila and her boyfriend were speeding down an icy stretch of highway between Port Austin and Cedar Point, the place of departure for the Nanticoke ferry.

Lloyd was familiar with the road, knew it swung sharply left before crossing Crabtree Creek.

Slow down, he tried to warn them. *For God's sake, slow down. You won't make that turn.*

But the driver hadn't intended to turn. When the highway bent left, he kept straight, maneuvering his pickup truck down a sandy road that burrowed deep into wild marshland. Suddenly Lloyd realized that Sheila wasn't sitting next to her boyfriend but was slumped against him. She was dead and the man was transporting her body to the marshes where no one would ever find it.

Just before waking up, Lloyd caught a glimpse of the driver's face—the same grinning visage he had seen in the *Tidewater Tidings*, that of Joel Crothers.

"Bastard," he muttered. "I should've killed you when I had the chance."

The effort caused him to gag, as though he were choking on his own words. His throat was parched and his body felt like it was on fire—his head, his neck, his back. Especially his back.

The room he occupied was windowless and tiny, smaller even than the bedroom of his trailer. Where the hell was he? He noticed a whirring sound, its pitch increasing as he inhaled, decreasing as he exhaled. Something scraped against his face, tubing of some sort stuck to his nostrils. He tried to pull it off but he couldn't move his arms. He began to panic.

When he finally realized where he was and why he was there, Lloyd screamed. The hoarse sound coming from his throat wasn't even loud enough to compete with the hum of the oxygen machine in the corner.

CHAPTER 1

Twenty-eight-year-old Abby Burlew wheeled her aging Toyota Corolla into the small parking lot, took up two of the three remaining spaces, half from each, and hurried toward the whitewashed cinderblock building that housed the *Scarboro Gazette*.

Although the paper's flextime policy allowed its employees to begin their eight-hour workday between six-thirty and nine, it was now nine-fifteen.

Sid Beckwith, the *Gazette*'s only investigative reporter, was smoking a cigarette in front of the building when he noticed Abby. He looked at his watch then at her then back at his watch.

"Fuck you, Sid. When I get here is none of your damn business."

"Geez, Abby. No reason to bite my head off. I was just teasing. I didn't even say anything."

She had already opened the *Gazette*'s front door when his words finally sank in.

Looking sheepish, she stopped and slowly turned around. "Sorry about that, Sid. I'm having one of those days—you know, when everything seems to have turned to shit, including me. I didn't mean to dump on you. Hope you won't hold it against me."

"Apology accepted. Hope the world looks better to you as the day goes along."

"It won't. But thanks anyway."

As she approached her cubicle on the second floor, Abby noticed a yellow post-it note attached to an envelope in her in-basket. *Read this and come see me*, the message said, and in the almost indecipherable flourish that looked all too familiar, it was signed *Charlene*.

"Whoopdedo," Abby muttered, sitting down at her desk. "Must be something really urgent—like bingo night at Antioch Baptist Church or some frigging flea market that just opened up."

"Maybe she's finally decided to make you a full-fledged reporter," replied the heavy-set young woman in the adjacent cubicle.

"Yeah, right. I don't get it, Becky. What did I ever do to offend that bitch?" Abby shook her head and heaved a sigh. "Besides having an occasional bipolar moment," she added with a rueful chuckle.

"Hang in there, Ab. Let me know when you find out what ole Attila the Honey is up to."

After firing up her computer, Abby picked up the envelope, surprised to see that it was addressed to Sid Beckwith. She removed the contents, a two-page letter written in shaky handwriting and signed *Lloyd Bostrum* and a clipping from a newspaper she had never heard of, the *Tidewater Tidings*. She glanced through the clipping, an article about a Joel Crothers who grew greenhouse tomatoes on Nanticoke Island. At the top was a picture of the young man proudly standing between two rows of waist-high tomato plants.

She wondered why Sid would give such garbage to Charlene instead of tossing it. Whatever the reason, she decided, it was a new low in trivial assignments.

Dear Sid,

I'm writing to you because you always side with the underdog, plus you've got a reputation for being a kind of dog yourself, a bulldog that keeps on digging until you find what you're looking for. Sid, I need you to find out what happened to my daughter Sheila who disappeared five years ago. Actually, I already know what happened to her. She was murdered. I even know who did it. At least I'm ninety-nine percent sure. It was Joel Crothers, the scumbag in the article I'm enclosing. He also killed Rhonda Tolbert the East Carolina coed who disappeared last April.

Abby caught her breath. She remembered reading about the Tolbert girl. Her body had been found on a country road near Greenville, and the murder, as far as Abby knew, was still unsolved. Why had Charlene given her this material? Had she read the clipping and not the letter?

Sid, if you check out what the papers said about the Tolbert girl like I did, you'll find she went to East Carolina University where she was studying to be a teacher and that she did her practice teaching on Nanticoke. What you won't find out is she spent a lot of time shacked up with Joel Crothers while she was on the island. I know that for a fact. I also know she dumped Joel after she finished practice teaching and went back to East Carolina to finish up her studies. A couple weeks before she would've graduated she was murdered!!!! The exact same thing happened between Joel and my daughter, Sid. After Sheila finished high school, she got a job waitressing at Captain Jack's, a restaurant in Bogue City where Joel was a waiter. She went out with him once or twice and he fell for her like a ton of bricks. Sheila got tired of him real quick, Sid. She told me so herself the last time I saw her. Soon after ditching the bastard, she disappeared. First my daughter then Rhonda Tolbert. Same pattern exactly!

No way could this be meant for me, Abby thought. She considered calling Sid Beckwith but decided to finish reading the letter first.

After figuring out Joel had to be the killer, I took my pistol over to Nanticoke and confronted the son of a bitch. He admitted shacking up with the Tolbert girl but swore up one side and down the other he never touched Sheila. He said they were just friends. The guy talked me out of pulling the trigger, Sid. I've done some rotten things in my time, but one thing I can't do is kill someone without being a hundred percent sure they deserve it. Like I said, I'm ninety-nine percent sure Joel murdered my daughter. I'm hoping you'll come up with the other one percent and turn the evidence over to somebody that'll make sure the bastard gets what he deserves. Please do this, Sid—for me and for the two innocent young women he killed.

Bostrum went on to say that after confronting Joel Crothers, he had taken the evidence he'd collected to Sheriff Mountcastle in Bogue City. The sheriff had promised to pursue it, but there was never an arrest, not even an indication that one was being planned.

Mountcastle keeps telling me these things take time, Sid, but obviously he's just stalling. Joel won't ever get arrested, at least not by Mountcastle, not after what I found out the other day. Guess who his chief deputy on Nanticoke is. Joel's older brother, that's who. Now how the hell can justice get done with a conflict of interest like that!

The letter continued for another half page, Bostrum launching into what a mess he had made of his life.

I'm fifty-three years old and I don't have a thing to show for it but a run-down trailer and a girlfriend with a face like a bull terrier and the breath to match. I'm sick and tired of trying to squeeze a living out of my half-assed machine shop and I'm too old to get a decent job. Booze and pot don't do a damn thing for me anymore and I'd rather hang it up than get hooked on meth or coke.

Then came the final paragraph, which gave Abby a jolt. She looked up Sid Beckwith's extension and dialed it. After identifying herself, she asked why a letter addressed to him from Lloyd Bostrum would end up on her desk with a note from Charlene Greer attached. "What's going on, Sid? Is this some kind of sick joke?"

"No joke," he told her. "I gave that letter to Charlene in case she wanted to assign it to somebody else. I'm leaving this rag in a few days, Abby. I was fortunate enough to land a job at the *Richmond Times Dispatch*."

"No kidding?" Amazed at Sid's good fortune and, apparently, her own, Abby congratulated him and wished him good luck. After ending the call, she went over to Becky's cubicle.

"Would you believe Charlene's note was attached to an absolutely juicy assignment? It's about a murder, actually two murders assuming the Bostrum girl is dead, which seems likely. This is way out of my league, Becky. But just in case I get a crack at it, would you run a check on a Lloyd Bostrum for me. His letter is postmarked Saturday afternoon. It was mailed from Bogue City, which must be where he lives—or lived. In the last paragraph, he said he was going to kill himself right after mailing it."

CHAPTER 2

Have a seat, my dear," said the woman with such cheerfulness that Abby thought there was no way she'd be given the assignment. Her boss was in too good of a mood.

A short, plump woman who wore rimless eyeglasses and was elegantly dressed in a navy blue suit and white silk blouse, Charlene Greer projected the demeanor of someone ready to take charge of whatever situation might happen to arise. At one corner of her desk were photographs of her three children. As everyone at the *Gazette* knew, the son was in his second year at Duke Law School and both daughters had been debutantes and were successfully married, one to a dentist in Charlotte and the other to a history professor at Wake Forest University.

Abby plunked herself down in the visitor's chair farthest from the pictures and prepared for the worst, the possibility that Charlene would ask her to check into Lloyd Bostrum's suicide attempt, after which the bitch would decide whether or not to assign the story. And to whom. It sure as hell wouldn't go to her.

"So what do you think? Would it be a waste of time to check out this Bostrum character's complaint?"

Not wanting to sound overly enthusiastic, Abby let a

few seconds pass before replying. "If he's right about Joel Crothers, this is front page news. Even if he's wrong, there's probably a story here. And I don't mean a feature about a Nanticoke lad and his crop of greenhouse tomatoes."

"I realize you've never tackled anything like this, but Sid Beckwith doesn't have the time or inclination to look into it. In case you haven't heard, he's leaving the *Gazette* at the end of the month. Would you like to give this a shot?"

"You bet," Abby said, trying to hide her delight.

"I know you have a young son. Can you leave him for a few days?"

"No problem. My mother will take care of him." The possibility that her mother, who had a full-time job, wouldn't be able to take care of Kevin didn't enter Abby's mind. Though better at thinking things through than she used to be, she still tended to ignore the chasms that lurked along her intended path. Or the need for bridges to cross them.

"There's something else to consider. This assignment could be dangerous. One young woman has been murdered and another has disappeared, possibly murdered. It's not like you'd be doing a story on, say, the debutante ball."

"That would be a lot more dangerous," Abby replied without missing a beat. "If I have to cover another one of them, I'll die of boredom."

"Really? If you'd been a debutante yourself, maybe you'd feel differently."

Abby bristled. She longed to tell her boss just how silly and pretentious she found the whole idea of *coming out* to be, but she recalled a similar situation that had turned out badly and resisted the impulse.

"What do those girls need to come out for, anyway?" she had remarked upon being asked to cover last year's debutante ball. "Most of them have already had sex with half the eligible bachelors in Scarboro."

Nodding toward the pictures at the end of her desk, Charlene had thanked Abby for setting her straight on the sexual proclivities of her daughters. Realizing her blunder, Abby had apologized, saying she didn't know what had come over her. Although Charlene appeared to accept the apology, the look in the woman's eyes told Abby she wouldn't soon forget the incident.

"Well, this assignment should be anything but boring. Any problem with your starting tomorrow?"

"None whatsoever."

"You've got the rest of the week to see what you can come up with. Be back in the office Monday and we'll go over your findings."

Although delighted to get the assignment, Abby wondered why Charlene had offered it to her, especially after so much time had elapsed since her plea for more meaningful work. "I'm very happy to be working at the *Gazette*," she had told Charlene several months earlier, making sure there wasn't a trace of whining or belligerence in her voice. "But I feel like I'm in something of a rut. I'd love the opportunity to prove to you that I'm capable of handling more challenging assignments."

"Sure, I'll keep that in mind," Charlene had said in a dismissive tone that made Abby suspect nothing would come of her request. And nothing had until now.

She wondered if Charlene had thought she would turn down the assignment, thereby providing evidence to the contrary if she complained again about the trivial nature of the work she was given. Or had Charlene hoped she would accept, thinking the assignment beyond her capability? If she bungled it, the woman could use that against her too. "What exactly do you expect of me?" she asked.

"I'd like to know if the sheriff really is dragging his

feet or ignoring evidence. More likely, though, Bostrum has blown everything out of proportion. If you find that out for sure, you'll have done your job."

Charlene opened a desk drawer and took out a North Carolina map. After folding it so only the coastal area was visible, she slid it across the desk. "Ever been to Nanticoke?"

"Nags Head is about as close as I got," Abby said, her response evoking a bittersweet memory of the rustic beach house her parents rented the summer she was ten. It was the last vacation her family would take together. Cancer claimed her father two years later, and three years after that, when Abby was a high school sophomore trying out for the girls' basketball team, her brother Matt was killed in a car accident.

"Not much out there this time of year," Charlene said. "Most of the motels are closed. And don't expect to find any department stores, night clubs, or fancy restaurants. I'd be surprised if there's even a doctor on the island. If you get sick, you'll have to take a ferry back to the mainland before you can get treatment. Still interested?"

"I'm not scared off that easily," Abby said and tried to hand back the map.

"Keep it. It might come in handy. I have two other suggestions. It would be a good idea to touch base with the sheriff at some point, but you'll have to decide when. If Joel Crothers is guilty and his brother the deputy is covering up for him, both will probably get wind of your visit if you contact the sheriff before going out to the island. But it's always possible the sheriff will be cooperative, in which case you'll save time by talking to him sooner than later. You'll have to use your own judgment about that."

Abby nodded, surprised that Charlene had actually given her credit for having any judgment. "And your other suggestion?"

"If we can believe Bostrum's final paragraph, the man is dead. But if he isn't, I'd keep my distance. He sounds like a loose cannon."

Focusing on the words *loose cannon*, Abby wondered if her boss had used the term as a dig at her. Charlene went on to discuss other aspects of the assignment, such as how much Abby's travel advance would be and the types and amounts of expenses she could claim upon her return.

When she finished she stood up and held out her hand. "You asked for a challenge. Now we'll see what you can do with one."

Abby stopped at Becky's cubicle on the way back to her own. "I got it," she said, barely able to contain her excitement. "I got the assignment."

"Congratulations. I hope you don't expect too much of yourself. You're not Bob Woodward just yet—or Sid Beckwith."

"Did you know Sid's leaving? He got a job at the *Richmond Times Dispatch.*"

"I'd heard rumors. Good for him."

"And lucky for me. Apparently, Charlene doesn't have anybody else to give this to. Did you find out anything about Lloyd Bostrum?"

"I did. Saturday afternoon he rammed his truck into a bridge abutment. He's still alive but not by much. I talked to one of the nurses at the Bogue City Hospital and it doesn't sound good."

CHAPTER 3

With a heavy heart, Lillian Webster listened to the long, rambling message on her voice mail. *Son of a bitch,* she thought. *We're right back to square one. That girl has been doing nothing but puff features and, all of a sudden, she's an investigative reporter hot on the trail of a double murderer.*

"Damn," she muttered. "She must've stopped taking her meds."

But the longer Lillian listened, the more she began to realize that maybe, just maybe, she was overreacting. The voice she heard didn't necessarily belong to a person in the throes of mania. Wasn't it possible that Abby was legitimately excited about a long-overdue assignment of substance, as farfetched as the nature of that assignment might sound? By the time the message ended, Lillian couldn't be sure. At least she felt a glimmer of hope, especially since Abby had concluded the message with the words "Don't worry, Mom. I'm still taking my lithium."

Steeling herself against the possibility that her daughter had suffered a major relapse, Lillian dialed Abby's number at the *Gazette*.

After clarifying the nature of the assignment for her mother, Abby spent the rest of the morning tidying up loose ends at her desk. She spent the afternoon in the *Gazette*'s morgue reading everything she could find about Sheila Bostrum and Rhonda Tolbert.

There were two articles about Sheila in the weeks following her disappearance, both repeating the same basic facts, and a follow-up story two months later stating that the police had developed no leads in the case. According to the articles, Jack and Mary Bethune, who owned the restaurant where Sheila had worked and the boarding house where she had roomed, weren't aware of anything out of the ordinary going on in her life. Mary Bethune, the last known person to see Sheila, said she seemed in good spirits the day she disappeared. Since it was Sheila's day off and she had previously spent nights away from the boarding house, Mary didn't think anything of her absence until Sheila didn't show up for the lunch shift the following day. When she failed to appear for the dinner shift as well, Mary contacted the girl's mother, who immediately called the sheriff.

The news articles about Rhonda Tolbert were more numerous, but the police seemed to have drawn a blank in that case as well. A senior at East Carolina University where she was a member of Chi Omega sorority, Rhonda had gone jogging one afternoon in May and didn't come back. When she hadn't shown up by bedtime, her sorority sisters grew worried and called the police. Two days later, her body was found near a dirt road a few miles east of Greenville. Her throat had been slashed.

According to one article, Rhonda had been engaged to be married. The Pitt County sheriff, whose jurisdiction included the Greenville area, had questioned her fiancé extensively and ruled him out as a suspect. The sheriff also had interviewed various students and faculty at the university as well as several people who had known Rhonda on Nanticoke Island.

Not a single person could suggest a motive for her murder.

⌀⌀⌀

The sun had almost reached the tree line when Abby pulled her Toyota into the parking lot of Oberlin Road Elementary School. As she hurried up the sidewalk, she felt a twinge of guilt about having to leave her son in Latch Key until such a late hour. But since both she and her mother worked and her ex-husband was long since out of the picture, there wasn't anything she could do about it.

On the way home, she gave Kevin a watered-down version of her assignment, sorry now that she hadn't given the same one to her mother, so neither would worry. Leaving out Rhonda Tolbert entirely, she explained that she would be spending the next few days in the Bogue City area trying to find out what happened to a young woman who disappeared several years ago.

"What if she was murdered and the killer tries to kill you?" Kevin asked.

"I don't think it'll come to that. But if it turns out she was murdered, I'll try to investigate in such a way the killer won't realize he's being investigated. Then I'll turn the information over to the cops and let them make the arrest."

Abby pulled into a left-hand turn lane behind a line of cars stopped for a red light. She could see their apartment complex in the distance, three dingy-looking brick buildings arranged in the shape of a horseshoe with a courtyard in the middle that invariably needed mowing.

"Your grandmother will be picking you up the rest of the week," she said. "You won't mind staying with her, will you?"

"No, ma'am. Granma's cool."

"She invited us over for supper tonight. How about a little one-on-one basketball when we get there? That way I won't have to go jogging."

Ever since Abby started taking her psych medication on a regular basis, she had tried to counteract the weight-gain side effects of her meds by jogging at least four miles a day. A half hour of one-on-one basketball wouldn't burn off nearly the calories that jogging would, but it would provide a chance for some quality time with her son.

"How many points do I get?"

"I'll spot you five baskets in a game of twenty. If we play a second game, we'll adjust according to who wins the first."

"What if we both win a game? How do we break the tie?"

"We'll negotiate that if and when the time comes. You'll be dead on your feet by then anyway, so it's a moot point."

"Yeah, right. Okay, I'll do it on one condition."

"What's that?"

"I get to call a foul whenever you do any trash talking."

"You mean I can't say something like you're slower than Bucky Dixon's grandmother who's ninety-years old and uses a walker?"

"That's right."

"And I can't even yell 'In your face, boy!' when I pull up for one of my beautifully executed jump shots?"

"Not without getting called for a foul."

"What the heck fun is that?"

"Take it or leave it."

Abby shrugged. "Okay. Guess I'll just have to kick your scrawny little butt in silence."

"That's a foul, Mom. You just put me on the free throw line and the game hasn't even started."

⁕⁕⁕

Shortly after five o'clock, Abby drove Kevin and his suitcase to her mother's house, a modest brick ranch in a working-class neighborhood on the east side of Scarboro. Attached to the garage was the weathered backboard Abby's father had installed when her brother was Kevin's age. Although Matt had been one of the best basketball players in the neighborhood, he hadn't been good enough to make his high school team. His sport had been track, and he still held Scarboro High's record for the fastest mile in competition.

Basketball had turned out to be Abby's sport. During her last two years of high school, she was her team's starting point guard, a position she had learned in neighborhood pickup games. In earlier years, she and her brother had played countless games of HORSE and one-on-one in the driveway, Matt spotting her fewer and fewer baskets the older she got. One afternoon when she was in the seventh grade, Matt had convinced some of his buddies that she was good enough to fill in for one of their pickup games at a nearby park. She played well enough to be asked back the next time a fill-in was needed. The following year, she was a fixture on the court and could trash talk with the best of them.

Abby won her first game with her son by a single basket while keeping her trash talk to a minimum. Kevin won the second, thanks to Abby's decision to launch most of her shots from long range, some questionable defense, and a slew of trash talk fouls. Kevin, it turned out, really was too pooped for a third game.

After supper while the boy was doing his homework

in Abby's old bedroom upstairs, she and her mother, a strawberry blonde in her mid-fifties, sat at the kitchen table, each nursing a cup of tea. At first, Lillian tried to convince Abby that her assignment was too dangerous, totally unsuitable for anyone not trained in police work or as an investigative reporter. When Abby categorically rejected that argument, her mother made her promise to be careful, to take her medication exactly as she normally would, and to call on a regular basis to report how things were going.

As she was getting ready to leave, Abby asked if she could borrow the pistol her mother purchased when the neighborhood was having a rash of break-ins. "Just in case I run into trouble," she said. "I'm sure I won't need it."

"That's not a good idea, Abby."

"Why not?"

"You don't know a thing about guns."

Abby glared at her mother. "That's not the real reason, is it, Mom?"

"Of course it is."

"It's because I'm bipolar, isn't it? You don't trust me to have sense enough not to have an accident. What if I get killed because I don't have anything to defend myself with? How will you feel then?"

Lillian's face clouded with concern. She went over and hugged her daughter. "I went through enough grief losing your father and your brother," she said. "I couldn't stand to lose you too."

"Then you'll lend me the pistol?"

"I can't, honey. I just can't."

CHAPTER 4

Abby slept fitfully, excited about her assignment and the possibility that if she performed it well, she could advance her career, yet fearful such an investigation might be beyond her capability. Waking up long before her alarm was set to go off, she lay in bed for a few minutes savoring the fact that she was pursuing a story Sid Beckwith normally would have covered. She showered, took her morning dose of lithium, ate a quick breakfast, put her suitcase and laptop computer in the car, and was on the road by six-thirty, glad to be getting an early start.

Knowing she needed to drink plenty of water while taking lithium, Abby took periodic sips from a water bottle as she drove, hoping she wouldn't need a bathroom any time soon. She had thought about wearing a Depends, but after reading about the female astronaut who wore adult-sized diapers while driving non-stop for hours to murder her rival, there was no way Abby would risk getting caught in a similar get-up.

Two hours of steady driving brought her to a gas station on the outskirts of Bogue City. After filling her tank, she used the restroom and then asked directions to the local hospital. In spite of Charlene Greer's advice, she had decided to begin her investigation with Lloyd Bostrum, assuming he was still alive. At some point, she would need to question him anyway, and the longer she put it off, the greater the risk he wouldn't be around to interview.

"I'd like to see Lloyd Bostrum," she told the hospital receptionist a few minutes later, a young woman with pale, freckled skin and bleached blonde hair who was entering data into a computer. According to the tag pinned to her blouse, her name was Gretchen.

"Visiting hours don't start until ten. Are you a relative?"

"I'm investigating his daughter's disappearance. I work for the *Scarboro Gazette*." The pleasure Abby took from saying those words rivaled the thrill she used to feel after making a clutch play in a crucial basketball game.

"You're a little late, aren't you? It's been years since anybody saw Sheila."

Abby explained that Bostrum had sent the *Gazette* a letter asking for help. "He must've mailed it shortly before his accident," she added, not wanting to risk getting sidetracked by revealing that the accident was, in fact, an attempted suicide. "Did you know Sheila?"

"We went to the same high school. She was a year ahead of me."

"What can you tell me about her?"

Gretchen shrugged. "Well, she was nice looking, I'll give her that. Actually, she seemed kind of spoiled. Always had to have her way, especially when it came to guys. If she wanted one, she went after him. And when she got him, she expected to be treated like the queen bee she thought she was."

"The guys put up with it?"

"Most did. She treated them pretty good in return, if you get my drift."

A young nurse and a candy striper strolled past, heading toward the snack shop down the corridor. Both waved to the receptionist.

"Leave some doughnuts for me," Gretchen called. Then she refocused her attention on Abby. "Why would Mr. Bostrum want the *Gazette* involved after all this time?"

"He's given up on the police and thinks we're his only chance of finding out what happened. Were you in contact with Sheila the summer she disappeared?"

Gretchen shook her head. "The last time we talked—other than to say hi in the hall, that is—was at the Monogram Club dance. We double dated that night."

"Really? Who was Sheila's date?"

"A football player named Gary Thompkins. He and my steady at the time were buddies. Gary had been going with Sheila for about three months, which for her was something of a record. They broke up that night. She ignored him most of the evening."

"What seemed to be the problem?"

"Same one she always had—staying serious about anyone other than herself for very long." Gretchen frowned and shook her head. "I shouldn't talk that way. Sheila wasn't a bad person. Just had some growing up to do." The telephone rang and Gretchen answered it. After checking her computer for a patient's room number, she transferred the call.

"How'd the breakup affect Gary?" Abby asked.

"I doubt he lost any sleep over it. Even if he did, he wouldn't have killed Sheila. Gary was an athlete and all, but he wasn't a jerk like a lot of jocks."

"Does he still live in the area?"

"Nope. He went to college and never looked back. I don't know what he's doing now or where he's doing it."

Again, the telephone rang. After Gretchen fielded a

question about visiting hours, Abby asked if any of Sheila's other boyfriends took breaking up with her particularly hard.

"Hard enough to want her dead? I seriously doubt it. She was nice looking and all but so are a lot of girls."

"Was some other guy in the picture when Sheila broke off with Gary?" Abby asked, not ready to give up on the possibility that unrequited love had been responsible for Sheila's disappearance.

"I have no idea. I didn't see her at all after school got out. I know she was working at Captain Jack's when she disappeared, but that's about all I can tell you."

"Do you know anybody else who worked at Captain Jack's that summer?"

"Seems to me Angie Dake did. Yeah, she and Sheila hung out a lot in high school. Last I heard, Angie is a hairdresser somewhere on the Outer Banks."

Abby opened her purse and took out a pen and a small notepad. After writing down the name *Angie Dake*, she asked if Gretchen knew Jack or Mary Bethune.

"Not personally. I know they own Captain Jack's and go south for the winter. Where exactly I couldn't say."

At Abby's request, Gretchen provided directions to the Bethune's boarding house. "Nobody will be there," the receptionist added. "It's just for restaurant workers and the restaurant is closed this time of year."

Abby started to ask if the name Joel Crothers rang a bell, but thought better of it. If it turned out Gretchen knew Joel, she might pick up the phone and call him. Even if she didn't know him, she might get word around that he was a murder suspect. "Do you know of anybody besides Angie Dake who might know what was going on in Sheila's life the summer she disappeared?" she asked.

Gretchen thought for a moment. "Seems like Bobby Musgrove worked at Captain Jack's that summer. He runs the Chevy dealership. Sold me a used car last year and I haven't had a lick of trouble with it. Yeah, try Bobby. If it turns out he didn't work at Captain Jack's, maybe he can tell you somebody who did."

Abby jotted down *Bobby Musgrove* and the directions to Musgrove Motors. Putting away her notepad, she asked Gretchen who she needed to talk to about seeing Lloyd Bostrum.

✑✑✑

Ten minutes later, a middle-aged woman with close-cropped salt-and-pepper hair introduced herself to Abby as the head nurse of the intensive care unit. "I understand you'd like to see Mr. Bostrum."

Abby told her about Bostrum's letter requesting that the *Gazette* find out what happened to his daughter.

"That's a tall order, considering how long ago Sheila disappeared," the woman said. "Everyone around here seems clueless about it."

"Don't people have theories?"

"Most folks assume she was abducted by a drifter. You hear about instances like that. A young woman crosses paths with a psychopath who abducts her, rapes or tortures her, then kills her."

"Is that what you think happened?"

"It's as good a theory as any, as far as I'm concerned. What do you hope to learn from Mr. Bostrum?"

"Whatever he can tell me about Sheila, especially her activities around the time she disappeared."

"I'm not sure how much help he'll be, if any. He's said practically nothing since regaining consciousness. Normally, I wouldn't allow an interview with someone in his condition, but in this case, I think I'll make an exception. Who knows, maybe talking to you will lift his spirits."

After thanking the receptionist for her help, Abby accompanied the nurse through a maze of corridors until they reached the intensive care unit. Inside, a nurses' station faced a line of curtained cubicles, each containing a bed, all but two of which were empty. In one, an elderly woman lay on her side, apparently asleep. In the other, a man with a bruised, puffy face lay staring at the ceiling. Tubes ran from his nostrils to a nearby oxygen machine. Another spiraled up from his right arm to an inverted bottle of clear liquid hanging next to the bed.

Abby followed the nurse into the man's cubicle. "Abby, this is Carolyn Rogers, Mr. Bostrum's friend," the nurse said, indicating an anxious-looking woman with too much makeup sitting in a far corner. The woman gave a nod and a faint smile, which Abby returned, wondering if she was the girlfriend Bostrum had described in his letter. She wasn't exactly a beauty but she wasn't a dog either.

"You've got a visitor, Mr. Bostrum," the nurse said. "This is Abby Burlew. The Scarboro paper sent her to investigate your daughter's disappearance."

The man's head moved slightly and his gaze slowly lowered until his eyes, which were red and swollen, fixed on Abby.

"Carolyn," he said in a guttural wheeze, barely above a whisper. "You and—Florence—Nightin—gale get lost."

The woman in the corner got up from her chair. "Sure, Lloyd. Whatever you say. I'll be in the waiting room."

After the two women left, Abby moved closer to the bed. "Do you feel up to answering a few questions, Mr. Bostrum?"

The way he looked at her reminded Abby of a wounded animal with nothing left except its suffering and a desire to inflict whatever damage it could, even on itself.

"Actually, there's only one question I really need to ask. The others aren't all that important."

Still no response.

"I'd like to know what Sheila told you the last time you saw her," Abby said, trying not to let her voice betray her anxiety. "According to your letter, she said something about breaking up with Joel Crothers. I'd like to know exactly what she said about that."

The man's lips pulled back in what might have been a snarl and he muttered something unintelligible.

Abby moved closer. "I'm sorry, I couldn't hear you."

"I said—where's Sid—Beckwith?"

"He got a job with another paper. The *Gazette* sent me in his place."

"You do the—same kinda—work?" Bostrum asked in a raspy whisper.

"Not exactly. I do features mostly."

"You do—what?"

"Write columns about topics of general interest."

"You don't have—any ex—experience—doing Sid's—kinda—work?"

Abby shook her head. "This is my first investigative assignment, but I don't think that'll be a problem."

A grotesque half-cough, half-choking sound welled up from Bostrum's throat. Abby thought he might be having a convulsion and was about to call the nurse when she realized the sound was laughter.

"Ask for—Clark—Kent," the man wheezed. "They send—Lois—fuckin'—Lane."

Abby's face reddened. "You could've done worse, Mr. Bostrum. I'm going to do everything I can to find out what happened to your daughter."

"Do something—really—useful, Lois. Get a—needle. Pump some—air in my veins."

Abby stood mute. "Can you at least tell me if Sheila's mother still lives in Port Austin?" she finally asked.

"Fuck—off," Bostrum said with casual contempt, his

gaze returning to the ceiling. After that, he refused to acknowledge her at all.

$\infty\infty$

"How'd it go?" Carolyn Rogers asked when Abby entered the waiting room a few moments later.

"It didn't. Except for a few choice obscenities, he had very little to say."

"I was afraid something like that would happen. Have a seat and tell me what you'd like to know. Maybe I can help."

Still reeling from the way Bostrum had responded to her, Abby sat down in a chair directly across from the woman and took a deep breath. "According to his letter to the *Gazette*, the last time he saw Sheila they talked about a waiter at Captain Jack's named Joel Crothers. I'd very much like to know the specifics of that conversation."

"I was with Lloyd that night. It was the first time he took me out for dinner. Sheila was our waitress."

Ah, Abby said to herself, recalling Bostrum's description of Sid Beckwith as a tenacious bulldog. *If ole Lois fuckin' Lane keeps on digging, she just might unearth a bone or two herself.* "Did she say anything about Joel?"

"As a matter of fact, she did. I remember she looked preoccupied and kind of stressed out and Lloyd kept asking her what was wrong. Finally, she told him she was having boyfriend troubles or something to that effect. 'That Crothers fellow?' Lloyd asked. Sheila seemed really surprised he remembered the name. I don't know why because a few weeks earlier she'd told Lloyd about a fishing trip Joel took her on. Anyway, whatever the problem, she brushed it off, said it was something she'd have to work out for herself."

"That's all she said about Joel?"

"All that I remember."

"She didn't mention anything about breaking up with him?"

"Not that I recall. To tell the truth, I wasn't really focusing on their conversation. It was the first time Lloyd had taken me anywhere and I was nervous. You know, concerned about making a good impression."

Disappointed at having reached what appeared to be a dead end, Abby asked if Carolyn knew whether Sheila's mother still lived in Port Austin.

"As far as I know. Her name is Horvath. Dorothy Horvath. Listen, I'll ask Lloyd what Sheila said about Joel that night. Don't get your hopes up, but I'll work on him. Maybe he'll open up with me. Where can I contact you if he does?"

Abby wrote down the words *Dorothy Horvath* in her notebook. "I don't know where I'll be staying when I get to Nanticoke, and I doubt my cell phone will work out there. Why don't you give me your number and I'll call you in a day or so."

Abby jotted down the number Carolyn gave her and put away the notebook.

"Don't be angry with Lloyd for not cooperating," the woman said. "It must be hell lying there in the shape he's in not knowing if he's going to live or die."

"I'm not angry at him," Abby said and stood up.

Actually, she felt sorry for the man. She also felt grateful because he had taught her a valuable lesson. During her periodic bouts with depression, she had often thought of suicide as her most viable option, though she had always chosen to hang in there because of her mother and Kevin. But if she ever did decide it was time to check out of her room at the hotel of life, she now knew to make damn sure to turn out the lights.

CHAPTER 5

The Bogue City waterfront bore little resemblance to the bustling, charming district Abby remembered from previous visits. Neptune's Alley, so alive and picturesque in summers past, now looked dreary, grimy, and uninhabited—a ghost town street with an ocean view. Nobody strolled the sidewalk, browsed the docks, or even maneuvered a car down the narrow winding pavement. The fishing boats lined up in their slips all seemed small and ordinary, barely resembling the impressive crafts that sparkled in her memory. Even the seagulls looked drab and dingy, their periodic shrieks eerie and vaguely unsettling on this bleak Wednesday in February.

The last time she visited Bogue City, Abby had been with her ex-husband and Kevin, a toddler at the time. They had spent a weekend at a cheap motel on Emerald Beach, just across the sound, and the three of them had swum, gone for walks on the beach, toured antique shops, and eaten enough seafood to gain ten pounds as a family. She and Mark had snorted enough cocaine to keep the fact that they no longer even liked each other from being a concern.

Abby hadn't been married long before she realized her marriage probably wasn't going to work. She had never considered her breasts a problem until Mark suggested she get implants, an idea she dismissed as ridiculous, telling him she would enlarge her boobs when he started wearing elevator shoes. Soon he began finding fault with other things about her as well, especially her housekeeping. Their apartment needed cleaning, the refrigerator was a mess, and her cooking was a disaster.

Some of his complaints were justified, Abby knew, but after a while, she just didn't give a damn. Mark wasn't exactly Prince Charming himself. A longhaired stoner who fancied himself an artist, he was barely as tall as she and seemed to shrink in stature the longer she knew him. By the time they separated, she wondered what she had seen in him in the first place.

She located Captain Jack's with no difficulty, a sprawling wooden structure that extended on stilts some hundred feet into the sound. *Best Seafood in the State*, boasted the sign on the front door.

Not an exaggeration, Abby reflected, her mouth watering as she recalled the broiled fish, coleslaw, tartar sauce and ketchup she had mixed together into an unrecognizable but delicious concoction that even Mark, whose table manners weren't stellar, found disgusting.

We open April tenth, another sign added. *Bring your appetite*. Unfortunately, there was no name, telephone number, or address where anyone associated with the restaurant could be reached.

The only evidence of human activity came from a corrugated metal building diagonally across the street where an old Ford Mustang and a ramshackle Chevy pickup truck were parked. Everything else in the neighborhood was closed down, boarded up, or simply vacated for the winter—the gift shops, the other restaurants, and the marina where small boats bobbed up and down in their slips. Noticing the flicker and flash of what she thought was a welding torch through the building's lone window,

Abby crossed the street and knocked on the door. Then she knocked again when nobody responded. Finally, a swarthy man with matted sweaty hair and muscular, tattooed arms opened the door.

"Yeah?"

"I'm looking for somebody connected with Captain Jack's," she said, nodding toward the restaurant. "I'd like to talk to the owner, but I'll settle for anyone who works there."

"You hafta settle for less than that, lady 'cause I dunno anybody works there." After saluting Abby with a grimy right hand, he shut the door.

She got back in her car and, after consulting her notes, drove to Second Street and turned left. Two blocks later she stopped in front of a hulking two-story dwelling, its sagging front porch and old-fashioned wooden shutters matching the description Gretchen had given of the boarding house where Sheila stayed the summer she disappeared. It looked deserted but Abby knocked on the front door anyway. When nobody responded, she tried the knob, which was locked. She went around back where she found a charcoal grill wrapped in a protective cover, a few wooden lounge chairs with flaking paint, and a horseshoe pit in need of fresh sand. The backyard was bordered by a tall ungainly hedge and, except for a single bulb above the porch door, there was no outside lighting. A person could meet with foul play out here, she thought, and nobody would be the wiser.

She drove back to Main Street and followed Gretchen's directions to Musgrove Motors. The showroom window featured a smiling yellow whale floating above dark blue lettering that doubled as water and proclaimed *At Musgrove you get a whale of a deal with service to match.* An American flag flapped overhead, snapping and popping in the wind like a whip.

A rope slapped against the flagpole, making a hollow, clanking sound.

"I'd like to talk to Bobby Musgrove," Abby told the man who greeted her in the showroom, a lanky fellow with long sideburns.

"I can show you our stock. My name's Mel."

"Thanks, Mel, but I need to talk to Bobby. It's not about cars."

The salesman gave her a quizzical look. "I'll tell him you're here," he said and disappeared down a hallway. A moment later he returned, accompanied by a clean-cut young man wearing tan slacks, a blue dress shirt, and a stylish maroon tie.

"I'm Bobby Musgrove. What can I do for you?"

Abby introduced herself, explaining that she worked for the *Scarboro Gazette* and was looking into Sheila Bostrum's disappearance. "I was told you might have worked at Captain Jack's the summer she disappeared, and I was hoping you could give me some leads."

"Afraid I won't be much help, but I'll tell you what I know. We can talk in my office."

He led her down the hall and into a small brightly lit room with a window overlooking the parking lot. Indicating two vinyl upholstered chairs near a desk piled with paperwork of various descriptions, he asked her to have a seat. Abby chose the one on the left. Bobby turned the other so it faced her and sat down.

"I was a waiter at Captain Jack's the first part of that summer," he told her. "Around the end of June one of the salesmen here at the dealership quit, and my father asked me to fill in until he could find a replacement. I sold so many cars Dad ended up hiring me full time. He retired last year and now I run the place." Bobby smiled apologetically. "I know you didn't come here for my life story, but I'm afraid that's about all I can tell you. I really didn't know Sheila very well. I don't have a clue what happened to her. Why the sudden interest after all this time?"

Abby told him about Lloyd Bostrum's letter asking the *Gazette* to investigate. "I just talked to him," she said. "Or tried to. He's in the hospital and wasn't very communicative."

"Sounds like he might not make it from what I've heard. Any change in his condition?"

"Apparently it's still touch and go. His letter mentioned a waiter named Joel Crothers. Does that name ring a bell?"

Bobby nodded. "He seemed like a nice enough guy. Got along well with everybody."

"Mr. Bostrum thinks he was in love with Sheila. Did you get that impression?"

"Not at all. They might've gone out together a couple of times, but I wouldn't even call it dating. It was more like a brother and sister relationship far as I could tell. Joel was from Nanticoke and had a girlfriend back home."

Abby wondered how there could be such a discrepancy between Bobby's perception and what Sheila had apparently told her father. "How old was Joel at the time?"

"Eighteen, maybe nineteen. He'd just finished his freshman year at East Carolina."

Abby had attended that university her first year out of high school, and she wondered if Joel could have been there then, deciding she probably would have preceded him by at least a couple years. Abby didn't like thinking about those days. She was about to ask Bobby another question when a heavy-set man with a ruddy face appeared in the doorway.

"Sorry to interrupt, but I just got an offer for the green Malibu." He handed Bobby a piece of paper. "I might be able to squeeze another couple hundred out of 'em, but I can live with that figure if you can."

"Go ahead and make the deal," Bobby said. The salesman nodded and left the office. "Dad thinks I'm too easy when it comes to price, but I believe a satisfied customer is a repeat customer. I want that young couple to buy their next car from me, not just this one. Sorry for the interruption—and the digression. It sounds like you think Joel might be responsible for Sheila's disappearance."

"Lloyd Bostrum thinks he is. Did Joel commute from Nanticoke that summer or live around here?"

"Nanticoke is too far to commute unless you want to spend half your day on the ferry. His sister lived here then. Joel stayed with her."

"She doesn't live here now?"

"I don't think so. I don't know her name. She's married—at least she was then—so it wouldn't be Crothers."

"Do you know Jack and Mary Bethune?"

"Yeah. Nice people. Jack was a ship's captain in his younger days. They spend their winters in Florida, so I'm afraid you're out of luck if you want to talk to them."

Disappointed the people she most wanted to question weren't available, Abby asked if there was anything else Bobby could tell her about Joel. "I'd like to find out whatever I can about him," she said. "His personality, interests, temperament, how he related to girls and other guys, anything that might give me some insight into the kind of person he was—and is. By the way, I'd appreciate it if you didn't tell anyone I've been asking about him. I don't want Joel knowing he's being investigated. And if it turns out he's innocent, I wouldn't want people thinking otherwise."

"Understood," Bobby said. He told her Joel seemed a little quieter than most of the waiters and waitresses at Captain Jack's, though he wasn't averse to hanging out with them and seemed to enjoy himself when he did. "I know the guy liked to fish. Every chance he got he'd wet a line down at Neptune's Alley or at one of the gravel pit ponds just outside of town. One time he asked some of us to go deep sea fishing on his brother's boat. I was all set to go but had to cancel out when Dad got shorthanded."

When there was nothing else Bobby could tell her about Joel Crothers, Abby asked him about Sheila Bostrum, starting with whether he knew her in high school.

"I did. We were in the same grade."

"What was she like?"

"She had a lot of boyfriends—and a reputation for being something of a hot number."

"Do you remember any of the boyfriends in particular?"

"None that would be any help to you now. Gary went off to college and lives out of state. Simon was killed in a boating accident. Rodney joined the Army and was stationed in Afghanistan the last I heard."

"Gary's last name is Thompkins?"

"Yeah. He got a football scholarship to Wake Forest."

"Any chance he could've killed her?"

Bobby chuckled. "He wouldn't hurt a fly unless it happened to be standing between him and the other team's quarterback."

Mentally crossing Gary off her almost blank list of suspects, Abby asked if Sheila went out with anyone other than Joel the summer she disappeared.

"I wouldn't know. I wasn't around her that much, and I didn't see her at all after I started working for Dad."

"Is there anybody else you're aware of who might've known what was going on in Sheila's life that summer?"

"Can't think of a soul."

"What about Angie Dake? I understand she and Sheila were friends."

"Yeah, they were. And now that you mention it, Angie did work at Captain Jack's that summer."

"Does she still live around here?"

"Seems to me she lives in Hatteras...or maybe it's Buxton. The sheriff could tell you for sure. You probably should talk to him, Abby. He could answer a lot of your questions that I can't."

Bobby gave her directions to the sheriff's office, and Abby wrote them down on her notepad. "One last question," she said. "Have you got any theories about what happened to Sheila?"

"Not really. Since nobody's seen or heard from her in all these years, I figure she must be dead. But if she was murdered, I don't have a clue who did it."

Abby thanked him for his time and got up to leave. Bobby accompanied her back to the showroom and then asked if she planned to spend the night in Bogue City.

"Depends on what I find out from the sheriff. What time does the last ferry leave for Nanticoke?"

"Four o'clock. But it leaves from Cedar Point, which is a half hour drive from here. You might be cutting it close if you have more people to see before you leave. If you decide to spend the night, I'd like to take you to dinner. There's a nice restaurant just opened up in Port Austin and there's a Holiday Inn there too. Getting a good night's sleep shouldn't be a problem, and you'd be five miles closer to Cedar Point."

Abby weighed the pros and cons of accepting such an offer. "Thanks, but I'm under pretty severe time constraints," she said. "I appreciate the invitation, though."

Bobby handed her his business card. "If you change your mind, let me know. Good luck with your investigation, Abby. Anything I can do down the road to help, just ask."

As she got in her car, Abby felt a twinge of regret for having been so quick to turn down Bobby Musgrove's dinner invitation. He seemed nice enough and he hadn't been at all pushy. But chances were he'd try something afterward, and she didn't want that kind of complication, at least not right now. Or did she? For a moment she entertained the notion of spending the night with a handsome young stranger, deciding the idea wasn't altogether unappealing.

"Good Lord, girl, get a grip," she told herself and started the car.

Making sure nobody was coming from either direction, she pulled away from the curb and sped back downtown in search of a place to eat lunch. She was hungry enough to eat a woolly mammoth.

CHAPTER 6

In contrast to the stone, white-columned courthouse nearby, the squat stucco building that housed the sheriff's department made Abby think of a trailer set up on the grounds of an old mansion. While eating lunch at Ralph's Barbeque in downtown Bogue City, she had decided there was little to gain—and possibly a lot to lose—by not consulting with the sheriff now, before leaving the mainland. The more she could learn from the man, the better her chances of determining Joel Crothers's guilt or innocence once she reached Nanticoke. Or so she hoped.

The only person in the outer office, a portly middle-aged deputy who seemed about to nod off at his desk, told Abby the sheriff was in conference. "Something I can help you with?" he asked, stifling a yawn.

"I want to talk to the head honcho," she said, on the verge of yawning herself because of all the barbeque, coleslaw, and hushpuppies she had eaten. "Any idea how long he'll be?"

The deputy shrugged. "You can wait over there if you want to." He indicated several metal folding chairs in a small waiting area near a window.

Abby sat down in one of the chairs and picked up a

newspaper, which happened to be the *Scarboro Gazette*. After scanning the headlines, she read what promised to be Sid Beckwith's final column, at the end of which he announced his decision to move on to the *Richmond Times Dispatch* and thanked his readers for their loyal support. Abby still found it intoxicating that she was pursuing something Sid normally would have handled, but considering her lack of experience, she had to admit that thinking of herself as an investigative reporter was a bit of a stretch.

She was about to doze off when she heard voices. Opening her eyes, she saw three males, two in police uniforms, heading down the hallway. The one in the lead, a short, wiry middle-aged officer who walked with a swagger, reminded Abby of a bantam rooster. The other cop, tall and lanky, was about the same age as the heavy-set young man in jeans and sweatshirt walking beside him.

Neither of them looked more than a year or two out of high school.

"Not a word about this to anybody, Terry," the older officer said. "Thanks for agreeing to help out."

"Glad to obloige, Sheriff," the young man replied in a quaint accent that made Abby wonder if it was the Nanticoke brogue she had heard about, a combination of old English and Southern redneck reportedly used by some islanders. "Moight need a favor from you sometoime."

Terry removed his coat from a hook near the door, gave a thumbs-up sign, and left the office. The sheriff turned to the young officer beside him. "I want you in place by noon tomorrow, Duane. You don't have a problem with that, do you?"

"No, sir. But I still think we oughta do this in shifts."

"There's less chance of you being recognized than any of the other deputies. Don't worry, you'll get paid for whatever extra time you put in, plus I'm giving you the rest of today off. I want you plenty alert tomorrow. No partying or boozing it up tonight, understand?"

Looking none too happy, the deputy nodded.

"Chin up, son. This is a real opportunity. Handle it right and you'll be in good shape come bonus time."

The deputy's face brightened. "I won't disappoint you," he said and headed for the coat rack.

"Somebody waitin' to see the head honcho," the other deputy announced, emphasizing the final two words.

The sheriff turned in Abby's direction, smiled, and strode over to where she sat. "Sheriff Leland Mountcastle," he said. "What can I do for you?"

Abby stood up and extended her hand, which the sheriff shook in a cordial manner. When she told him she was a reporter for the *Scarboro Gazette* and wanted to talk to him about Sheila Bostrum and Rhonda Tolbert, Mountcastle's air of relaxed cordiality was replaced by a look of surprise that bordered on shock.

"Hell, Sheila disappeared five years ago. That's not news, it's ancient history. Why's the *Gazette* interested in her now?"

Abby's explanation about Bostrum's letter brought a scowl to the sheriff's face. "Let's go in my office," he said. "Hold my calls, Leon. All of 'em."

She followed Mountcastle down the hallway and into a room cluttered with filing cabinets and folding chairs. On one wall hung a map of the county, and on another, interspersed with pictures of law officers and other officials, were two wooden placards. One said *Pardon your breathing while I smoke* and the other *The whippings will continue until morale improves.*

The sheriff pointed toward the haphazard semicircle of chairs next to his desk and told Abby to have a seat. "Might as well let me see the letter."

She withdrew it from her purse, handed it to him, and

sat down in the closest of the folding chairs. She watched him read it, saw his face register interest only as he was finishing the second page.

"So the guy actually was trying to kill himself," Mountcastle said, returning the letter to Abby and then sitting down at his desk. "It figures. Excuse my French, but that letter is bullshit pure, plain, and simple. He's been giving me the same crock for months. Bostrum is alive, you know."

Abby nodded. "I just tried to talk to him. He didn't have much to say."

"You're further ahead than if he'd jawed a blue streak. The man wouldn't recognize the truth if it jumped up and bit him on the ass."

"Your French has gotten worse," Abby said, beginning to agree with Bostrum's assessment that Mountcastle was the wrong person to be investigating Sheila's disappearance.

"It tends to get that way when people waste my time."

"Then you must think Sheila is still alive."

"I don't know if she is or not. I do know, if she's dead, it wasn't Joel Crothers killed her. Joel might seem guilty if all you've heard is Bostrum's side of the story, but he didn't take into account all the facts."

"Such as?"

"Joel's relationship with the Tolbert girl for starters. Bostrum claims Joel was heartbroken when she left the island, but that's not true. Joel already had a girlfriend when Rhonda came on the scene. He'd gone with Beth for years and had no intention of breaking up with her. His fling with Rhonda was what you might call a brief indiscretion while his true love was temporarily unavailable."

"What's this true love's last name?" Abby asked, annoyed by the sheriff's cocky attitude.

"Harker. She lives in Hatteras but right now she's a student at Chowan College."

Abby winced, feeling a sudden sting of shame. After flunking out of East Carolina, she had applied to Chowan and had been accepted. At first, the school seemed a good fit, especially since it didn't take her long to become a starter on the girls' basketball team, something she hadn't been able to do at East Carolina. Eventually, however, she'd had several manic episodes at Chowan, the last of which left the college little choice but to send her home.

"That's in Murfreesboro, isn't it?" she asked, attempting to buy a little time while she tried to regain her focus on the here and now.

"Yeah, far enough away so Joel didn't have to worry about Beth showing up unexpectedly and catching him in the act."

Abby's final week at Chowan had started out great. In a game at Ferum College, she scored sixteen points, handed out thirteen assists, and hauled in eleven rebounds, her first ever triple double. Back on campus, she glided through the next few days as though on her way to an uncontested layup. She made new friends, was more talkative with her old ones, even participated in her classes, something she hadn't done before.

Tuition at Chowan wasn't cheap and, like many students there, Abby had a part-time job to help defray the costs. Assigned to work in the dining hall two days a week and during special events like Founder's Day and Homecoming, she was scheduled to help serve meals that Friday evening at a banquet celebrating the induction of new members into Chowan's Athletic Hall of Fame. Earlier that day, she had almost singlehandedly carried the discussion in her English class.

Back in the dorm, she told her roommate "I don't know why I wasn't exempt from having to take freshman

English. Obviously, I know as much about the subject as Dr. Potter."

The roommate took issue with Abby, said she had been acting weird lately, and asked if she was feeling all right.

"I feel great!" Abby snapped. "What the fuck do you mean I've been acting weird?"

When the roommate tried to explain that Abby had been staying up all hours of the night and had been saying things that didn't make sense, Abby cut her off, accusing her of being jealous. Later when the roommate tried to talk her out of working at the Hall of Fame banquet, suggesting she call in sick, Abby would have none of it.

"Sick hell," she said as she headed for the dining hall. "I'm back and better than ever!"

An hour later, as she was helping serve food to those gathered for the induction ceremony, it suddenly occurred to her that she herself was one of the honorees and therefore should be seated at the table of honor.

Setting aside her tray, she hurried to the front table, introduced herself as the best point guard Chowan ever had, and sat down. She began chatting with the inductees on either side of her, a tall black guy who had been a star forward at Chowan before playing a few seasons in the NBA and an older white guy whose beer belly and double chin belied the fact that he held Chowan's record for most touchdown passes.

When Abby strode to the podium to give her acceptance speech, insisting that the master of ceremonies had overlooked her name, two members of campus security appeared and forcibly hauled her away—

"You still with us?" Mountcastle asked, picking up a long-stemmed pipe from his desk. "Or are you taking a not-so-short trip to Bermuda?"

"Sorry. I was just thinking. The fact that…uh…that

Joel had relationships with two young women who ended up missing or dead—that's more than a coincidence, don't you agree?"

Mountcastle fished a kitchen match from his shirt pocket, scraped the match against his shoe, and touched the flame to the bowl. "I would, if Joel actually had relationships with both those women." He sucked on the stem, giving the pipe his full attention until smoke curled around his head. "He didn't have a relationship with Sheila Bostrum."

"They went out together. Joel even took her on a fishing trip. Didn't you read that part of Bostrum's letter where she complained about Joel falling for her?"

"I read it. I also heard Bostrum say it when he dumped this same so-called evidence in my lap. Either he made up that part or he was confused. There was nothing going on between Joel Crothers and Sheila Bostrum. I checked it out with people who knew 'em both."

"What people?"

"Sheila's friend and co-worker at Captain Jack's for one. Angie Dake would've been the first to know if Sheila and Joel were an item. Angie will verify everything I've told you. She works at a beauty shop in Buxton, a place called Mane Street Salon. It's spelled just like the hair on a horse's neck. You might also talk to Roy Pendleton, the Pitt County Sheriff. Roy'll give you all the details you want about Rhonda's murder." Mountcastle reached for the telephone on his desk. "I'll let him know you're coming."

"Whoa," Abby said, holding up her right hand. "I don't want to talk to him yet. Who else told you there wasn't anything going on between Joel and Sheila?"

"Other restaurant workers, college kids mostly. None of 'em live around here. The good news is they wouldn't help you clear up anything because there's nothing to clear up, at least not as far as Joel Crothers is concerned. He's innocent."

Disappointed with the way the conversation was going, Abby had a strong suspicion that the sheriff wasn't telling her all he knew about Sheila Bostrum's disappearance and Rhonda Tolbert's murder, especially as they pertained to Joel. "Did you talk to the Bethunes about Sheila?" she asked.

"I did. They said her relationship with Joel was strictly platonic."

"Did they say whether Sheila went out with anybody else that summer?"

"I asked about that, and they didn't think so. Mary did mention Sheila talking kind of lovey-dovey to somebody on the phone. She said she thought the guy's name was *Ron*, but she couldn't be sure. When she kidded Sheila about it, Sheila said she was just joking around with some guy she knew in high school. I checked out the boyfriend angle myself, Abby. There wasn't a guy in Sheila's life that summer, Ron or anybody else."

"What about Bobby Musgrove?" Although Abby no longer considered Bobby much of a suspect, she thought Mountcastle's response might reveal his own ineptitude if nothing else.

"Bobby didn't work at Captain Jack's more than a few weeks," the sheriff replied. "I did check him out. There wasn't any connection between him and Sheila."

"Which brings us back to Joel," Abby said, reluctantly acknowledging that she might have underestimated Mountcastle's capabilities. "Did he have an alibi for the afternoon Sheila disappeared?"

"He didn't need one."

"How can you say that? Even if Lloyd Bostrum doesn't have all his facts straight, there's still a lot of evidence pointing to Joel."

The sheriff sucked on his pipe but there was no smoke. He fished another match from his pocket, struck it on his shoe, and drew flame into the bowl. "You still don't get it, do you? The problem is Bostrum himself. The guy never got anything right in his life. He had a nice wife and left her for a floozy who ended up ditching him. He had a good job at a company with a future, and he quit in order to start up a rinky-dink machine shop that never made him a dime. Last Saturday, he tried to commit suicide by driving his truck into the side of the Neuse River Bridge. Turns out he botched that too. The dumb turkey was wearing his seat belt."

It took a moment for the Sheriff's last sentence to register. "You're kidding."

Mountcastle shook his head. "It's possible he in-tended to end up in the river, in which case wearing his seat belt might've made sense. But either way he messed up. Instead of driving out on the bridge where there's nothing but a low guard rail between him and the water, he drove smack dab into a concrete abutment. If he hadn't been wearing his seat belt, he'd have died on impact and saved himself a lot of grief."

Abby thought of the pathetic, rage-filled man lying helplessly in the emergency room cubicle. "I don't see how Bostrum's ineptitude is relevant to Joel's guilt or innocence," she said.

"It's relevant because that letter he sent the *Gazette* fits the same pattern. It makes about as much sense as the other things he's done. If I were you, I'd forget the whole thing. Otherwise, you'll be wasting your time and the *Gazette*'s money. Hell, as far as I know, Sheila Bostrum is alive, well, and living in San Francisco or some such God-forsaken place. But if she is dead, I guarantee you one thing—Joel Crothers didn't have a thing to do with it."

"Okay, you've made your point," Abby said grudgingly. "I have to wonder, though, just as Mr. Bostrum did, whether you're capable of being objective when Joel's brother is one of your deputies."

She expected the sheriff to get angry, maybe even fly off the handle. The opposite occurred; he seemed to get calmer, more in control of himself. "The fact that Joel and Steve are brothers has nothing to do with this," he said, looking Abby straight in the eye. "Nothing whatsoever. Sooner or later, you'll realize that. Anything else, or can we put this interview to bed?"

"I've got two more questions," Abby said, resigned to the likelihood that her time spent with Mountcastle was going to be less than productive. "When Joel worked at Captain Jack's, he stayed with his sister. Do you know where she lives?"

"Tennessee the last I heard. Her husband works for K-Mart. They made him manager of a store out there. What's your other question?"

"Can you give me Dorothy Horvath's address and phone number?"

"Be glad to." Mountcastle got up from his desk. "I'll get you Angie Dake's and Roy Pendleton's numbers while I'm at it. I'll even throw in the number where Jack and Mary Bethune can be reached in Florida at no extra charge."

What a jackass, Abby thought as she got up from the chair. But she had to admit the sheriff had done a pretty good job of defending his position and had seemed to enjoy himself in the process.

CHAPTER 7

The man who answered the phone said Dorothy was at work and asked if he could take a message. When Abby explained her reason for calling, his manner turned chilly.

"There's nothing she can tell you she hasn't already told the sheriff. You'll be opening old wounds for no reason."

"I understand how you feel," Abby said. "But I'm sure your wife would want to do whatever she can to help solve her daughter's disappearance."

"Is there any new evidence?"

"There is, but I'd rather not go into it on the phone. Could you give me Dorothy's work number? I need to talk to her as soon as possible."

"I don't want you bothering her at work. If you absolutely have to contact her, she gets home around four-thirty."

The man hung up before Abby could reply, leaving her to decide whether an interview with Dorothy Horvath—assuming the woman allowed one—would be worth spending the night on the mainland.

Deciding to postpone going to Nanticoke until the next morning, she drove the four miles to Port Austin, a picturesque waterfront community with a minimum of strip malls, fast food joints, and condo complexes. After checking out the lodging situation, she decided on the Holiday Inn, a two-story structure that hadn't been there when she last visited the town. It had a nice view of the sound and its off-season rate seemed reasonable.

When she got to her room on the second floor, it was much too early to call Dorothy, so she unpacked a few things and then got out the list of phone numbers the sheriff had given her. She tried Angie Dake first. After two rings, a young woman's voice came on the line: "I'm not home, so leave a message, please. If that's you, Mike, don't say a word and don't call again. It's over, asshole. Sorry, Mom."

With a chuckle, Abby hung up then tried the Bethune's Florida number, only to get their answering machine. After unpacking a few more things, she went jogging, something she did almost every day, ever since her therapist recommended it in the strongest terms. "Exercise is absolutely crucial," Dorene Milsap had told her. "Right up there with taking your meds. In fact, that's one of the reasons you need to do it. Lithium increases a person's appetite, so if you take it on a regular basis, which you damn well better unless I prescribe otherwise, you'll probably start putting on weight. *Unless...*" Dorene further emphasized the word by stretching it out. "Unless you make exercise a top priority. Do it every day possible, Abby, even if you feel so rotten you can hardly drag yourself out of bed. Actually, if you're feeling depressed that's all the more reason to exercise. It's the best way to raise the serotonin level in your brain. It reduces depression with the added benefit of burning off calories. You've got a nice figure now, but you won't keep it unless you run your butt off—and I mean that literally." Dorene had paused, giving her words a chance to sink in. "That's two of the four best pieces of advice I can give you, Abby. Take your prescribed medication every single day, and get your ass out there and pound the pavement." When Abby asked what the other two pieces of advice were, Dorene said she'd get to them eventually. "Right now you've got enough on your plate. Start your exercise program and get used to taking your meds on a regular basis."

Abby had liked Dorene from the start and had tried to heed her advice. It hadn't been easy. There were plenty of days when the mere thought of jogging revolted her, but she always felt better after doing it, physically and mentally. At best, it gave her a buoyant feeling similar to the way she used to feel during her early marijuana days. At the very least, it took the edge off her depression.

She jogged for almost an hour in Port Austin and, in the process, covered practically the entire town, including the residential areas. Her only problem was a large Rottweiler that roared up behind her on a quiet street, causing her to gasp and her heart rate to soar. Slowing to a walk, she tried to appear calm, doing her best to ignore the dog, who seemed to be deciding whether or not to attack her. Eventually, he lost interest.

When she got back to the motel, she showered, dressed, and tried the Horvaths' number. Dorothy answered on the first ring. After Abby identified herself and explained the nature of her assignment, the woman readily agreed to a meeting.

"Apparently my husband was rude when you called earlier," she said. "He was just trying to protect me, Abby, probably afraid I'll start obsessing about Sheila again. Don works the night shift at the post office and leaves here about quarter to eight. You're welcome to come over any time after that."

Abby wrote down directions to Dorothy's house and said she would be there around eight. She then tried Angie

Dake's and the Bethunes' numbers again, getting the same pre-recorded messages. She put on her jacket and walked the three blocks to the Golden Dragon, a Chinese restaurant she had noticed earlier that afternoon.

After a meal of sweet and sour chicken that included some of the best shrimp-filled egg rolls she had ever tasted, Abby felt almost as bloated as the whale on Bobby Musgrove's car dealership window. On her way back to the motel, she noticed an open gift shop across from a marina and decided to take the opportunity to buy souvenirs for her mother and Kevin. After browsing a while, she bought her mother a large vanilla-scented candle on a sea shell-encrusted holder that, according to the tag, was hand decorated by a local craftsman. She got Kevin a model of a clipper ship, along with a poster of the Harlem Globetrotters. Abby had always been a Globetrotters' fan, though there was an incident involving the team that made her cringe every time she thought of it. Against the advice of her mother, who could tell that Abby was manic at the time, she had driven all the way to Raleigh to watch the Globetrotters play. And, against her mother's strenuous objections, she had taken Kevin with her.

As she watched the game, Abby found herself focusing more on the Washington Generals' ineptitude than on the Globetrotters' magic. She knew the Generals weren't supposed to win, but to Abby's way of thinking their lack of resistance was so blatant it diminished the Globetrotters' performance. She began yelling at the Generals, demanding they play better defense. Toward the end of the game, she was in such a funk she took Kevin by the hand and hurried to the locker room area, determined to give the Generals' point guard a piece of her mind. When she spotted the guy, she proceeded to get in his face the way an irate baseball manager might argue an umpire's blown call. Eventually, a security guard intervened, containing Abby long enough for the player to escape into the locker room. When she finally calmed down enough to gather up Kevin, the boy was nowhere to be found. Abby panicked, soon reaching full-fledged hysteria.

A half hour later, a police officer found the boy in a men's restroom. Kevin had locked himself in a stall and was quietly crying. By the time the officer determined that he was physically unhurt and led him to a waiting squad car, Abby was strapped to an ambulance gurney and on her way to Rex Hospital in Raleigh, one of several hospitalizations that had resulted from her bipolar disorder, her drug addiction, or a combination of the two.

Abby's first hospitalization had occurred a few days after the incident at Chowan College. At the dean's insistence, she left Chowan and returned to her mother's house, where she became increasingly belligerent and irrational. After several days of volatile behavior—during which she kicked a hole in her bedroom door, smashed two of her mother's most cherished antique vases, and actually shoved her mother for suggesting that Abby needed psychiatric help—Lillian reluctantly called the police. Abby was taken to the Scarboro hospital's BSU, where she was diagnosed as bipolar.

After a three-week hospital stay, Abby returned home fairly well stabilized on medications. She refused to believe, however, that she was actually mentally ill and accused the hospital doctors of being the crazy ones. She hated the side effects of her medication, especially the sluggishness and the weight gain they tended to cause, and eventually stopped taking them, telling herself she really didn't need them anyway. As a result, she ended up in the hospital again—a cycle that would repeat itself several times.

It was the Globetrotters' incident that finally caused Abby to take her bipolar disorder seriously. The relief she felt after learning that Kevin was safe and the undeniable fact that she alone had placed him in real danger woke her up to the reality that she did, indeed, have a mental illness and needed to deal with it. When Rex Hospital's psychiatrist suggested Abby start seeing a therapist well-versed in bipolar disorder, she readily agreed. And when the hospital's social worker told her she would have to clean up her act if she wanted to keep Kevin, Abby not only didn't object but thanked the woman for giving her another chance. "I'll do whatever it takes," she'd said, and this time they were more than just words.

COCO

Too loaded down with packages to continue her walk, Abby returned to the Holiday Inn where she watched the news on TV until time to leave for Dorothy Horvath's house. She had no trouble finding it, a modest well-maintained brick ranch in the subdivision where she had encountered the dog.

The porch light was on, and a woman with a slightly wrinkled but otherwise pretty face opened the door just as Abby was about to ring the bell. "I'm Dorothy," she said and ushered Abby into a small but attractively furnished living room where a brown-eyed girl with dark curly hair was sitting on the rug in front of a monopoly board. "Abby, this is my daughter Susan."

"Time for me to skedaddle," the girl said and stood up. "Mom said you want to talk about my missing sister and that's not the kind of thing an eight-year-old should listen to. It's a drag being a kid."

"Your daughter is adorable," Abby said after she and Dorothy were situated on the black leather sofa next to the picture window that overlooked the front yard.

"I'm scared to death something will happen and I'll

lose her too," Dorothy replied and then, as though embarrassed by what she had just said, she looked down at her hands, which were clasped tightly in her lap. "What new evidence do you have about Sheila?"

"Actually it's something your ex-husband provided." Abby opened her handbag and withdrew Bostrum's letter. "He sent this to the *Gazette*. It pretty much explains everything."

Dorothy took a long time to read the letter. When she handed it back, there were tears in her eyes. "It occurred to me that Lloyd's wreck might not have been accidental. Things haven't gone well for him lately."

Abby explained that she had been to the hospital to see Bostrum and that he hadn't responded to her questions. "I'd like to know more about what was going on between Sheila and Joel Crothers," she said. "Did your ex-husband ever talk to you about Joel?"

Dorothy shook her head. "The last time Lloyd and I talked was at Sheila's memorial service, which was over two years ago. She'd been missing so long he presumed she was dead and thought a service might bring some closure. It hasn't worked out that way for me. Apparently, it hasn't for him either."

"The sheriff seems convinced Joel didn't have anything to do with Sheila's disappearance, but I'm not so sure. Is there anything you can tell me that might support either position, the sheriff's or Mr. Bostrum's?"

"I don't recall Sheila ever mentioning a Joel Crothers, Abby. That doesn't mean Lloyd is wrong. Sheila didn't live at home that summer, so I wasn't as aware of her comings and goings as I once was."

"Did she move out because of problems at home?" Abby asked, wondering if Dorothy's second husband might have been a factor.

"I think she just wanted to try living on her own. She

was planning to move back in after Captain Jack's closed in the fall, assuming she hadn't found another job in the meantime."

"Did you have any contact with her once she moved out?"

"She called a few times, maybe once a week. Occasionally I'd stop by the boarding house to see her. Don and I never ate at Captain Jack's or any other restaurant that summer because Susan was quite young then and we didn't know any good baby-sitters. Up until then Sheila had been our baby-sitter."

"Did she seem upset about anything when you talked to her?"

Dorothy paused in reflection. "The first month or so she was fine. Toward the end—the last few weeks before she disappeared—she seemed kind of preoccupied."

"Had she ever acted that way before—while she was living at home, I mean?"

"Yes and no. Like most teens, she had her occasional moods. They never lasted long, though. Sheila was generally a happy person. But the last few times we talked she seemed...well, distracted."

"She never let on what was bothering her?"

"Not to me. I thought it might have something to do with her job, so I asked if she'd like to quit and come back home to live. She told me she liked being a waitress and living at the boardinghouse. Whatever her problem was, I didn't think it was anything serious, so I didn't press her. I didn't want her to think I was meddling. Now I wish to God I had."

Noticing tears in Dorothy's eyes, Abby slid over next to her on the sofa. "I know a little of what you're going through," she said, putting a hand on Dorothy's shoulder. "I never lost a child thank goodness, but I did lose a father and a brother. I know talking about this can't be easy."

Hoping she hadn't overstepped her bounds, Abby withdrew her hand and moved back to the other end of the sofa.

"Thank you for telling me that," Dorothy said, wiping her eyes with a tissue. "Go ahead and ask your questions. I want to help if I can."

Abby explained that earlier in the day she had talked to two people Sheila went to high school with and both said she had a lot of boyfriends, none of whom she stayed interested in for very long. "Do you think one of them might have had something to do with her disappearance?"

Dorothy shook her head. "They all seemed nice enough. None struck me as being vindictive or unstable."

"Did you get the impression that Sheila had a boyfriend the summer she disappeared?"

"No, I didn't. She never mentioned anybody."

"What about Bobby Musgrove? He was one of the people I talked to this morning."

"The name rings a bell. It seems to me Sheila might have gone out with him at some point. I could be mistaken."

"Could they have dated in high school or while she worked at Captain Jack's? Bobby was a waiter there that summer."

"I...I don't think so. I don't know why the name sounds familiar."

Abby continued to question Dorothy, but none of the woman's responses resulted in any information that suggested Bobby Musgrove, Joel Crothers, or anyone else was responsible for Sheila's disappearance. Eventually, Abby decided it wouldn't serve any purpose to continue the interview. Before ending it, however, she had one final question.

"Dorothy, have you got any idea—maybe a theory of some sort—about what happened to Sheila?"

The woman sighed and her eyes took on a far-away

look. "As a matter of fact, I do. I know it isn't plausible, but I've always had the hope that she's still alive. She was upset when her father and I divorced, and she and my second husband never hit it off very well. I don't mean there were any serious problems between them. It's just that Sheila was always the apple of Lloyd's eye. I know it hurt her to see his life going downhill the way it did, especially his heavy drinking. I think it's possible she left the area to get away from all that. I know it sounds silly. After all this time my mind tells me she's dead. But in my heart, I still feel there's a chance she's out there somewhere, and someday she'll let us know she's safe."

ℰↄℰↄ

Back in her room, Abby gazed at the lighted street and the dark water of the sound beyond, thinking about what she had learned so far. Not all the smoke blown in the sheriff's office, she reflected, had come from Mountcastle's pipe. He had expressed such concern that she not waste time going to Nanticoke, and yet he would have her drive some fifty miles southwest to interview the sheriff of Pitt County and even farther northeast to interrogate Angie Dake. Mountcastle, it seemed, wanted her to go anywhere but east, the direction she would soon head.

Though she had learned very little from Mountcastle and nothing from Lloyd Bostrum, Abby felt her investigation hadn't been a complete flop. Carolyn Rogers had shed some light on Sheila's conversation with her father at Captain Jack's, and Dorothy Horvath had confirmed Bostrum's assertion that something had been troubling Sheila the last few weeks before she disappeared. Dorothy had also revealed an interesting tidbit of information—the possibility that Sheila had gone out with Bobby Musgrove at some point. If that were true, why hadn't Bobby mentioned it? Could he be hiding anything else? And more importantly, was he somehow involved in Sheila's disappearance?

Abby wondered if she should check out Bobby Musgrove more thoroughly. Mulling it over, she decided to leave for Nanticoke first thing in the morning. Time was short and there was no real evidence implicating Bobby. Perhaps his name sounded familiar because Dorothy had seen it a thousand times on the sign outside the Chevy dealership.

As she gazed at the choppy dark water of the sound, Abby realized there was, in fact, a way she might learn more about Bobby Musgrove without prolonging her stay on the mainland. First thing tomorrow, before leaving for Nanticoke, she would call Bogue City Hospital and ask Gretchen if she remembered Bobby ever going out with Sheila.

Not bad strategy for a fledgling reporter with a mental illness, she reflected as she got up from the chair and closed the curtains. As she began getting ready for bed, however, she reminded herself that it was much too soon to pat herself on the back. Considering how far she was from figuring out whether Joel Crothers was guilty or innocent, she'd have to be manic to do that.

CHAPTER 8

With a long blast of horn that sent two pelicans flapping from nearby pilings, the ferry eased from the dock and made for open water, trailing a frothy wake that glistened in the early-morning sun. It was a wide boat with a bulkhead separating four rows of cars, two on each side.

Abby stood at the starboard railing and watched the waves roll past, rumples in a gray-green blanket. The ferry ironed them out, keeping a steady deck.

Earlier, while waiting at the dock, she had called the Bogue City hospital on her cell phone and asked Gretchen if Sheila Bostrum had ever dated Bobby Musgrove.

"Not to my knowledge," the young receptionist replied after a brief pause. "Somebody told you she did?"

"Sheila's mother said the name sounded familiar."

"I know Sheila went out with a lot of guys, but I'm almost positive Bobby wasn't one of them."

"That's good enough for me. Thanks again for all your help, Gretchen."

After the ferry had been under way a while, Abby decided to call Carolyn Rogers. The woman told her that Lloyd Bostrum had been so depressed last night that she didn't have the nerve to ask him about Sheila and Joel. She hoped he would be in a better frame of mind today. If so, she would broach the subject then.

After ending the call, Abby gazed at the receding shoreline and hoped life would be kind to Carolyn Rogers. There was something both admirable and pitiful about the woman's devotion to Lloyd Bostrum. Mostly pitiful, Abby decided. Then she felt a twinge of guilt for rendering such a harsh verdict when she herself had a history of behavior that was downright crazy at times. At least Carolyn didn't seem like a nutcase.

Abby slipped the cell phone back into her purse and got out of the car. As she gazed at the horizon, she thought of her son, hoping whatever had caused her mental illness wasn't hereditary.

The mainland receded into a jagged pencil line separating water from sky, reminding her of an etching that hung on a wall of Dorene Milsap's office.

"Quite a ways from home, aren't you?"

The voice caught Abby unawares and she turned toward it. The man who had waved her onto the ferry and chocked her tires was standing a few feet away. Handsome in a rugged sort of way, he had an aura of confidence that made her wonder what he was doing in such a menial job.

"Just where do you think my home is?"

"Scarboro, of course."

"How'd you know that?"

"Your license plate holder. It's got a Scarboro dealership written on it. How long are you going to be on the island?"

"That depends."

"On what?"

Abby decided this was as good a time as any to try out her cover story. "How long it takes to do my research. I work for the *Scarboro Gazette* and I'm doing a feature on Nanticoke in winter."

The man seemed amused. "Just what do you expect to find out there this time of year?"

Abby shrugged. "Whatever makes it unique—the geography, the inhabitants. I'm sure I'll find lots of interesting things to write about."

"Afraid you're in for a big disappointment. Even in the summer, nothing much happens on Nanticoke. This time of year you might as well forget it."

A gust of cold spray struck Abby's face. "I like a challenge," she said, wishing she had been able to come up with something witty. She took a tissue from her coat pocket and wiped away the spray.

"Well, you've sure got one. Where are you staying?"

"Don't know yet."

"Want a recommendation?"

"Sure—as long as it's not run by Norman Bates."

The man chuckled. "Don't worry, we don't have any psychos on the island, at least none I know about. I'll need a little background information. Three or four questions should do the trick. Let's start with what you like to do when the workday is over. In other words, what kind of night life do you enjoy?"

"I didn't think there'd be much to choose from."

"If you like country music and have a taste for beer, the possibilities are limitless. Otherwise, I'm afraid you're in for a dull time."

"I didn't come out here for entertainment. I have a job to do."

"Duly noted. Do you like seafood?"

"Sure do—except for oysters. Clams I can do without too. But most anything that goes with tartar sauce, cole-slaw, and French fries I like. I adore shrimp, regardless of how it's prepared."

"So far so good. How about moonlight boat rides?"

"Never been on one."

"Maybe we can change that. Do you play pool?"

"Afraid not."

"You sure have led a sheltered life. Are you married?"

"What's that got to do with places to stay on Nanticoke?"

The deckhand smiled. "I need to know if I'm going to guarantee my recommendation."

"Well, if you must know, I'm divorced. Haven't you used up your allotment of questions?"

"Just one more. What's your name?"

"Florence Nightingale," Abby said, recalling Bostrum's instructions to Caroline Rogers and the ICU's head nurse. "My friends call me Flo."

The deckhand's eyes narrowed. "You're putting me on—aren't you?"

"Why would I do that?"

He shrugged then stepped back and seemed to size Abby up before making a final decision. "For you, Flo Nightingale, or whatever your name is, I'm going to recommend a motel uniquely suited to a very pretty, though sheltered, feature writer like yourself. I recommend the Inlet Inn."

"Why that particular place?"

The man laughed. "It's the only motel open this time of year. Everything else closes after the channel bass and blue marlin season. They don't open up again until spring."

Abby sighed. "I'm glad I didn't pay in advance for that recommendation," she said, not knowing whether to be amused or put off by the deckhand's brand of humor.

"Actually, the Sand Dollar is still open. But it's at the north end of the island away from everything. I'm sure you'll like the Inlet Inn. It has all the amenities, yet it's homey and quaint. Glen and Mavis go out of their way to make their guests feel comfortable. Just follow Lake Street two blocks north of the ferry slip. It's right across from the post office. You can't miss it."

The wind gusted and Abby brushed back a lock of hair that had fallen over her forehead. "Thanks. I'll check it out."

"If I can be of further help while you're on the island, don't hesitate to ask. My office is a block and a half north of the Inlet Inn, same side of the street."

"Your office?"

"My apologies for not introducing myself, but I was having too much fun." The man extended his hand. "I'm Steve Crothers, the island's chief deputy. They don't pay me much, but if somebody needs a cop, I'm the guy they call."

Abby looked at him in astonishment. "I thought you were a deckhand."

"Right now that's exactly what I am. When you've got child support payments like I do, you pick up extra cash whenever and wherever you can."

Trying not to appear flustered, Abby took his hand and told him her real name, wondering if he already knew about her from Sheriff Mountcastle.

"Your hand's cold, Abby," Steve said. "Let's go inside where it's warm." He pointed toward a door in the ferry's bulkhead. "There's a snack bar in there and the coffee is pretty good. I'll give you a list of places to check out for your feature. It's a package deal—no charge."

Abby didn't detect anything furtive in the deputy's manner, no indication that he had advance notification of her visit. He seemed to be a guileless flirt, genuinely interested in her and her project.

"I'll join you on one condition," she said, brushing back another lock of hair.

"What's that?"

"Your list of places to see is longer than your list of places to stay."

Steve laughed again, full and easy, his eyes, which Abby suddenly realized were the same grayish blue as the ocean, showing considerable mirth.

"Don't expect it to be much longer. I wasn't kidding when I said there's not a lot going on this time of year. Nanticoke in winter is like an old bear during hibernation. It takes quite an effort just to locate its pulse."

CHAPTER 9

The ferry slowed then entered a narrow channel that soon widened, as Steve had said it would, into an irregular-shaped lake. There were boats of various sizes and descriptions along the shoreline and a few larger ones anchored in the middle. In the distance, Abby saw houses and other buildings, the most striking of which, a cone-shaped lighthouse, rose high above the others.

"I'll show you why this is called Diamond Lake if I get a chance," Steve said as the ferry's motor began decelerating. "In the meantime, good luck with your feature." He gave her a wave and headed for the front of the boat.

Abby stood at the railing a while longer, taking in the scenery and hoping, in spite of herself, that she would see more of this deckhand/deputy. When the dock loomed close, the ferry's motor churned into reverse and she returned to her car.

The Inlet Inn was easy enough to find, a sprawling two-story wooden structure that apparently had once been a private residence. Deciding to have a look around the town before registering, Abby continued down Lake Street past an ancient-looking church with paint peeling from its steeple to a downtown area comprised mainly of small shops. What impressed her most was the fact that there were no stoplights or fast moving traffic. In fact, there was hardly any traffic at all. The streets were narrow and winding, most of them at least partially covered by sand. Some of the houses had strange outbuildings, and Abby made a mental note to ask what they were. The village had the atmosphere of a sleepy college town between semesters, but it looked like no town she had ever seen or imagined.

By the time she returned to the Inlet Inn, she had fallen in love with it.

Entering the lobby, she encountered a series of intense, repetitive, high-pitched noises. Clearly made by a blonde-haired girl standing near the registration desk, the sounds had an urgency about them, but they weren't a warning or a plea for help or, as far as Abby could tell, an attempt to communicate anything at all. The only thing they even remotely resembled, she thought, was a bad impersonation of a car that wouldn't start.

"Yuheeee, yuheeee, yuheeee…"

The girl looked to be in her mid-to-late teens, and her activity was as bizarre as the noises she made. She was twirling a bright flannel shirt, which slapped and flopped against the hardwood floor as though alive, a florid fish newly out of water. Hovering intently over the shirt, the girl could have been a juvenile witchdoctor delivering an incantation or a demented cowgirl spinning a rope.

"Yeeeeee," she shrieked. "Yeeeeee, yeeeeee…"

A tall middle-aged man with a wide forehead and deep-set brown eyes emerged from behind the registration desk. "Let's trade, Jelinda," he said, handing the girl a rumpled teddy bear and in the same motion gently taking the shirt. "How about playing with this old friend for a while?"

Without looking up or acknowledging the man in any

way, the girl began chewing on the bear's feet. "Yahgi," she said in a less urgent tone.

"In case you're wondering, my niece is autistic," the man said to Abby.

Of course, she thought. I should have known. "Last fall I did a feature on autistic kids in the Scarboro area," she told him, recalling the one assignment of substance she had been given while working at the *Gazette*. "Your niece reminds me of some of them."

"A feature?" the man asked, returning to the desk.

"I'm a feature writer for the *Scarboro Gazette*. I came out here to do a story on Nanticoke in winter."

He gave her a quizzical look. "There's not much going on this time of year."

"So I was told by a deckhand who turned out to be a deputy sheriff. If you think about it, that's pretty unusual in itself."

The man nodded. "Actually, you picked a good time if what you're after is a close-up look at us islanders, the permanent residents, I mean. You'd probably get a distorted view in the summer when the place is swamped with tourists. Right now, what you see is pretty much who and what we are. I assume you'd like a room. Our off-season rates are in effect, forty dollars a night unless you want the bridal suite, which is ten dollars more."

"A regular room is fine. I'm not sure how long I'll be staying. At least two nights, maybe three."

"I'll put you down for two, but you're welcome to stay as long as you like. I'm Glen Turpin. My sister Mavis Gilbert and I run the place."

Abby shook his hand and introduced herself.

"You don't happen to play bridge, do you, Abby?" Glen asked, handing her a pen and a registration card.

"I used to," she said, recalling the many games she played in her East Carolina dorm for a tenth of a cent a point. Not only did those games cost her precious spending money but also they hastened her academic demise.

"The inn hosts a duplicate game every Thursday night. My sister's partner has the flu, and as far as I know, she hasn't found a replacement. Interested?"

"I'm not very good."

"As long as you know the basics, you'll be fine. We don't play for blood. I doubt Mavis will give a hoot if the two of you come in dead last."

"Then I'll play. What time do you start?"

"Eight o'clock sharp right here in the lobby. I'll let Mavis know she's got a partner."

An object whizzed past Abby's arm and struck the counter with a soft thud—the teddy bear. Jelinda shrieked and began jumping up and down, flailing her arms. "Yahggeeee!"

"What's the matter, honey?" Glen asked. "Give me a sign."

Jelinda's right hand fluttered up to her mouth, fingers coming together in a point that tapped her lips.

"She's either thirsty or hungry," Glen said, taking a key from a board on the wall and handing it to Abby. "I'm going to take her to the kitchen. If you'll fill out that card and leave it on the counter, you can make yourself at home. Your room is on the second floor at the end of the hall. Number eight. Mavis will be up shortly with your linens and such."

Abby's room turned out to be spacious and cozy, replete with a Victorian Golden Oak double bed, dresser, and chest of drawers plus a comfortable easy chair with a floral slipcover. A radiator quietly hissed beneath a window framed by gold brocade draperies.

She had just finished unpacking her clothes when there was a knock on the door and a tall woman, with the same deep-set brown eyes as Glen, entered the room carrying towels, washcloths, soap, and two rolls of toilet paper.

"I'm Mavis Gilbert," she announced, taking the items into the bathroom. "Hope my brother didn't have to twist your arm to be my bridge partner."

"Actually I'm glad for the chance to meet some of the islanders," Abby replied, a little surprised at how easily she had slipped into the persona required by her cover story. "It should help with my feature."

Returning from the bathroom, Mavis withdrew a piece of paper from her shirt pocket, unfolded it, and handed it to Abby. It was a map of the island, a copy of a hand-done effort, carefully drawn and full of detail. "I'm afraid us islanders are a dull bunch, especially in the winter."

"I've already got a lead on someone interesting—Joel Crothers. Not many people grow tomatoes this time of year. I don't see his greenhouse on this map."

"It's easy enough to find." Mavis went to the window and pointed toward an expanse of spruce trees in the middle distance. "Just past those evergreens the land slopes down to an open field. The greenhouse is in the middle. Normally you could walk there, but you'll be better off driving. We've had a lot of rain lately and the ground is soggy. Just follow Lake Street past the ferry dock and the coast guard station and then turn right at the first road you come to. It'll take you to Joel's trailer, which is a stone's throw from the greenhouse."

"I'll check it out after lunch. Does the inn serve meals?"

"We do. Our menu is limited to the staples, but I've been told the food itself is excellent. The dining room is just off the lobby in the north wing. Lunch is from 11:30 to 1:00. Any other questions before I leave you to your explorations?"

"Well, I am curious about Jelinda," Abby said. "Glen told me she's autistic. I did a feature on autistic kids in the Scarboro area, and I was amazed at how gifted some of them are."

"My daughter doesn't fall in the gifted category," Mavis said, an edge to her voice. "Actually she's at the opposite end of the spectrum."

"Well, she's sure a pretty girl," Abby said, deciding to drop the subject.

"Pretty doesn't count for much when your main activities are spinning objects and playing with your spittle. I'd trade her looks for a normal brain in a heartbeat."

"I wouldn't mind having one of those myself," Abby said. During the awkward silence that followed, she realized how ridiculous and inappropriate her comment was and sought some way to repair the damage. "Did you know there are autistic centers around the state?" she asked. "There's even one in Greenville."

"Jelinda spent two years in their program. They weren't even able to toilet train her. You're not thinking of using her in your feature, are you?"

"I hadn't even considered it."

"Don't." Mavis turned to leave. At the door she hesitated and then slowly turned back around. She took a deep breath, let it out, and took another. "You had a right to enquire, Abby," she said. "I'm sorry I snapped at you. Are you still interested in being my bridge partner tonight?"

"Sure…as long as you're not expecting a whole lot. I've forgotten most of the conventions. Blackwood and Stayman are my limit. I'm not even sure I remember Stayman."

"The old-fashioned Goren method is fine with me. I'll meet you in the lobby a few minutes before eight."

"Sounds good."

As Mavis was leaving the room, Abby noticed that the

woman wasn't wearing a wedding ring, and she wondered what had become of the husband. *One thing for sure*, she told herself; *it'll be a long time before I ask Mavis Gilbert any more personal questions.*

CHAPTER 10

The waitress had upper arms as big as thighs and a torso to match, but she walked easily about the dining room, her movements agile, even graceful for such a large woman. She had just brought Abby's lunch when two young men burst through the doorway, each holding an uncapped bottle of beer. The shorter one also carried the remainder of a six-pack, and with a start, Abby realized he was the same heavy-set young man who had been in Sheriff Mountcastle's office the previous day. He even had on the same sweatshirt. The other resembled a young, thin version of Steve Crothers, except for his hair, which was tied back in a ponytail. When he passed the waitress, he gave her a smack on the rump.

"What's the matter with you, Joel Crothers? You gone plumb loco?"

"We're celebrating, Juanita. This is a great day for tomato growers."

"Hector know you mommuck me, he cut you in strips and use you for shark bait. What you doin' with that beer? You know Mr. Turpin don't allow booze in here."

"Go tell him we're breaking his rules," Joel said and tilted the bottle to his mouth, draining its contents. "Tell him that's not all we're breaking either." He flung the empty bottle against the wall where it exploded in a shower of glass.

An elderly couple whose meals hadn't yet arrived got up and headed for the door. Abby's inclination was to do the same, but since the apparent perpetrator of this bizarre scene was her number one suspect, she decided to stay.

The waitress hurried after the old couple, apologizing for the disturbance. The young men sauntered over toward Abby. Joel blew her a kiss as he passed, and Terry grinned, showing no sign of recognition.

"Bring us a menu, Juanita," Joel called as they sat down at the corner table. "We don't have all day."

"Yeah," Terry said and banged his bottle on the table, spewing out some of its contents. "You don't keep tomato barons waitin'."

The only other person still in the room, a bald middle-aged man who had eaten most of his meal, got up and, after giving Joel and Terry a look of disgust, headed for the door. As he passed the cash register, he placed a ten-dollar bill on the counter.

"Hope my dad doesn't get wind of this," Terry said, barely loud enough for Abby to hear. "He'll kick my butt harder than Hector Creef's gonna kick yours."

"We can explain things if we have to," Joel told him in a low voice.

A moment later Glen Turpin, followed by the large waitress, entered the open doorway. After taking a quick look around, Glen went over to the young men.

"What's wrong with you boys, carrying on like this?" he asked, his voice showing more surprise than indignation.

"We're celebratin', Mr. Turpin," Terry said. "Pull up a chair and join us?"

"Alcohol isn't allowed in here and neither are people under its influence. You'll have to leave."

"Chill out, Glen," Joel said. "For your information, Terry and I just made a big business decision. We're putting up another greenhouse."

"Roight next to your property loine," Terry chimed in. "Earl's gonna dig up the area Monday and put in the drainage system. Someday that whole field's gonna be covered with greenhouses. We moight buy this inn of yours and make it our corporate headquarters."

"You're drunk, Terry. You're both drunk and I want you to leave."

"We're not going anywhere until we finish celebrating," Joel said. "Tell ham hocks over there to bring us a menu."

"Want me to call Steve?" the waitress asked. "He'll cool down these clabborheads."

"I'll call him. Just keep an eye on things. Anybody else comes in, just tell them we're closed until dinner."

Glen hurried from the room and the waitress stationed herself near the door. "You fellers oughta stick to weed. You don't handle beer so good." Noticing the ten-dollar bill on the counter, she picked it up and put it in the cash register.

"Pipe down, Juanita," Joel told her. "We don't need advice from you."

"That's roight," Terry added. "You don't show us some respect, we'll meet hubby at the dock this evenin' and rough him up a bit. Send him home ta big mama with tears in his eyes."

"You must be eatin' the stuff instead of smokin' it, Terry Pitts. You look cross-eyed at my man, he kick your asses so hard you'll have to take off your shirts to shit." She noticed Abby sitting at the nearby table. "Sorry, missy. All I can say is those two clowns better enjoy themselves while they can. Steve'll close down their act real soon."

A few minutes later Glen Turpin re-entered the dining room accompanied by Steve Crothers, who was wearing a police uniform similar to Mountcastle's. He had a holstered pistol strapped to his waist.

"Never thought I'd respond to a situation like this," he said as he approached the corner table. "Don't you guys have anything better to do?"

"Got plenty to do," Joel told him. "We're just taking a little time off to celebrate."

"We're expandin' our business," Terry added, holding his bottle aloft. "We're puttin' up a second greenhouse."

"Last I heard you didn't have enough market for the one you've got."

"You always have been out of touch," Joel said, his voice tinged with hostility. "We're getting more orders than we can fill. We got the location all picked out—the southeast corner of the field right next to Mr. Turpin's property line."

The look of amusement on Steve's face faded. "Don't you realize how swampy it can get down there?"

"Won't be a problem after Earl puts in the drainage system."

Steve shook his head in disbelief. "If you're going to build another greenhouse, why not put it next to the first one?"

"The closer to the hill, the more protected it is from the wind," Joel explained. "We should've started there and worked back. If things work out like we plan, we'll eventually have a line of greenhouses halfway across the field."

"Where the hell do you think the market will come from?"

"The mainland, of course. Not many grocery stores over there know about our tomatoes. But they will."

"Gonna be rich someday," Terry said. "Why don't you and Mr. Turpin sit down and we'll drink a toast."

"The celebration is over," Steve said. "You guys are leaving."

"Aw, come on, big guy," Terry pleaded. "Cut us tomato barons some slack."

"Now!"

Joel stood up and gave Steve a mock salute. "Better do as he says, Terry. We don't want big brother going ballistic."

"What a shame that'd be. Sorta like the Wright brothers gettin' gunned down 'fore their plane got off the ground."

Abby watched them collect their remaining beer bottles and head for the door. "Hasta luevesta," Terry said when he passed Juanita. "I wouldn't count on hubby gettin' home in one piece tonight."

"You full of it, Terry Pitts. Better hope my Hector don't get wind of your shenanigans."

"Want to file a complaint?" Steve asked Glen.

"No, I don't think so. They didn't do any damage other than break a bottle or two."

"Consider yourselves lucky," Steve called after the young men. "Next time you have an urge to celebrate, do it at the Salty Dawg—assuming you've got enough money left to afford a pitcher." He walked over to Abby's table. "Maybe I should've recommended the Sand Dollar after all."

Abby chuckled. "I thought nothing exciting ever happens on Nanticoke."

"What you just saw is probably the most excitement you'll encounter your entire stay on the island." Steve glanced at his watch. "Assuming those two don't cause any more trouble, I don't have anything pressing the next couple of hours. How about letting me show you around?"

Abby was tempted but decided her investigation should come first. "Thanks, but I'm hoping for an interview with the chief tomato baron. I'll give him a few minutes to sober up before going over to see if he's ready to meet the press."

"How about tonight then? I'm sure there are plenty sights you haven't seen and probably won't see unless I show 'em to you."

"Tonight I'm playing in the Inlet Inn bridge tournament," Abby said, sorry now that she had agreed to be Mavis's partner.

"Damn. I haven't struck out this much since I played high school baseball. I hope Joel is more cooperative with you than he's been with me lately. I'll check with you later to see how things went."

As she finished eating her lunch, Abby thought about the incident she had just witnessed. There had been something strange about Joel's and Terry's behavior, even beyond their apparent desire to hold a mid-day celebration. They hadn't seemed in an especially festive mood, particularly Joel. It was almost as though they had been seeking a confrontation with Glen or Steve or both, yet when the opportunity presented itself, neither had taken particular advantage of it.

"More coffee, missy?" the waitress asked after cleaning up the mess the young men had made.

"No thanks."

"Sorry 'bout the disturbance. Mr. Turpin say no charge for the meal."

"I enjoyed it in spite of the commotion. Just bring me the check as you normally would."

"No can do. Boss's orders."

"In that case, thanks. By the way, Juanita, how well do you know Joel and Terry?"

"I thought pretty good 'til now."

"They don't usually act like this?"

"Definitely not, missy. Them two fellers are a long way from bein' saints, but I never seen 'em this far off-shore."

CHAPTER 11

Between the Inlet Inn and the coast guard station, Abby encountered two vehicles, one of them a bicycle. Following Mavis's directions, she turned right at the first opportunity, a dirt road that narrowed to little more than a path as it wound through prickly ash and yaupon so thick she couldn't see more than a few feet to either side. After about a hundred yards, the vegetation thinned, replaced by live oaks and pines, which allowed greater visibility. Up ahead on the right, she saw a house trailer and, some fifty yards beyond in the middle of a rutted field, a polyethylene-covered greenhouse. She bumped her way across the field and parked next to an ancient black Chevy Monte Carlo with a rear bumper sticker that proclaimed, "I'm so horny even the crack of dawn looks good."

As she approached the greenhouse, she heard periodic buzzing noises that reminded her of an old-fashioned telephone's busy signal. She knocked on the plywood door, waited, and then knocked again, louder. The buzzing stopped and a moment later Terry Pitts opened the door.

"Is Joel here?" Abby asked, eying the cylindrical object in the young man's hand, which except for the metal prong at one end resembled a flashlight.

"Left a few minutes ago. Say, didn't I see you at the Inlet Inn?"

"I stayed for the entire performance. You seem to have sobered up fast."

"I—I weren't really drunk. What you wanna see Joel about?"

"That kiss he blew me. I was hoping it was his way of inviting me over for an interview." Abby introduced herself, giving her standard line about doing a feature on the island in winter. "Growing tomatoes in February seems like a novel idea. I'd like to learn more about the young entrepreneur and his tomato business."

Terry chuckled. "You're the second person this month wantin' to interview Joel. You'd think he was *Billy* Joel or somethin'."

"Somebody else interviewed him?" Abby asked, feigning ignorance.

"The guy's article made it sound like Joel's the only one doin' any work around here. As you can see, that's not exactly the case."

Abby nodded. "I tell it like I see it, Terry, and right now I see you're the one working. When do you expect Joel back?"

"Not 'til suppertoime. He went on a tomato run to Hatteras. I'll be glad to show you around."

"Well, I really wanted to talk to Joel, but—"

"I know as much about this business as him. You don't smoke, do you? Tobacco Mosaic can really mess up a crop. I couldn't let you in if you smoke—or chew."

"I don't do either."

"Then step right in and make yourself to home."

As she entered the greenhouse, Abby noticed a sudden rise in temperature and humidity. Five double rows of tomato plants ran the length of the house, taller than in the clipping Bostrum had sent the *Gazette*, almost shoulder high. Each plant had been pruned to a single stem and was supported by twine attached to its base and looped several times around the stem before being tied to an overhead wire.

The lower clusters contained mature fruit, some ripe enough to eat.

"Impressive," Abby said with genuine admiration.

"The greenhouse was Joel's idea, but like I said, I do at least as much work as he does." Terry held up the cylindrical object. "Ever see one of these gizmos?"

"What is it?"

"A pollinator." Terry touched the prong to an open flower cluster. There was a buzzing sound and the blossoms quivered, spilling a fine yellow powder. "Garden tomatoes get pollinated by the wind and bees, but it's all closed up in here so we gotta do it ourselves."

"Must take a long time."

"About an hour if I hustle. If I'm really pressed for toime, I just whack those wires every few feet with a stick, which shakes a lot of the pollen loose, especially on the upper clusters. That method works okay when the plants get big, but when they're small or even this soize, we need to pollinate by hand."

"Couldn't you introduce some bees and save yourself some work?"

Terry shook his head. "We need to use insecticoide to keep down the aphid and whitefly population, and that would kill off the bees."

For the next few minutes, Terry pointed out and explained various pieces of equipment, including a squirrel cage motor in the greenhouse peak that blew air between the two layers of polyethylene, separating them and causing a storm-window effect, which, according to him, cut their fuel oil bill by a third. Finally, he demonstrated the watering system, which consisted of collapsible, perforated polyethylene tubes running between each double row of plants.

"What's back there?" Abby asked, pointing to the Homasote partition at the far end of the troughs. It had a small door in the middle, which based on what she had seen from the outside, must lead to at least another twenty feet of greenhouse space.

"That's our storage area. You know, pots and fertilizer and such."

"Mind if I take a look?"

"It's locked and Joel has the key." Terry reached down and plucked a large ripe tomato from near the base of one of the plants. "For your eatin' pleasure," he said, handing it to Abby. "Remember who gave it to you. Last name is spelled P-I-T-T-S, just like it sounds."

"I'll make sure I spell it right. How well do you know Joel, Terry?"

"Pretty good, I guess. We been friends since we were kids."

"What's he like?"

The young man shrugged. "Smarter'n the average bear. He can be a bit of a loner, but he'll party with the best of 'em when he's in the mood. Most of the toime, though, he'd rather read a book than party. He even writes poetry."

"Really? Ever read any of his poems?"

"Naw. If it's not in the funnies or the *National Enquirer*, I generally don't mess with it."

"What else does Joel do besides raise tomatoes, read books, and write poetry?"

"He loikes to fish. He'll cast for hours down at Diamond Lake. Don't seem to matter if he catches anything or not."

"From the way he was throwing bottles around at the Inlet Inn, he seems like a bit of a hothead. Am I wrong about that?"

"He can get mad if somebody pushes him too far. But mostly he's a pretty laid-back dude."

"How can he be pushed too far?"

"You know, some jerk at the Salty Dawg gets in his face and gives him a hard toime—that kinda thing."

"Guess he wouldn't take any crap from a woman, would he?" Abby asked, hoping Terry wouldn't notice anything odd about her question.

"Are you kiddin'? He's a big pussycat with Beth. That's his girlfriend. They'll probably toie the knot after she finishes college. She wants to be a nurse."

"A tomato baron and a nurse, huh. That sounds like an interesting combination." *Now if I can just slip this next question past him, I might make some real progress.* "Have there been other women in Joel's life besides Beth?"

Terry gave her a puzzled look. "You sure you don't work for the *Inquirer*?"

Before Abby could respond, there was a low rumbling noise, which she thought might be thunder. Terry cocked his head as though listening, an anxious look on his face. The noise grew louder and he went to the door and opened it. "Oh, shit."

Abby followed him outside and saw a backhoe bouncing across the field. It stopped a few feet from her car, and a burly man with a scruffy beard switched off the motor and jumped to the ground.

"That pipe for the Crocker job ain't in yet, Terry. I figured I'd get started here."

"We don't want the work done yet, Earl. Didn't Joel tell you we wanted the job done Monday?"

"He didn't say I couldn't start earlier. I can see the plot's all laid out."

Looking flustered, Terry seemed to search for words. "We—we're just not ready yet," he said.

"If you're short on cash, that's not a problem. I won't bill you guys 'til the end of the month. And I'll give you a reasonable time after that to pay."

"It ain't the money. We need toime to—to decoide for sure where we wanna put the darn thing."

Hands on hips, the big man sighed and slowly shook his head. "Joel didn't sound undecided to me. I wouldn't have driven over here if it hadn't sounded like a done deal. You guys need to shit or get off the pot."

"I'm sorry, Earl."

"Tell Joel to let me know when he makes up his mind. This time he's gonna give me a deposit. If I drive back over here and the same thing happens, I'll keep the money and you can get somebody else to do the work."

"I'll tell him."

Earl climbed back onto the backhoe and started the motor, almost clipping Abby's rear bumper as he backed up. After a grinding of gears, the vehicle lurched forward and began bumping across the field.

"I gotta get back to work," Terry said, clearly upset. "Anything else you want to know, ask Joel."

"Will he be here tomorrow morning?"

"Probably. He usually starts work between seven and seven-thirty."

"I'll drop by early then. Thanks for the tour, Terry—and the tomato."

The young man nodded vaguely and withdrew into the greenhouse, closing the door behind him.

Abby considered walking to the far end of the building to see what was behind the Homasote. Not wanting to upset Terry any further, she decided against it. Knowing there wasn't enough room to pass the backhoe until it reached Lake Street, she waited another minute or so before getting in her car and starting the motor. As she drove across the field, she noticed someone in the front window of Joel's trailer, a young man staring in the direction of the receding backhoe. As soon as he saw her, he disappeared from view.

Although the person looked familiar, Abby was sure he wasn't Joel. It wasn't until she reached Lake Street and began maneuvering her car around the slow-moving backhoe that she realized the guy was Duane, the young deputy she had seen yesterday in Sheriff Mountcastle's office.

CHAPTER 12

"Over here, partner," a voice called.

More than thirty people had gathered in the lobby, most of them occupying the two rows of card tables that stretched from the registration desk to the front door. The voice belonged to Mavis Gilbert, who was waving from one of the middle tables where she sat with two older women. Abby threaded her way toward them.

"Abby Burlew, this is Jeannette and Estelle Dromgoole. Aside from being excellent bridge players, they own the best antique shop on the island. I told them about your project and they've been dying to meet you."

"Indeed we have," Jeannette, the younger of the sisters, said as Abby sat down. "How wonderful that you're doing a feature on us." A plump woman with fair skin and lustrous white hair, she looked to be in her early seventies. "There's so much rich history here that most people on the mainland aren't aware of. Our wild ponies, for instance. Have you heard about them?"

"I haven't," Abby replied, hoping her lack of knowledge about Nanticoke wouldn't compromise her credibility as a feature writer.

"It's still a mystery how they got here," Estelle said. More slender than her sister, she had neatly coiffed blue-gray hair. Both wore dresses in contrast to all the other women in the room, who had on jeans or slacks. "It's my belief they were put ashore by Sir Michael Broughton's ship the *Leopard* in the late 1500s."

"And I think they swam ashore from a Spanish shipwreck," Jeannette interjected. "But it's all conjecture. The only thing known for certain is they came from Spain, a fact proven by their number of ribs and vertebrae."

Estelle nodded her assent. "I'm sure you've heard of Graylock, the pirate who made Nanticoke his primary lair. He was killed just off our southern tip in 1720 by Lieutenant Thomas Oldham of the Royal Navy."

"Estelle, if you're going to deluge Abby with facts, you should at least make sure of their accuracy. Oldham killed Graylock in 1718."

Damn, Abby thought. I've been plunked down in the middle of a fucking *Walton's* episode with the recipe sisters.

"I stand corrected," the older sister replied with a good-natured smile. "There's also the *Chesapeake*, the American freighter sunk off our shores by German submarines in..." She glanced at her sister.

"In 1942," Jeannette said. "Before we provide Abby any more tidbits of island lore, we should find out how she plans to use them. We don't want her beating us to the presses with her own book about the island."

A look of concern crossed Estelle's face. "You're not that kind of writer, are you? You're not planning to do a book about us?"

Abby shook her head. "Just a feature. You're working on a book?"

Jeannette nodded. "Whether it'll ever be published—or even finished—remains to be seen. Antiques are our first love and they consume most of our time and energy."

"Attention everyone!" a male voice boomed.

Glancing around, Abby saw Glen Turpin standing near the front desk. The few people not already seated went to their tables and sat down.

"Before we start, I'd like to introduce a newcomer to our game. Abby Burlew will be my sister's partner tonight. She's doing a feature on the island for the *Scarboro Gazette*, so it's possible she'll be interviewing some of you in the next few days. I'm sure she'll be making mental notes tonight, so we'd better be on our best behavior."

"She's probably a ringer Mavis imported so she can finally win," someone suggested, and there was considerable laughter.

"Don't respond to that," Mavis said. "Let's keep 'em guessing."

"They won't have to for long. As a card shark I am barely more than a minnow."

There was more good-natured laughter followed by a few more announcements. Then play began.

It soon became evident Abby was right about her bridge-playing abilities.

She misplayed the first hand by not drawing trumps quickly enough, allowing her opponents a needless rough, and she botched the third hand by drawing them too quickly, thereby losing a trick she could have ruffed on the board.

Her defense wasn't much better. Against Jeannette's four-heart contract, Abby led away from her ace of spades, which eventually died in her hand.

The Dromgoole sisters, on the other hand, took advantage of mistakes and played almost flawlessly. At the end of each board, Jeannette suggested how they could have played or defended even more effectively, but she was as critical of herself as she was of her sister.

After the final hand's post mortems, the Dromgooles

invited Abby to visit their shop. "We have all kinds of glassware," Jeannette told her. "As far as cut glass goes, we have no peer on the Outer Banks."

"Our collection of art glass isn't too shabby either," Estelle added. "I'd say we're an oasis of quality in what's fast becoming a desert of...what word am I looking for, Sister?"

"Try *shit*," a beefy man with bushy eyebrows muttered at the adjacent table just loud enough for Abby to hear. "That's the word I'd use to describe all that antique junk."

"Herbert!" the middle-aged woman across the table scolded. "Watch your mouth."

"How about *crassness*?" Jeannette said, smiling at the man. "It's equally applicable to objects and people."

Glen called for the second round and Abby and Mavis moved to the next table. Their new opponents, two young fishermen named Scoggins and Jetmore, had tanned, leathery faces and hands that looked more suited to heavy lifting than sorting cards.

Although they were friendly enough, Abby could sense they took the game seriously. During one three no-trump contract, she brought relief to their faces by failing to unblock a suit Mavis had established.

After the hand, Abby apologized for her mistake.

"Don't give it a second thought," Mavis said. "For me bridge is a pleasant diversion. It doesn't matter in the least if I win or lose."

After that, Abby's game improved. At least she avoided making any more glaring errors. There was little time for conversation until after a round with two coast guard officers who excused themselves for a quick smoke outside.

"How'd the interview with Joel go?" Mavis asked.

"He wasn't there. Terry Pitts showed me around the

greenhouse. I'm going back in the morning to see if I can talk to Joel."

"I heard about the disturbance in the dining room. This isn't the first time I've had to wonder about Joel's character."

Abby's ears perked up. "From what I've heard, that wasn't typical behavior," she said, hoping Mavis would go into detail about Joel.

"A year ago I might have agreed. But not after the way he carried on with—" Mavis hesitated, as though not sure she wanted to continue. "—with that Tolbert girl."

"The student teacher who was murdered?" Abby asked, delighted for an opportunity to discuss Ronda's murder without having to broach the subject herself. "Was something going on between her and Joel?"

"The same thing that happens between rabbits in mating season."

"Oh?" Abby waited for Mavis to elaborate.

"I wouldn't have minded if they hadn't used her room for their frequent couplings. If you happened to be in the lobby at the time, you'd have to be deaf not to hear wild moaning and the squeaking of bedsprings. Finally, I told her no more visitors or she'd have to find a room some-where else."

"Did she end the relationship with Joel?"

"Hardly. Before she left the island, she made a point of telling me that fucking—her word, not mine—was a lot more enjoyable in his trailer than under the noses of old prudes like Glen and me."

Before Abby could ask more questions, Glen an-nounced the next round, and she and Mavis had to move.

The final few rounds proved uneventful. Mavis chat-ted amiably but didn't mention Joel again, and Abby found no opportunity to bring up the subject. At the last table, which was occupied by Glen and his partner Josephine

Devereaux, the principal of Nanticoke's elementary school, Mavis seemed to run out of conversation. Glen too appeared subdued.

The last four hands went quickly. Abby played one of them, making a three-spade contract that might have been defeated had Josephine's opening lead not been a trump, thereby allowing a free finesse of the spade queen. After the hands were over, Mavis thanked Abby for playing and got up from the table.

"I can't stay for the tally. Juanita is watching Jelinda and she's already put in a full day."

Glen too excused himself and began collecting the score sheets, taking them to the registration desk. Several players gathered around to watch the tabulations.

"Is it my imagination or are those two mad at each other?" Abby asked Josephine, a tall rawboned woman with a ready smile.

"Glen and Mavis? They did seem a bit preoccupied. What do you think of Nanticoke so far, Abby?"

"I love it. How long have you lived out here?"

"Almost a decade. I was looking for a change of scene, and I answered an advertisement for a teaching job. I figured I'd stay a year, two at most, but now you couldn't blow me out of here with a keg of dynamite."

"Wish I felt that way about my job."

"For me it's not the job so much as the island itself, though I do like my job."

"Is it a lot different from being a principal on the mainland?"

"Yes and no. Nanticoke isn't exactly what you'd call the real world, though it's real enough for those of us who live out here. But when our kids get bussed to Buxton for middle school or leave the island for whatever reason, they're headed for the real world. I try to make sure they've mastered the fundamentals and are ready."

"How many teachers have you got?" Abby asked, feeling a twinge of guilt that she was laying groundwork for bringing up the subject of Rhonda Tolbert.

"Six—one for each grade."

"I remember reading about an East Carolina student who did her practice teaching here. Wasn't she murdered?"

"Yes. That came as quite a shock."

"Any idea who might've killed her?"

"Not the slightest. I hope you don't plan to mention Rhonda in your feature. I really don't think her murder had anything to do with Nanticoke. If you're looking for somebody interesting to write about, you might consider that man over there." Josephine nodded toward the registration desk. "Glen seems so unassuming and self-effacing, but there's a lot more to him than meets the eye. Bet you didn't know he's a life master bridge player."

"I had no idea. What's he doing playing with the likes of us?"

"Oh, he's not remotely interested in winning our little tournament. He just wants everyone to have a good time. He'll satisfy his competitive urges this weekend at the Eastern Regionals in Raleigh."

"Will you be his partner there?" Abby asked, trying to think of a way to return their conversation to Rhonda Tolbert without being conspicuously obvious.

"Heavens no. If the game of bridge were a ladder, Glen would be standing on the top rung and I'd still have one foot on the ground. He'll find a partner in Raleigh. Apparently the larger tournaments attract a certain number of good players who come by themselves."

Josephine went on to tell Abby that Glen had once been a teacher himself, at a girls' preparatory school in Virginia. "I never quite understood why he gave up teaching, but then I quit trying to figure him out years ago. Looks like he's finished with the scores."

"Quiet, please," Glen said as he stepped out from behind the registration desk. Gradually the room fell silent.

"Tonight our second place winners are...Randy Jetmore and Alan Scoggins."

A cheer broke out and the two fishermen gave each other high fives.

"It's the first time they've placed," Josephine said, applauding. "Mavis got them started last year when she taught a class for beginners."

"Now for tonight's first place pair," Glen said when the applause subsided. "It's none other than...Estelle and Jeannette Dromgoole."

There was a mixed response, a few groans interspersed with light clapping. The sisters were all smiles as they waved.

"Hoity and Toity win again," Herbert said. "I'm surprised they aren't blowing kisses to the crowd."

"They're good sports when they lose," his partner replied. "Try being one yourself for a change."

People began leaving, many of them stopping to wish Abby good luck with her feature. After collecting the boards and storing them behind the front desk, Glen rejoined her and Josephine.

"You and Mavis were right in the middle," he told Abby. "Not bad for never having played together. By the way, Steve Crothers would like a word with you. He said he hopes he doesn't have to cart you off to jail."

"Jail?" Abby said. She turned and saw the deputy standing near the registration desk. "What the hell for?"

The corners of Glen's mouth lifted in a wry smile. "Refusing to cooperate with a law officer."

CHAPTER 13

I'm getting ready to make my rounds," Steve said. "Figured I'd give you one last chance to see Nanticoke the right way—with me as your guide."

"It's a little late for sightseeing, isn't it?" Abby replied, deciding to put up a token resistance.

"I thought you city gals had stamina."

"We do but most of us require something you islanders apparently don't need much of—you know, sleep."

Steve glanced at his watch. "I'll have you back by eleven and I guarantee you'll see at least one sight worth putting in your feature."

"Fair enough. I'll get my coat."

The air was crisp and frost had formed on the grass, making crunching noises underfoot. Unobstructed by clouds, the moon cast a soft luminescence over the village.

"I can drive if you'd rather not walk," Steve told her. "The tour is about a mile and a half round trip."

"Let's walk," Abby said, deciding not to pass up an opportunity to burn off a few calories, even though she knew exercise this close to bedtime wasn't conducive to sleep, and a good night's sleep was especially important to someone with bipolar disorder.

"Good. There's something really nice about a moonlit walk on a clear cold night. How'd the interview with Joel go?"

"I had to settle for Terry Pitts. Joel was off delivering tomatoes."

After passing a few houses, they came to a cluster of shops. Steve tried each door, shining his flashlight inside, making sure nothing looked disturbed. At one called "Vanishing Americana," Abby asked him to wait while she examined the merchandise in the window.

"The Dromgooles were right," she said. "They've got some really nice glassware."

"Did they give you a history lesson or the lecture on how antiques help keep society from going to the dogs?"

"I got the history lesson."

"Those two don't live in the same century we do. But they do add character to the island."

"They don't sound like islanders, at least not what I thought most islanders would sound like."

"It's hoi toide on the seund soide?" Steve said.

"Yeah. As far as I could tell, the Dromgooles could just as easily live on the mainland. So could you for that matter."

"The Nanticoke brogue has all but died out," Steve told her. "Only some old timers and a few diehards talk that way anymore."

"Juanita does."

"Her folks have lived here for two hundred years. So have her husband's. Those two families seem to feed off each other's dialects."

"Terry talks a little that way too."

"Terry is something of a good ole boy. I think he considers the brogue a kind of status symbol." Steve shined his light across the street. "See that grocery store over there? My parents owed it back in the day. I spent many an afternoon bagging for customers and putting up stock."

"Do your parents still live here?"

"Dad died quite a few years ago. Mom lives in Florida now with her sister. She stayed on the island just long enough to make sure Joel got all the college he wanted, which was two years at East Carolina."

"Why didn't he keep going?"

"Officially he got tired of the academic life. Unofficially I think he was homesick. Nanticoke is in his blood just like it's in mine."

"Have you ever lived anywhere else?"

"When I was in the army. Those three years let me know just how special Nanticoke is. I like having the ocean all around me—its beauty and power and its subtle and not-so-subtle changes. And I especially like the fact that it insulates us from negative stuff like pollution and jammed-up freeways and crime. Of course, we're limited as far as shopping goes, and our night life leaves something to be desired. But you can take a walk like this and not have to worry about being mugged, even if you aren't accompanied by a cop."

"Sounds like your job is a piece of cake."

"In the winter, it pretty much is. It gets tougher during the tourist season, but we normally don't have a lot of problems, even then."

The only downtown establishment still open was a small bar with "Graylock's Lair" printed on the sign over the door. The sound of The Eagles singing "Lyin' Eyes" drifted into the street.

"How about a beer?" Steve asked.

"No, thanks. I thought you were on duty."

"Things are a little more flexible out here. That's another reason I like living here. Earl and I don't have to do everything by the book."

"Earl?"

"My assistant."

"A big bearded guy with a backhoe?"

"That's him."

"I saw him at Joel's greenhouse. He wasn't too happy when Terry wouldn't let him do any digging."

"I thought Earl wasn't starting that job until Monday."

"That's what Terry told him. Apparently Joel didn't make it clear he couldn't start earlier."

Steve shook his head. "I swear they barely got enough market for the tomatoes they raise now. But you can't tell Joel anything. At least I can't. If I told him fire burns, he'd find a reason to disagree."

After a while, they came to a small brick building with two windows, one containing vertical bars.

"That's my office," Steve said. "As you can see, it's also the jail."

"It's so tiny. What would you do if you had to arrest more than one or two people?"

"The coast guard has a holding facility I can use. I've only needed it once—when a motorcycle gang got too rowdy."

The business district ended and so did the sidewalk. The street, unpaved now and covered with sand, curved uphill and to the right, toward the ocean. The first house they came to had a series of downspouts that ran from its eaves to a rectangular brick formation in the side yard. Behind the house stood an outbuilding that looked too large for a shed and too small for a garage.

"What are those brick structures?" Abby asked.

"The one out back is a detached kitchen. A lot of the older homes have them, especially those built in the early 1800s. That little building next to the house is a cistern. I've got one attached to my house. We can't sink wells very deep out here or they get contaminated with salt water. The more rainwater we use, the less strain on our wells."

The street narrowed and eventually a wooded area rose up on their right, blocking the moon, throwing much of the surrounding area into shadow.

"Keep an eye out for Graylock," Steve warned. "His ghost has been known to prowl this part of town. The guy never did have much respect for the law. I understand he liked feature writers even less."

"Well, if you can't handle him, I'll whip out my pad and pen and threaten to interview him."

Presently they came to a small park-like area with a British flag at the entrance. At the far end, bathed in moonlight, stood four stone slabs.

"Did the Dromgooles tell you about this place?" Steve asked.

"No. What is it?"

"The British cemetery. The men buried here were part of an antisubmarine fleet England loaned us during World War II. Their boat got torpedoed near Cape Hatteras and their bodies washed ashore. Our navy buried them here." Steve opened the wrought-iron gate and led Abby past a gnarled oak tree toward the headstones.

"It's beautiful," she said. "Somebody takes good care of it."

"The coast guard does the maintenance. You'd be surprised at the number of visitors to these graves, locals and tourists. Folks really appreciate what these men did." Steve touched Abby's arm. "There's something over here I'd like to show you."

She followed him past the headstones to a tall hedge then through a narrow gap in the foliage. The ground dropped off sharply to the water below, which shimmered in the moonlight like countless shards of broken glass.

"That's why it's called Diamond Lake," Steve said.

The objects Abby saw—boats tied here and there along the shoreline, the ferry docked at its slip, even the lake itself—appeared exquisite in their clarity and symmetry. "It's like stepping into a painting," she said.

"Two things need to happen before this scene really comes alive. The moon has to be full and pretty much where it is now, about three quarters up in the sky. And you've got to be standing right here. You can't get the same effect from anywhere else on the island. See those boats near the marina where the lake starts curving back toward the ferry?"

"I do."

"One of them is mine. You can't tell which from here, but it's white with red trim and has *Jesse II* written on the stern. Originally, it belonged to my grandfather, who named it for my grandmother Jessica. Dad inherited it and left it to me. I've made a few improvements so it's still a darn good boat. I'd like to take you out on her sometime, Abby. Are you interested?"

"Maybe."

"How about tomorrow night? There's a restaurant at the north end of the island that's got really good seafood. We'll use the *Jesse II* for transportation."

"Sounds like fun."

"Can you be ready by four-thirty? We leave any later, it'll be too dark to take advantage of the scenery."

"I'll be ready." Abby glanced at her watch. "Speaking of time, you've got exactly fourteen minutes to get me back to the Inlet Inn."

"What if we don't make it?"

"Guess I'll have to file a complaint with the local police. Word has it they enforce the law with an iron fist."

"That's true," Steve said. "But the chief deputy went off duty at ten-thirty, and his assistant is probably snoring his head off right now and won't hear the phone."

⌒⌒⌒

When Abby got back to the Inlet Inn, the card tables had been put up and the lobby was back to normal. Glen Turpin was seated behind the front desk. As soon as Abby closed the front door, he got up and hurried toward her.

"I understand you were asking about Rhonda Tolbert," he said in a low voice.

"So?"

"Jo said your interest seemed more than casual. Why exactly are you here, Abby? Are you really doing a feature on Nanticoke?"

Although her initial reaction was to stick to her cover story, she wondered if it might be to her advantage to confide in Glen. There was an aura of trustworthiness about him, and she could definitely use a knowledgeable confidant to help with her investigation.

"Why is it so important to you what I'm doing?" she asked, still not sure whether to take the man into her confidence.

"I'd like to see Rhonda's killer brought to justice. Is that why you're here, Abby—to investigate her murder?"

Hoping she wasn't making a mistake, she decided to act on her hunch. "Actually I'm here to find out what happened to Sheila Bostrum. I have reason to believe there's a connection between her disappearance and Rhonda Tolbert's murder."

Glen started to speak, stopped, started again, then took Abby by the arm and led her to a sofa in the corner of the room nearest the front door. "Have a seat," he said. "and tell me about this. But keep your voice down. Mavis has a heart condition and I don't want her hearing a word of what we're saying."

CHAPTER 14

Abby tossed and turned during much of the night, and when her alarm clock went off at six forty-five the next morning, she felt so groggy she was tempted to reset it. Not wanting to risk missing Joel again, she dragged herself out of bed and into the bathroom. Five minutes in the shower did little to revive her, and she considered forgoing her morning dose of lithium since the stuff would probably make her even more sluggish.

She took it anyway, deferring to Doreen Milsap's admonition that "a barge with a rudder functions a lot better than a yacht without one."

Once dressed, she headed for the dining room for a much-needed cup of coffee. Although Dorene had suggested she give up caffeine, Abby had drawn the line at coffee, feeling she needed at least one cup every morning to jump start her brain, which today felt like a set of rusted gears clogged with sand.

It was almost seven-thirty when she parked next to a Ford pickup truck that looked only slightly younger than Terry's decrepit Monte Carlo. She knocked on the plywood door of the greenhouse, waited a moment, and knocked again. Finally, the door opened and Joel Crothers appeared, wearing a respirator and carrying a spray tank on his back.

Still feeling more groggy than usual, Abby introduced herself and began explaining that she worked for the *Gazette* and was writing a feature on the island.

"I know why you're here," Joel said, pulling down the respirator. "You'll have to wait. I've got two more rows of tomatoes to spray." The door closed behind him.

Muttering a series of expletives, Abby decided to take a closer look at the proposed site for the new greenhouse. Something about its location hadn't seemed quite right yesterday, and as she approached the staked area she remembered what it was: the entire plot had been in the shade.

Right now, the area was in the sun, though not by much. Abby glanced at the sky, estimated the sun's path for the next few hours, and then examined the nearby trees and the contour of the land. Just beyond the crest of the hill, she saw the top of what looked like a large house—or inn.

Turning her attention back to the staked area, she noticed that one part of it looked different from the rest, as though someone had dug there recently and then smoothed out the dirt. She had just started over for a closer look when she heard the greenhouse door swing open. Seeing Joel, minus the respirator and spray tank, emerge, she headed in his direction.

"We can talk out here," Joel told her, zipping up his jeans jacket. "The air in the greenhouse won't be fit to breathe for a while."

"What about your trailer?" Abby asked, curious if Duane was still there. "It's kind of nippy out here."

"It's either here or in my truck, Abby. I've got work to do."

"Here's fine," she said, pulling her coat up around her neck.

"So what's on your mind?"

"You. Feature stories generally focus on one person and…well, I think you might make a good centerpiece for mine."

Joel chuckled. "I don't believe you're writing a feature, Abby. Terry said you were more interested in my love life than anything else. What exactly do you want from me?"

Caught off guard by the young man's directness, Abby didn't know what to say. At least Joel's tone hadn't been abrasive or antagonistic. There was none of the hostility she had sensed during his encounter with Steve at the Inlet Inn.

"You think I killed somebody?"

She started to feign ignorance, but the knowing look on Joel's face told her that would be a waste of time. "A few days ago Lloyd Bostrum sent the *Gazette* a letter asking us to investigate his daughter's disappearance," she said, wishing she had drunk a second cup of coffee. "I'm here to check into that."

"I'm surprised he didn't accuse me of killing Rhonda Tolbert too."

"Actually, he did. I'm investigating that too."

"Well, you can investigate all you want. I didn't kill anybody."

Focus, Abby told herself. Her brain seemed like an old mule she was trying to urge forward. "You did have an affair with Rhonda Tolbert, though. Didn't you?"

"I'd call it more of a fling. She was looking to spice up her life before settling into the routine of middle class suburbia. I was looking for…well, I guess that's obvious. After a while we realized we didn't even like each other very much."

Abby pushed a lock of hair back behind her ear and shifted weight from one foot to the other, waiting for her brain to catch up. "You must've liked something about Rhonda."

"I did—her body. We slept together a few times and that was it. I was glad when she left the island. If we'd kept it up much longer, somebody I do care about might've found out."

Abby tried to dredge up the name of Joel's girlfriend from Hatteras. "Beth...Parker?" she finally said.

"Harker."

"Are you sure she didn't find out?"

"I'm positive. Beth's no murderer, if that's what you're getting at."

The edge in Joel's voice let Abby know she had struck a nerve. She wondered if it would be better to pursue the Beth Harker angle now or wait until she covered other ground. "Tell me about Sheila Bostrum," she said, deciding to wait. "What kind of relationship did you have with her?"

"We worked at the same restaurant. She was a waitress and I was a waiter. That's about it."

"You went out together, though, didn't you?"

"A couple of times. I took her to a movie and we played some miniature golf."

The difference between the deliberate way Abby posed her questions and the rapidity with which Joel responded to them reminded her of the story of the hare and the tortoise—the hare on speed and the tortoise on lithium. She doubted a second cup of coffee would have helped. "What about...the uh...fishing trip?"

"There were four of us—Sheila and me and another waitress and a busboy named Doug. My brother took us out in his boat."

"And?"

"We spent the afternoon fishing and then had a cookout on the beach."

Slowly Abby nodded. "What about after the cookout?"

"We spent the night here on the island. The next morning we caught the ferry back to the mainland. And no, there wasn't any hanky panky. Doug and I stayed at my mother's house. The girls stayed at the Inlet Inn."

So far Joel's answers, though coming faster than she would have liked, seemed straightforward enough. He didn't seem overly concerned about her questions. "Did Sheila go out with anybody besides you that summer?"

"I never saw her with anyone. But I did get the impression she was seeing somebody. As the summer wore on, she got more and more on edge. Certain things she said made me think she'd fallen for some guy and he was giving her a hard time."

"Yeah? What kind of things did she say?"

"I don't recall anything in particular. It just seemed to me she was having boyfriend problems."

"It seemed that way to her father too," Abby said after only a brief pause, thinking maybe her mule of a brain had actually started inching forward. "And he's convinced you were that boyfriend."

"He couldn't be more wrong. Sheila wasn't interested in me, other than as somebody to pal around with when she didn't have anything better to do."

Keep up the pressure, Abby told herself. Don't let him off the hook. "That bothered you, didn't it—the fact that Sheila didn't have the same feelings for you that you did for her?"

The calm way Joel shook his head told her there was no hook as far as he was concerned. "You're missing the point, Abby. I had a life of my own that summer. I had a job that kept me busy and friends I hung out with and I spent a lot of time fishing. I had a girlfriend—Beth Harker, not Sheila Bostrum. And you may find this hard to believe, but I actually like to read in my spare time. I didn't sit around pining for Sheila or waiting for her to give me a morsel of attention. That's just not the way it was. She was a looker but she was also self-centered and shallow."

"So are you saying you actually disliked her?"

"I'm just saying I didn't see her as girlfriend material. She didn't have a thought in her head that didn't revolve around clothes, makeup, shopping, or guys. And she was one of those girls who knew she was pretty and expected everyone to kowtow to her because of it. This was just my private observation. It didn't bother me because Sheila and I weren't close enough for it to matter. We got along fine as co-workers and casual friends."

Abby imagined herself as a juror listening to Joel's testimony during his trial for the murders of Sheila Bostrum and Rhonda Tolbert. If he is guilty, she reflected, he's a smooth talking son of a bitch. Giddyup mule, she said to herself, deciding it was time to push a little harder. "How long have you known Beth Harker, Joel?"

"Since middle school. We started going together when we were in the eleventh grade."

"Were you still going together the summer you worked at Captain Jack's?"

"Yeah. But it was hard to get together with Beth living in Hatteras and me working in Bogue City."

"Did she know you were going out with Sheila?"

"I doubt it. There was no reason for me to mention it. It wasn't like I was being unfaithful."

"Maybe she found out anyway and considered Sheila a threat. And if she did find out, it seems to me she had reason to want Sheila Bostrum *and* Rhonda Tolbert out of the way."

"That's bullshit. Look, I don't have a clue who killed

those girls. I know Beth didn't and I know I didn't. There's really nothing else I can tell you." Joel turned toward the greenhouse.

"Please don't go yet," Abby said, sorry now she hadn't waited longer to focus on Beth. "There's something else I need to ask you. It's about greenhouse tomatoes."

"Make it fast. I've got things to do."

"They require a lot of sun, don't they?"

"Yeah. The more the better."

"Then why put a greenhouse up next to those woods?" She pointed toward the four stakes. "In another few hours that area will be completely shaded."

Joel looked flustered. "If lack of sun is a problem, we'll cut back some of those trees."

"That land belongs to Glen Turpin, doesn't it?"

"We'll get his permission before we do the cutting. Are you done?"

"Not quite. Do you know a guy named Duane?"

"No."

The denial, Abby thought, came too quickly, faster even than Joel's normal responses. "Yesterday afternoon I noticed a guy standing at the front window of your trailer. He's the same person I saw the day before yesterday at the sheriff's office talking to Terry. His name is Duane and he's one of Mountcastle's deputies."

"So? Guys come here all the time to see Terry and me. Whoever you saw probably asked Terry if he could use the bathroom. From a distance he must've looked like that deputy you saw." Joel took two steps toward the green-house and then stopped. "I hope you're not going to talk to Beth about any of this," he said in a subdued voice.

"It all depends on what else I find out—and when."

"She won't tell you anything you don't already know. If she finds out about Rhonda, we could be history."

"Maybe you should have thought about that before

you had your fling," Abby said, expecting an angry retort but not getting one.

"You're right. Unfortunately, there's nothing I can do about that now. You realize Beth doesn't live around here anymore."

Abby nodded. "She's a student at Chowan College."

"Murphreesboro is a long way to drive just to talk to somebody who won't be able to tell you anything you don't already know. You probably wouldn't be able to find Beth anyway."

Abby resisted the impulse to tell him that she knew the campus like the back of her hand. "I'm sure someone at the college will help me locate her."

Joel gazed into the distance, looking troubled. "If you absolutely have to talk to Beth, will you at least wait until Sunday?" he said, giving Abby a plaintive look. "If she's going to find out about Rhonda, I'd like it to be from me. I have a date with Beth Saturday. If I can dredge up the nerve, I'll tell her then myself. At least give me that much time. Please."

Abby knew what the sensible response to Joel's request should be, but she couldn't bring herself to make it. "All right," she finally replied, against her better judgment. "I'll wait until Sunday."

CHAPTER 15

Back in the Inlet Inn's dining room, Abby mulled over her interview with Joel as she ate a modest—by her standards—breakfast of one egg and two pieces of toast. No sense piling on the calories when, in all likelihood, she wouldn't be able to do nearly her normal amount of jogging while on the island. She wished she hadn't told Joel she would wait until Sunday to contact Beth Harker. That had been stupid. She wondered how she could have seriously thought herself capable of investigating one murder, let alone two. She had no idea what Sheriff Mountcastle, Terry Pitts, and the deputy named Duane were involved in—or even whether their plan, scheme, or whatever it was, had any connection whatsoever with Joel's and Terry's weird behavior yesterday at the Inlet Inn. What was the point of that little performance anyway, assuming it was a performance? Who was the intended audience? Glen? Steve? Herself? And more importantly, were these bizarre incidents in any way connected with Sheila Bostrum or Rhonda Tolbert? The more she wrestled with these questions the more ridiculous her current status as an investigative reporter seemed.

"Good morning, Abby."

Looking up, she saw Glen Turpin approaching her

table. "Hi," she said, not especially glad to see the man after the bizarre way he had acted the previous night.

Glen glanced around the nearly empty dining room, as though making sure no one was in hearing distance. "After we talked last night, I kept thinking I'd seen the name Sheila Bostrum somewhere. This morning something told me to check the inn's register, and there it was. Sheila stayed here the summer she disappeared."

"I know."

"You do?"

"She and Joel and two other workers at Captain Jack's came over for some deep-sea fishing. Sheila and the other girl spent the night here."

"Did you know that's not the only time Sheila stayed here?"

It was Abby's turn to be surprised. "I had no idea there was another time."

"Actually there were two other times. Come to the lobby when you finish eating and I'll show you."

"I'm finished now," Abby said, pushing back her chair. She left enough money on the table to cover the cost of the meal and a tip and then followed Glen to the lobby. A large hardcover book rested on the registration desk counter.

"This is our register from five years ago," he said, opening it to a page marked by a slip of paper. "These people stayed here on June twenty-fourth." He pointed to an entry near the bottom of the page. "There's Sheila's signature. No mistaking the name, is there?"

"Or Angie Dake's below it," Abby said. "What other days did Sheila stay here?"

Glen turned a few pages and again pointed to Sheila's signature. "July first," he said. "Apparently she was by herself this time." He turned more pages. "July sixteenth. Again she was by herself. What do you make of it, Abby?"

"Joel told me about the first visit, but he didn't mention any others. I'll ask him about it—and Angie Dake as well."

"You know her?"

"She works at a beauty shop in Buxton with a quirky name. I've got it written down somewhere."

Glen put the register back under the counter and pulled out an Outer Banks telephone directory. He opened it to the yellow pages.

"Ah, here it is—Mane Street Salon. It shouldn't be hard to find. We can take my car."

"What about your bridge tournament?"

"I can always take a later ferry. Right now I'm more interested in finding out what happened to Sheila than getting an early start for Raleigh."

"I'm meeting Steve at four-thirty," Abby told him. "We're going out to dinner."

"You'll be back in plenty of time. The Hatteras ferry runs every half hour and Buxton isn't far from Hatteras."

Abby weighed the pros and cons of having Glen accompany her. "I appreciate your wanting to help," she said. "But I need to do this myself."

"I won't get in your way. I won't even get out of the car if you don't want me to."

Abby shook her head. "I'm sorry."

Clearly disappointed, Glen closed the phone book and slid it back under the counter. "I've got a favor to ask unrelated to Angie Dake," he said. "I know this will sound strange, Abby, but—"

A door closed nearby and footsteps sounded in the hallway.

"That's Mavis," Glen said in a low voice. "I told you about her heart condition. It would upset her to know a murder investigation is going on and the victims were guests here. Remember—not a word about any of this."

Abby nodded her assent. "You were about to ask a favor?"

"It can wait," Glen whispered. In his normal voice, he asked where Abby and Steve were going for dinner.

"A restaurant at the north end of the island. I don't remember the name."

"Sawyer's Crab," Glen said as Mavis entered the lobby. "Delicious seafood. Whatever you order, you can't go wrong."

"I could use some help, Glen," Mavis said as she approached the counter. "Jelinda's bath water took a long time to drain out. Before you leave for Raleigh, will you make sure the tub isn't plugged up?"

"I'll do it now," Glen said. "Abby was just telling me she and Steve are having dinner at Sawyer's Crab tonight. Keep an eye out for the wild ponies, Abby. Make sure Steve shows you their pen."

Abby said she would and wished Glen good luck at the bridge tournament. After he left the lobby, Mavis asked how the feature was coming.

"Too early to tell. I'm starting to get a feel for the island, though. At least I think I am."

"Anything I can do to help, just ask." Mavis turned to leave but before reaching the door, she stopped. "I know you didn't ask for any advice, Abby, but I'm going to offer some anyway. For whatever it's worth, Steve Crothers would make a lousy husband."

Abby was taken aback. "What makes you think I'm looking for a husband?"

"I didn't say you were. I'd just hate to see you taken in by his charming ways and regret it later. Steve is a heartbreaker. More than one woman around here has found that out the hard way."

"I'll keep that in mind," Abby said. She turned and headed for her room.

After putting on her jogging shoes, she went outside. Still annoyed by Mavis's gratuitous advice, she walked around to the back of the inn, intent on finding a direct route to the greenhouse. Before questioning Angie Dake, she wanted to confront Joel with the fact that Sheila Bostrum had spent additional nights on the island.

The backyard sloped gently past a swing set and a sandbox to the tree line then dropped off sharply. Noticing a path near the sandbox, Abby followed it down the hill, almost losing her footing a few times on wet, slippery leaves. Halfway to the bottom, she could see the field. A few steps farther, she caught a glimpse of the greenhouse through a tangle of pine tree branches.

At the bottom of the hill, she had to cross a swampy area where her shoes made sucking noises and accumulated a layer of mud almost up to the laces. Regretting her decision to walk, she didn't notice that Joel's truck was gone, replaced by Terry's car, until she was on dry ground. Disappointed, she went over to the proposed site for the new greenhouse and took a closer look. Digging had definitely taken place there. Somebody had gone to the trouble of smoothing it out, making the ground appear almost undisturbed. The staked area was half in the shadows.

When she had seen enough, she headed for the greenhouse, stepping into sunshine as she walked, feeling its warmth on her neck. Almost as soon as she knocked, Terry opened the door.

"Oh, it's you again," he said, showing none of the friendliness he had exhibited a day earlier. "Whadaya want?"

"I need to talk to Joel."

"He said he told you all he knows 'bout those girls."

"There's something he didn't tell me."

"Well, he ain't here. Now if you don't moind, I got work to do."

Abby decided there was no longer any reason to keep up her cover-story charade. "What were you doing at the sheriff's office day before yesterday, Terry?"

The young man looked startled but quickly regained his composure. "Deliverin' tomatoes," he said. "We take a box to Mr. Mountcastle whenever we go to Bogue City. He's one of our better customers."

"You weren't delivering tomatoes when I saw you. You were talking to Mountcastle about an undercover operation involving you and a deputy named Duane. Yesterday after you showed me the greenhouse, I saw Duane looking out a window in Joel's trailer. What's going on, Terry? What the hell are you guys up to?"

"Oh, I'm 'bout five noine. Joel's a couple inches taller."

"That's not funny."

"It's definitely not as funny as you sayin' you saw me talkin' to Sheriff Mountcastle about an undercover operation or seein' one of his deputies in Joel's trailer. The guy you saw is a buddy of moine. I gave him the key so he could use the head."

"The person I saw was Duane, one of Mountcastle's deputies."

Terry shrugged. "Then I'd say you got yourself a problem. Maybe you been smokin' too much dope or maybe you need glasses. A hearin' aid wouldn't hurt either. Now if you'll excuse me, I gotta get back to work."

"Where can I find Joel?"

"Joel who?" Terry said and closed the door.

Abby tugged at the handle but the door wouldn't budge. When there was no response to her flurry of knocks, she considered going over to the trailer and pounding on its door to see if Duane would appear. Deciding that wasn't a good idea, she walked to the rear of the greenhouse and took a look around. She couldn't see well enough through the double layers of polyethylene to tell what was inside. The rear wall was constructed of Homasote just like the partition.

Walking back across the field, she found some relatively dry ground where she didn't have as much problem with mud. When she neared the top of the hill, she heard what sounded like Jelinda's voice, and, as the trees thinned, she saw the girl playing in the sandbox. Juanita was standing guard nearby.

"Mornin', missy. Out for your daily constitutional?"

"Something like that."

"From the looks, you better take hip boots next toime. Awful wet down there."

"Yeeeee," Jelinda said, picking up a handful of sand. An intense, almost rapturous look on her face, she watched the grains sift through her fingers. "Yeeeee…"

"Only place she rather be is the beach," Juanita said. "I take her there sometoime but you hafta watch her like a hawk. She love the water and can't swim a lick."

Abby squatted down. "Hello, Jelinda." She started digging in the sand, doing the same thing with her hands that the girl was doing. Without looking up, Jelinda pushed her away, knocking her off balance.

"She's strong."

"Like a young ox. That's why Miss Mavis give me the job of watchin' her. I can stop her if she decoide to run off or get some other offshore notion. Jelinda not a bad girl, just in her own little world."

Abby stood up. "Does she talk?"

"Nary a word. She not even toilet trained, missy. Wears special diapers Miss Mavis buy on the mainland."

The image of the disgraced astronaut flashed through Abby's mind, almost threw her off track. "How much does she understand?"

"Hard to tell. Sometoime she don't seem to know

sickum. But if you around her long, you realize she know a lot more'n she let on. It all a matter of what interest her. This morning, for instance, when Miss Mavis wanted to give her a bath, she didn't call Jelinda's name when the tub was ready because the girl wouldn't paid a bit of attention. She just said the word *bath* and Jelinda was right there in no toime. That girl love the feel of water. But you let Miss Mavis or anybody else call her or tell her to do somethin', it's like tellin' that lighthouse over yonder to grow feet and walk 'cross town. Many the toime me or Miss Mavis hafta pick her up and carry her 'cause she refuse to budge."

"She's such a big girl. I'm surprised Mavis could do that."

"That woman's strong as I am."

"Even so, I wouldn't think a person with a heart condition should be doing heavy lifting."

Juanita looked puzzled. "What you talkin' 'bout, missy? Mavis Gilbert ain't got no heart condition. Where you get that idea?"

"From Glen. He told me not once but twice."

"Well, if he say she got one, I reckon she must. Sure had me fooled. Here I been workin' for her all these years and I thought she fit as a fiddle. You sure you hear Mr. Glen right?"

"I hear just fine, Juanita. And I haven't been smoking dope either. Speaking of which, how long have Joel and Terry been growing marijuana in their greenhouse?"

"Say what?"

"Yesterday when they were raising hell in the dining room, you as much as said they were growing weed."

"I did no such thing, missy."

Feeling a knot of dread in her stomach, Abby wondered if she was starting to lose it again. Was she imagining things? Distorting reality? "I heard you, Juanita." *Didn't I?*

Juanita gave her a strange look. "Then either you hear me wrong or I got tangled up in me words. I tend to do that every now and then. I never would've said that 'bout those two fellers, missy. They act high on weed sometoime, but it never entered me noggin they be growin' it."

CHAPTER 16

As she scraped mud from her jogging shoes, Abby decided that she wasn't losing her mind. She was taking her meds as prescribed, jogging almost every day, getting plenty of sleep. Well, maybe not plenty. But seven hours a night was enough for any normal person, wasn't it? Realizing the ludicrousness of the question, she almost laughed.

She knew stress could bring on a manic episode. Although her investigation had definitely been stressful, it wasn't a bad kind of stress. She was finally working an assignment of substance and, as far as she could tell, doing a decent job of it. Actually, she felt pretty good about things. Damn good really. The fact that she tended to feel the same way when manic gave her pause.

As Dorene Milsap had explained, someone in the clutches of mania is the last person to realize she has a problem. She thinks everything is wonderful. She's smarter than everyone else, more capable. She has things completely under control. Anybody who thinks differently is stupid, jealous, or crazy.

"So how can I tell if I'm manic?" Abby had asked her therapist.

"You can't. Not unless someone tells you and you

believe that person, which you probably won't."

"Then there's no hope."

"Of course there is. But you need to have at least one person you trust. I mean really, really trust. Someone you know for an absolute certainty has your best interest at heart and would never, under any circumstances, mislead you."

"Matt. My dead brother."

"Who else?"

"My mother. Except…"

"Except what?"

"She'd probably lie to me if she thought it would keep me out of trouble."

"I don't really think that's a problem. If you're manic, you're already in trouble, and you'll only get worse until you get help. What you need most when you're manic is for someone to tell you the truth about yourself and for you to believe that person. By the way, that's my third credo. It's probably the hardest one to implement because, if you're manic, you think you've got the world by the tail and the last thing you tend to take seriously is somebody saying you're not in your right mind—unless you have complete and total faith in that person."

"Do you have such a person, Dr. Milsap?"

"Call me Dorene, Abby. And yes, I do. I wouldn't be here now if I didn't."

Although Abby didn't always see eye to eye with her mother, she had no doubt concerning Lillian's loyalty and devotion. Not only did she have Abby's best interests at heart but she wasn't reluctant to speak up whenever Abby was getting manic. Since her mother wasn't around at the moment to express her opinion, Abby took consolation in the fact that she was questioning her own behavior, something she knew people in the throes of mania rarely, if ever, did.

Abby decided it was as good a time as any to call the Pitt County sheriff. From her pocket book she fished out the number Mountcastle had given her and dialed it. After identifying herself to the person who answered the phone, she was put through to Roy Pendleton, an affable-sounding man who seemed happy to share what he knew about Rhonda Tolbert. As the sheriff explained it, Rhonda had lived in a sorority house on the edge of campus and had returned there after finishing her student teaching on Nanticoke. Normally, she went jogging after her final class of the day, and, according to her sorority sisters, that's what she did the day she disappeared. When she didn't return for supper, her sisters grew worried and went looking for her. About eleven that night, they reported her missing. Two days later a farmer found her body in a ditch next to a dirt road a few miles east of Greenville.

"According to the coroner's report, Rhonda was unconscious at least fifteen minutes before her throat was slashed," the sheriff said. "That suggested to me whoever killed her must have waylaid her while she was jogging, knocked her out, and then slit her throat right after dumping her in the ditch. There was a lot of blood next to the body but none leading up to it. Rhonda always stayed close to campus when she jogged, so it's unlikely she'd been out alone on a country road. Since nobody reported seeing a scuffle, I have a theory she knew her attacker and got willingly in his car."

"Any idea who this attacker might be?" Abby asked.

"Unfortunately, no."

"Did you ever suspect Joel Crothers?"

"Actually, he was our only real suspect. By *our*, I mean Sheriff Mountcastle and myself. Since Nanticoke is in his jurisdiction, we conducted a joint investigation. He told me about Sheila's relationship with Joel."

Abby wondered if Mountcastle had let Sheriff Pendleton know she might be calling, deciding he probably had. Regardless, it was a welcome change having a conversation with a sheriff who was not only cooperative and forthcoming but didn't seem full of himself. "Is Joel still a suspect?" she asked.

"Not really. Do you have any reason to think he killed either of those girls—other than Lloyd Bostrum's allegations? I know what he told Mountcastle. We both took it into consideration but we never came up with any evidence whatsoever against Joel."

Deciding she had probably reached a dead end, Abby asked if there were any suspects besides Joel.

"For a while I thought Rhonda's fiancé might've killed her," Pendleton said. "I checked him out, and I'm convinced he didn't know Rhonda was cheating on him. But even if he did, he was in Chapel Hill at the time of her murder. Only thing I can figure is some psycho saw her out walking and for whatever reason decided to make her his victim. I'm not real comfortable with that theory. Normally in a case like this, the murderer rapes the victim or does some other perverse act to her before or after he kills her. In Rhonda's case, there was no evidence of anything like that. And like I said, I think she might've known her attacker and got willingly in his vehicle."

"What kind of person was Rhonda?" Abby asked, wanting to find out if the sheriff's impression coincided with what she had already learned.

"She was popular, especially with her sorority sisters. She liked to have a good time, but she was a good student too. All in all, she seemed to be a decent sort, maybe a little on the wild side."

"In what way was she wild?"

"She got engaged about a month before she started student teaching, but up until then she was quite a party girl. Apparently she could drink most guys under the table and wasn't shy about doing just that or about sleeping with whoever she wanted to at the time."

"Could any of her lovers have wanted her dead?" Abby asked.

"As far as I could tell, she didn't have any enemies on campus or anywhere else."

"What about Joel's long-time girlfriend? Supposedly Beth Harker doesn't know about his affair with Rhonda, but maybe she found out."

"I wondered that too. Mountcastle was convinced Beth isn't the kind of person to commit a murder. He checked her out just like I did Rhonda's fiancé. That was good enough for me."

Abby thanked the sheriff for his time and ended the call. She glanced at her watch, saw it was just nine-thirty, and decided to try for a quick interview with Josephine Devereaux. Assuming she could wrap that up in a half hour or so, she should be able to interview Angie Dake and still get back in time to go jogging before her date with Steve.

After changing her slacks, she drove to the elementary school, a one-story corrugated metal building at the end of a cul-de-sac near the jail. A handful of cars and a lone school bus were the only vehicles in the sandy parking lot.

Entering the building, Abby heard children engaged in a game of some sort, their enthusiastic voices emanating from a classroom down the corridor to her right. In front of her was a large bulletin board filled with announcements and pictures, and to her left was an office suite with the word "Principal" on the door. She went in, finding a middle-aged woman with close-cropped gray hair and a ruddy complexion sitting in front of a computer.

"May I help you?"

Abby introduced herself and was about to ask if Jo

Devereaux was available when the woman herself appeared in the doorway on the far side of the room.

"I didn't expect to see you again so soon, Abby."

"I've got more questions for you. Have you got a few minutes?"

"Sure. Karen, if anybody calls for me, please take a message."

The principal's office was filled to overflowing with a desk, two chairs, three filing cabinets, and several open boxes, some containing folders, others stacks of papers. The desk was cluttered with books and papers of all descriptions.

"Have a seat and please excuse the mess," Jo said, closing the door. "My filing system leaves a lot to be desired aesthetically, but it works for me." She went behind her desk and sat down. Abby chose the closest visitor's chair.

"I'll get right to the point. As you apparently surmised last night, I'm not really doing a feature on Nanticoke. I do work for the *Scarboro Gazette*, but I'm investigating a possible connection between Rhonda Tolbert's murder and the disappearance of a young woman from the Bogue City area."

"Sheila Bostrum. I remember reading about her."

After explaining that Sheila and Joel Crothers worked at the same restaurant the summer she disappeared, Abby listed Lloyd Bostrum's reasons for thinking Joel murdered both his daughter and Rhonda Tolbert. "I told Glen all this last night. I wasn't prepared for the strange way he reacted."

"Strange? How?"

"For one thing he asked me not to mention any of it to Mavis. He said she's got a heart condition and is highly excitable."

"That's news to me."

"It was to Juanita too, and she's worked at the Inlet Inn for years. Doesn't it strike you as odd that neither Glen nor Mavis ever mentioned a heart condition?"

Jo shrugged. "Mavis has never been one to seek sympathy. I've never heard a word of complaint about how hard it must be to take care of Jelinda. Most mothers would have put her in a group home long ago."

"It's not just the heart condition," Abby said. "Glen seems so intense about everything. This morning he practically begged me to take him along when I interview a friend of Sheila's in Buxton. And whenever we talked, he seemed terrified Mavis would overhear us."

"I don't know what to tell you, Abby. As I mentioned last night, Glen is something of an enigma. He's very intelligent and well-spoken, and yet he left teaching to run an inn out here in the middle of nowhere. Why on earth would he do that? Nanticoke has its appeal, but Glen seems capable of being much more than an innkeeper."

After glancing at her watch, Abby told Josephine what she had learned from Joel, that he and Rhonda were having a "fling" as he called it, but that he was actually glad when she left the island. "Does that square with what you know about their relationship?"

"As a matter of fact, it does. Rhonda was quite open about her affair with Joel, at least with me. But I rarely saw them together, so I don't know what went on between them other than the obvious."

"Did you know Rhonda had a fiancé?"

Josephine nodded. "I didn't approve of what she was doing in that regard, but there was a certain innocence about the way Rhonda approached life. I think she was, basically, a decent person. She had an excellent rapport with the kids and obviously had their best interests at heart. There's no question in my mind but she'd have made a good teacher. I think she probably would have made a good wife too. What she and Joel were doing, well, it was kind of a last hurrah, a final fling as you called it, before they both settled down with the person they hoped to marry."

"Couldn't Joel have been more serious about Rhonda than he let on?"

"From what I gathered, he and Rhonda were both involved in a relationship neither expected nor wanted to last any longer than it did. Of course, I could be wrong about Joel. As I said, I rarely saw them together. I don't know Joel well enough to say what he is or isn't capable of. I know his brother Steve a lot better."

Abby had started to get up from her chair but sat back down. "Tell me about Steve," she said, feeling more than a little foolish. "He's taking me to dinner tonight."

Jo's eyebrows lifted ever so slightly. "Well, I know we're lucky to have him as our chief deputy. He loves the island and works hard at his job. He's always accommodating when I ask him to teach safety courses here at the school. It's obvious he likes kids, and he goes out of his way to teach interesting and informative classes, everything from swimming and boat safety to staying away from strangers during the tourist season."

"Mavis told me he's a heartbreaker and suggested I watch my step," Abby said, not sure if she was looking for a confirmation or a negation of that assessment.

"That might not be a bad idea," Jo replied with just the hint of a smile. "Depending on what it is you're looking for."

CHAPTER 17

The Hatteras ferry was less than half the size of the one Abby had taken from the mainland, but its motor was louder, a shrill whine that didn't lessen appreciably when she closed her car window shortly after departure. The water was calm and the trip across the sound uneventful, the boat winding its way back and forth on a course marked by buoys, steering clear of the tiny, uninhabited islands that cropped up here and there. The deckhand who chocked her tires and later waved her onto the dock at Hatteras was younger than Steve and lacked his good looks.

It took less than five minutes to put the town behind her and another twenty-five to reach the outskirts of Buxton where a cylindrical structure with spiraling stripes slid past on her right, a massive edifice that she recognized from pictures as the Cape Hatteras lighthouse. She stopped at a convenience store and asked directions to Mane Street Salon, which turned out to be in a nearby strip mall containing such diverse enterprises as the Sandwich Shop, the Gingerbread House, and Randy's Surf and Tackle.

The two beauticians were a study in contrast. The one nearer the door, the older by at least two decades, looked conventional in every way, including her neatly coiffed auburn hair. The other, a slender young woman with spiked purple hair, a nose ring, and tattoos on both arms, looked like a biker chick.

"Be with you in a jiffy, hon," the older woman said. "Have a seat."

"I'm looking for Angie Dake," Abby told her. "Any chance that's her working the next chair?"

"Darn good chance," the woman said, turning to the young operator, who was setting an elderly woman's hair with small metal rollers. "You keep getting referrals like this, Angie, and I might have to give you that raise you've been pestering me about."

"I'm not here as a customer," Abby told the younger woman. "I'd like to talk to you about Sheila Bostrum."

"Sheila? Why?"

"I'm trying to find out what happened to her. I work for the *Scarboro Gazette*."

The woman gave Abby the once over. "You'll have to wait 'til I get Mrs. Hudgins under the dryer." She nodded toward the row of plastic chairs in the empty waiting area. "You can sit over there."

Abby sat down and began leafing through a magazine, occasionally glancing up to see how the young operator was progressing. Angie finished setting her charge's hair in less than ten minutes, led her to a chair with a dryer attached, adjusted the dryer, and turned it on.

"How much is the *Gazette* paying for interviews nowadays?"

"Unfortunately nothing," Abby said, standing up. "But if necessary, I'll give you something for your time. How much do you have in mind?"

"Depends on how much of my valuable time you need. I'm not easy but I'm cheap. Linda can attest to that. Why're you investigating so long after Sheila's disappearance?"

"Her father sent the *Gazette* a letter asking for our help. I've already talked to the sheriff. He suggested I contact you."

"He did, huh? Well, let's go have our chat. I'm taking my break now, Linda. Okay?"

"No problem—just so long as you fill me in on all the juicy details."

"And me," said the woman Linda was working on, an elderly lady who reminded Abby of Estelle Dromgoole, except her hair was white. "I remember reading about that Bostrum girl. Don't you dare let Hazel burn up under the dryer."

"I wouldn't do that to a steady customer," Angie replied as she headed toward a door on the far side of the room. She opened it and turned to Abby. "You've got exactly fifteen minutes of free interview time. If you need more after I finish up with Mrs. Hudgins, we'll have to re-negotiate my fee. Better bring your coat. It's colder than an Eskimo's dick in there."

Abby picked up her coat and followed the young woman into a small, windowless area where Angie flipped a wall switch. Light from an overhead bulb revealed a sink with a coffee pot on the adjacent counter, a tiny refrigerator, a card table, three folding chairs, and a wall calendar featuring a hairy-chested Mr. February wearing little more than a smile. There was also a small space heater, which, Angie explained, had stopped working a few days ago.

"Have a seat and be thankful it's not summer," she said, putting on her coat. "You think it's uncomfortable in here now, you should be here in August. It's like a sauna."

Abby introduced herself as she pulled on her jacket. "Are things going any better between you and Mike?" she asked, sitting down in the chair directly across from the calendar.

Angie did a double take. "How'd you know about him?"

"I called the other day and got your answering machine. He must've really pissed you off."

"He did and he's not getting a second chance, even if he falls on his knees and begs. Better have some coffee. Fifteen minutes in this freezer and you'll feel like a block of ice. What would you like in it?"

"Whiskey."

"Unfortunately, there's none available."

"Milk and sugar is fine, heavy on the sugar."

Angie fixed two cups and handed one to Abby. Then she sat down across the table, her back to the calendar. "What would you like to know that the sheriff hasn't already covered?"

"The main thing is whether Joel Crothers could've had anything to do with Sheila's disappearance."

"I doubt it." Angie took a sip of coffee. "Like I told Mountcastle, there wasn't anything going on between those two."

"But they did go out together. Joel admitted it."

"Strictly a platonic relationship. Of course, with guys, you can never be sure. They tended to fall for Sheila in droves. But I didn't see anything to suggest Joel was one of 'em."

Abby drank some of her coffee, finding it hot and to her liking. "I understand you and Sheila were close."

"Yeah, we were."

"Close enough to know what was going on in her life that summer?"

"Depends on what you mean by 'going on.' We worked at the same restaurant and shared a room at a boarding house. If you're asking whether there was a guy in Sheila's life that summer, that's not an easy question to answer. I do think there was somebody. I never saw him and Sheila never talked about him. But the signs were there."

The chill Abby felt at the base of her spine had nothing to do with the room temperature. "What signs?"

"Mainly her moods. Normally Sheila was pretty up-beat, but as the summer wore on she acted down, more so than I'd ever seen her. I remember thinking at the time she seemed like a love-smitten teenager. I even joked about it once or twice and she got real touchy. That wasn't like her either."

"Couldn't Joel have been the reason?"

"I'm ninety-nine percent sure he wasn't. If they'd been lovers, there wasn't any reason to keep it a secret."

"But if she was seeing somebody other than him, why keep that a secret?"

Angie shrugged. "Good question. Normally Sheila was open about things like that. In high school she told me everything about the guys she dated. I don't know why she was so secretive that last summer—assuming she really was seeing someone."

"Were there other indications that she had a lover?"

"Well, there were a couple of times she disappeared for a day or so. When I asked where she'd been, she more or less told me to mind my own business. That definitely wasn't the Sheila I knew. Like I said, up until that summer, she'd pretty much shared everything with me."

Abby drank more coffee. Her mind seemed much clearer now than it had earlier in the day, not sluggish at all. She'd had no trouble keeping up with Angie, who was neither dull witted nor slow talking, and that boded well for later in the day.

The last thing Abby wanted was to act like a zombie during her date with Steve. "Any idea why the big change all of a sudden?"

"Believe me, I've asked myself that a lot over the

years. But I've never been able to come up with a satisfactory answer."

"When Sheila pulled these vanishing acts, did Joel happen to be gone too?"

"You know, I'm not real sure," Angie replied after a pause. "I think he was working those days but I can't swear to it."

"I'm pretty sure Sheila went to Nanticoke during those disappearances," Abby said after a moment. "Her name is in the Inlet Inn's register on three separate occasions. The first time was June twenty-fourth, which is the day you two went with Joel on the fishing trip. He said a guy named Doug made it a foursome. Is he right about that?"

"Yeah. Doug was a busboy at Captain Jack's."

"Could he have been the guy Sheila was seeing?"

Angie shook her head. "Too young. Plus, he wasn't cool or sexy enough to have interested Sheila. Seems to me he was a last minute full-in."

"For Bobby Musgrove?"

"You seem to have done your homework, Abby."

"Could Sheila have been seeing Bobby that summer? Her mother told me she thought they might have dated in high school."

"She's wrong about that. Bobby wasn't Sheila's type and she wasn't his."

Abby nodded. "Then I'll scratch him off my suspect list once and for all." She swirled the coffee around in her cup, staring at it, trying to decide what to ask next. "Tell me about the fishing trip, Angie. Did Sheila meet somebody that weekend who could be the mysterious boyfriend?"

"I don't recall us meeting anybody other than the people who ran the inn where we stayed, Mavis somebody and her brother."

"Glen Turpin. Could he have been the guy in Sheila's life?"

"You're kidding, aren't you? He seemed like a nice man, but Sheila wouldn't have been remotely interested in him and vice versa."

Abby asked if Sheila might have met somebody while on the ferry trips to and from the island or on the fishing trip itself.

"I don't remember meeting anybody on the ferry, and the four of us were the only ones Steve took out."

Abby caught her breath. "You don't suppose Steve was the guy—"

"He's a hunk—at least he was then—but he didn't show the slightest interest in us girls. There wasn't a thing going on between him and Sheila."

Though relieved, Abby was angry with herself for caring one way or the other. "What did you do after the fishing trip?" she asked.

"Sheila and I registered at the inn, and the guys went off by themselves. Later we had a cookout on the beach. Then Sheila and I went back to the inn, and Joel and Doug spent the night at Joel's mother's house."

"Was Steve at the cookout?"

Angie shook her head. "Just the four of us."

Abby nodded, feeling even more relieved. "Were you with Sheila the whole day?"

"Pretty much. She went off by herself for a little while after we registered at the inn. I told her I was ready for a nice long shower and she said to go ahead, she wanted to check out some of the shops downtown. She wasn't gone very long."

"Could she have met somebody during that time?"

"Who?"

"I don't know…Joel, Steve, Glen, some guy named Ron?"

"Ron?"

"Sheriff Mountcastle said Mary Bethune overheard Sheila talking kind of sexy on the phone to somebody whose name she thought was Ron. Was there ever a Ron in her life?"

"She never mentioned one to me. I think you're barking up the wrong tree, Abby. I didn't notice anything out of the ordinary that weekend, nothing at all to suggest Sheila fell for some guy or met up with one."

"Then why did she go back to the island two more times? And why was she so tight lipped about it?"

"I don't know. I admit it's puzzling."

Abby pulled her coat up tighter around her neck. "One thing for sure, several people, including Sheila's father, think she was involved with a guy that summer. And those same people noticed that she wasn't herself the few weeks before her disappearance. Her father said she even told him that Joel was becoming a problem."

"Mr. Bostrum said that?"

"In his letter." Abby explained that Lloyd Bostrum had been in a recent car accident and refused to talk to her. "I did have a long conversation with his girlfriend. Carolyn was with him that night at the restaurant. She remembered Sheila saying Joel was coming on too strong."

"Well, like I said, I didn't see any evidence of it. I don't know this Carolyn, so I can't comment about her credibility. But I wouldn't put much faith in anything Mr. Bostrum said. From what I know about him, he's a messed-up dude, more capable than most of seeing things that aren't there and missing those that are." Angie looked at her watch. "My break's almost over. Anything else you want to ask before I rescue Mrs. Hudgins?"

"Well, I was wondering about Sheila's stepfather. Her mother said he and Sheila didn't get along well. What can you tell me about him?"

"The guy had a rod up his butt, at least according to Sheila. You know the type, straight-laced and moralistic. I think the main reason she didn't like him was she thought he came between her mother and father, making it impossible for them to get back together."

"Do you think they would have gotten back together if Dorothy hadn't remarried?"

"I doubt it. She was well rid of Lloyd Bostrum if you ask me. I don't see how she put up with him as long as she did. But Sheila was blind to her father's faults, at least most of 'em."

Abby took a final sip of coffee and set the cup on the table. "One last question. Have you got an opinion about what happened to Sheila?"

"Not really."

"Not even an idea or a theory?"

Angie stood up and put the cups in the sink. "I don't have the slightest idea what happened to that girl, Abby. I wish I did. I'd like nothing better than to see her killer get what he deserves."

"Then you do think she was murdered?"

"To me that's pretty obvious. Sheila never said or did anything to make me think she'd light out for parts unknown. But who killed her or why, I don't have the foggiest notion."

CHAPTER 18

It was twelve-fifteen when Abby got back to Hatteras, time enough, she decided, to have a quick lunch and still make the one-thirty ferry. She found a small, well-maintained restaurant, the Sea Breeze Café, about a block from the ferry terminal, parked her car, and went inside. To save time she told the waitress she didn't need a menu and ordered iced tea and a turkey club sandwich, hoping such a meal was available. It was.

Her table was next to a window where she could see the ferry slip and the sound. As she waited for her lunch, she thought about Sheila Bostrum, wondering why the girl had been so secretive about whomever she was seeing the summer she disappeared. Abby was convinced now, after talking with Angie Dake, that there had been a man in Sheila's life that summer and their relationship had not been going well. But why keep the relationship a secret?

The waitress brought her tea, and, as Abby sipped it, she wondered if Sheila could have been pregnant. An unwanted pregnancy might account for her moodiness, but it didn't explain why she was so secretive about the prospective father. Why wouldn't she want people knowing about him?

There were two possible explanations, Abby finally

concluded after the waitress brought her triple-decker sandwich, which was surrounded by a generous serving of potato chips and a large dill pickle. Either the guy was married or Sheila was too ashamed of him to let anyone, including her best friend, know his identity. Since Sheila didn't seem like the kind of person to be easily ashamed, Abby decided it had to be a married man.

She wondered if the man was Steve Crothers, not a pleasant thought. But if it was Steve, why had Sheila talked on the phone in a sexually provocatively way with somebody named Ron? That name didn't sound at all like Steve—or Joel or Glen or Bobby, for that matter. It didn't resemble the name of anyone Abby thought might be responsible for Sheila's disappearance.

As she started on her final sandwich wedge, she glanced at her watch and saw it was one-twenty. The next ferry wasn't yet visible on the horizon.

"Can I get you anything else?" the waitress asked. "Some dessert maybe?"

Abby looked longingly at the slice of pecan pie displayed on the counter but decided she needed to save room for her dinner with Steve. "No thanks," she said. "That was a delicious sandwich. My compliments to the chef."

The woman seemed pleased. "That would be my youngest son Don. He just started working for us this week."

As she paid for the meal, the name "Don" resonated in Abby's mind, but she didn't think any more about it until after getting in her car. As she turned the ignition key, she realized the name's significance. Shutting off the motor, she hurried back into the restaurant and asked to see a phone book. After writing down the number of Sheriff Mountcastle's office, she returned to her car and dialed the number on her cell phone, only to discover that the call wouldn't go through. She tried again with the same result, concluding that she was too far from the mainland for her cell phone to work. Noticing a pay phone at the gas station diagonally across the street, she exited her Corolla and hurried toward it.

The woman who answered had a raspy voice that reminded Abby of Rod Stewart. "You're in luck," she said. "Mr. Mountcastle just got back from lunch. Hold on and I'll connect you."

Abby told the sheriff she had just talked to Angie Dake and it was clear now that Sheila Bostrum had been seeing someone the summer she disappeared and had protected his identity. "Either he was married or she was ashamed of him. The person I've got in mind satisfies both counts. He also passes the Mary Bethune test."

"The what?" Mountcastle said, clearly annoyed.

"Mary told you she heard Sheila talking lovey-dovey to a guy whose name she thought was Ron. Well, that person's name could have been Don—Don Horvath. Did you ever consider him a suspect?"

"Absolutely not. He didn't have a motive."

"How about keeping Sheila quiet about the fact that they'd been sleeping together?"

The pause at the end of the line was followed by a sigh of exasperation. "You're wasting my time again, Abby."

"It makes sense, Sheriff. The name 'Don' plus the fact that Sheila was so ashamed of what she was doing she didn't even tell her best friend. Up until then, she'd always shared the details of her love life with Angie Dake."

Another pause. "Well, at least there's some good news here. Apparently, you've gotten beyond the notion that Joel Crothers killed Sheila. That's progress. The bad news is you're engaging in pure speculation. You don't have a shred of actual evidence that Horvath and Sheila were lovers, do you?"

"I haven't had a chance to check it out yet. I was

hoping you'd tell me something either way that might be helpful."

"I will. Forget it. Don Horvath didn't have any more to do with Sheila's disappearance than Joel did. They didn't get along. If you don't like somebody, you don't choose that person for a lover."

"Sheila could have seduced Horvath for a lark," Abby persisted. "Or she might've done it to break up her mother's marriage. Either way, the guy had reason for wanting her dead."

Mountcastle sighed again, this time in resignation. "Well, if you feel that strongly about it, go ahead and check it out. If you come up with any evidence, something that actually links the two as lovers, let me know. Anything else you wanted to say?"

"I guess not. You're not one for offering encouragement, are you?"

"Not when somebody's headed down a blind alley. I try to steer 'em back on the right path so they don't waste any more time—theirs or mine."

After hanging up, Abby looked up the number of Mane Street Salon and dialed it on her cell phone. After three rings, Linda answered and told her Angie was busy with a customer and would be tied up for another half hour.

"I need to speak to her now. It's important."

"So's her job. You'll have to leave your number or call back later."

Abby saw that the ferry had reached the dock and was in the process of loading. "I'll call back," she said, switched off her cell phone, and hurried toward her car.

✄৩৩

When Abby pulled into the Inlet Inn's parking lot

forty minutes later, she once again dialed the number of Mane Street Salon on her cell phone. Again, Linda answered, but this time Angie was available and came on the line almost immediately.

"What's up? Decide to increase the interview fee you were planning to send me?"

"I want to get your take on an idea, Angie. I know it's a long shot but couldn't something have been going on between Sheila and her stepfather the summer she disappeared?"

"You mean like them sleeping together?"

"Yeah."

"Absolutely not. Sheila thought the guy was a jerk."

"A woman doesn't have to like someone to sleep with him. Sheila could've done it to show Horvath what a shit he is, you know, not having enough character to resist his stepdaughter. Or she might've wanted to break up his marriage. It's pretty clear she was devoted to her father and was hurt when he and Dorothy split up."

Angie didn't respond for a moment, long enough for Abby to think they might have been cut off. "Angie?"

"I was thinking about what you said. Actually, it never occurred to me Sheila might've slept with Horvath. I still don't think she did, but it would explain why she was so tight lipped about everything. It took a lot to embarrass Sheila Bostrum, a hell of a lot. But even Sheila would've been embarrassed to tell me about that."

Abby thanked Angie for her time and promised to let her know if anything came of her investigation. Switching off the cell phone, she got out of the car and headed for her room, wondering just how she would go about investigating Don Horvath. She couldn't ask Dorothy about him because that would make her suspicious of a man who could be innocent. It might even destroy their marriage, and Abby didn't want that on her conscience. She couldn't ask Horvath about it either, not without some kind of supporting evidence. He'd probably laugh in her face.

Once in her room, Abby changed into sweatpants and a sweatshirt. It wasn't until she was tying her running shoes that she noticed the envelope on the bed. It was propped against the pillow, her name written in large letters on the front. She tore it open and read the note inside.

> *I pride myself on being able to remember the Inlet Inn's guests, especially those who stay here more than once, but for the life of me I can't recall Sheila Bostrum. Can you possibly get me a photograph of her, preferably one in color? I imagine the* Gazette *would have one in its files. I know this must sound like a strange request, Abby, but it's important to me.*
>
> *See you Sunday afternoon or evening, depending on how long the tournament in Raleigh lasts and whether I do well enough to stick around for the results.*
> *Glen*

CHAPTER 19

With Steve at the helm, the *Jesse II* motored across Diamond Lake toward the passageway to the sound. Standing beside him and holding onto the padded captain's chair with her right hand, Abby watched the lighthouse glide past, its upper quarter bathed in sunlight. It had been in full sun when she jogged past earlier in the afternoon. Now it was the only visible object not completely in shadow.

"Reminds me of an upside-down ice cream cone," she said. "It's a runt compared to the one in Buxton. I saw that one—" She caught herself, realizing she was on the verge of saying something stupid. The last thing she wanted was Steve knowing where she went today. It would be hard to explain in light of her cover story. "—when I was a kid. It looked like a huge barber pole."

"Still does. I like this one better. Before they shut it down a few years ago, it was the second oldest working lighthouse in the country."

"No kidding?" Abby said, relieved her mid-sentence correction had apparently gone unnoticed. "Where's the oldest?"

"On Lake Michigan, I believe." Steve throttled down as the boat entered the narrow channel, its sloping sides lined with riprap. "Were you able to interview Joel to-day?"

"Yeah—finally."

"How'd it go?"

For an instant Abby considered telling him the truth. Now that Joel knew her real reason for being on the island, it was just a matter of time before Steve would know also, assuming he didn't already. Though Joel was no longer her main suspect, he was still on her list, and there was always the possibility Steve would reveal something incriminating about his brother. "Not as well as I'd hoped," she said, deciding not to tell all just yet. "I'm hoping to use Joel as the centerpiece of my feature, but so far he hasn't revealed much about himself."

"Did he say anything about that new greenhouse he plans on building?"

"Very little. I pointed out that it wouldn't get much sun next to the hill, but he didn't seem concerned. I couldn't really argue the point when the only thing I've ever grown successfully is a cactus plant."

The channel ended and the boat entered open water, bobbing up and down in the waves as it headed for the southern tip of the island. The vegetation along the shoreline thinned, soon giving way to a sandbar that narrowed to a point. The sun swung into view, a huge orange ball floating in the sound.

"Where'd that come from?" Abby asked in amazement.

"Don't look at it too long. One time I stared at a sunset for more than a few seconds, and when I looked away everything had turned blue—the sand, houses, and people, whatever I tried to focus on. Scared the hell out of me."

Steve maneuvered the boat in a wide semicircle, heading it toward the island's western edge. To her right, Abby saw what looked like a miniature battleship moored in front of a row of Quonset-style buildings. "What's that?"

"The coast guard station. That's their cutter at the dock."

The sun slid across the *Jesse II's* bow, and soon the boat was heading north, following the island's contour. Steve pointed out other landmarks, including the dirt road leading to Joel's trailer and greenhouse, its dusky surface barely visible in the distance.

"Ready to take over?" he asked as the village receded from view.

"Not unless the coast guard is prepared for a quick rescue."

"Just turn the wheel the way you want to go. Here's the throttle. Push it forward to speed up. Pull it back to slow down. Nothing to it."

Steve vacated the padded chair and Abby slid into it, taking the wheel with her left hand and the throttle with her right."

"Move the wheel back and forth a little to get the feel of it...that's good. Now open the throttle...good. You're doing fine, Abby. Guess I'll go below for a nap."

"I guess you won't. Stay right where you are, mister."

"Aye aye, captain."

Soon Abby was able to control the boat with no difficulty and her apprehension subsided. On impulse, she pushed the throttle several notches forward, feeling a sense of exhilaration as the *Jesse II* shot ahead, bumping across the waves. "If I'm going too fast, arrest me," she said, the wind whipping through her hair.

"I'm off duty," Steve replied, holding on to the back of the seat for support. "You'll have to reign yourself in."

Abby eased back on the throttle until the boat slowed to a normal speed. For a while the only visible reminder of the village was the lighthouse. Then it too disappeared.

The sun melted into the water and a vague moon materialized in the east, a pale yellow disk in a darkening sky.

"We're getting close," Steve said.

"To what?"

"They're small and shaggy and their ancestors came from Spain."

"Graylock's illegitimate children in desperate need of a haircut?"

"The wild ponies, silly. Unless they're near the beach, we won't see them. Slow down some more and head toward that cove. The quieter our approach, the better."

Abby did as instructed, pointing the boat toward a concave curve in the shore.

Steve pointed toward a wire fence jutting into the water. "That's the boundary of their pen."

"Where? Oh, the fence."

"Better let me take over now. These shallows can be tricky."

Abby stood up and moved to her left, and Steve slid behind the controls. "Bet I spot one before you do," he said.

"You're on."

"I've already seen two."

"Where?" Abby saw only sand, bushes, and gnarled, leafless trees, nothing resembling an animal. Finally, she saw them, two small horses grazing near the beach. "They blend right in with the landscape."

The *Jesse II* slowed to a crawl. For a while the ponies continued to graze, but as the boat drifted closer, they began making their way toward the woods.

"I've seen ten on the beach at one time," Steve said. "Keep looking. There might be others."

"I don't see any more."

"One's lying down near that pile of driftwood."

Only after the two original ponies had disappeared

into the woods did Abby spot the third. Smaller than the others, it struggled to rise as the boat moved closer, front feet pawing.

"He's hurt, Steve. He can't get up."

"Sometimes the colts get frisky and run up and down the beach. He probably stepped in a hole."

"Can we help him?"

Steve switched off the motor. "We'll run aground if we try to get any closer. I'll have to swim the rest of the way."

"It's February, Steve. The water is freezing."

"Good for the appetite—assuming I survive the shock."

He lowered the anchor over the side and then hurried below deck, emerging a few moments later wearing a wet suit. Opening a compartment next to the instrument panel, he took out a pistol and handed it to Abby butt first. "If his leg is broken, I'll have to shoot him. We'd be lucky to get a vet out here by noon tomorrow."

Carefully holding the pistol, Abby watched him climb over the side. There was a muted splash followed by a yell that sounded like part curse, part laughter. For a while Steve treaded water, sucking in breaths. Then he reached for the pistol.

Abby handed it to him, holding onto the railing as she leaned over. "How are you going to swim and carry that too?"

"Hopefully I'll be able to touch bottom soon."

She watched him swim awkwardly, holding the pistol above the water with his left hand, stroking with his right. Less than halfway to shore he was able to wade, but after a few steps, he lost his balance and almost fell, barely managing to keep the pistol above water.

Abby saw the pony lift its head as Steve approached then make a frantic attempt to stand. Eventually it gave up and rolled onto its side. Steve bent down to get a better look at the creature. Then he slowly raised the pistol. There was what could have been a brief clap of distant thunder, and Abby looked away as the sound echoed across the water.

She thought of the afternoon she and her ex-husband were on their way to a party in Carsonville, a town some eight miles east of Scarboro where some of the teachers at the community college lived. Out of nowhere, a Labrador retriever ran in front of their car.

The dog lay whimpering on the road's shoulder. Blood covered its flank, and its left hind leg was splayed out at a grotesque angle.

"Nothing we can do," Mark said and started back to the car.

"We can take him to a vet."

"We're not driving back to Scarboro just for a dog that's probably going to die anyway."

"Maybe there's one in Carsonville."

"Not a good idea, Abby. We try to move that dog, he'll bite the shit out of us."

"We can't just leave him here." She pointed toward a farmhouse in the distance. "Somebody there might be able to help."

The old man who answered the door told them the dog wasn't his and he didn't know who the owner was.

"Is there a vet in Carsonville?" Abby asked.

"There's one about a mile east of town. I don't think they're open on Sunday but I'll call and see."

He returned a moment later and told them the clinic was closed until tomorrow morning. "The answering machine gave a number to call in case of an emergency. It's the clinic in Scarboro that stays open twenty-four hours a day."

"Forget it," Mark said. "You pay through the nose at a

clinic like that." He turned to the old man. "How about calling the state police. Tell them a dog's lying on the highway."

"They'll just shoot the dog," Abby said.

"That's what they're supposed to do. Come on. We're not wasting any more time on an animal too stupid to stay out of the road."

At the party in Carsonville, Abby tried cocaine for the first time. Her misgivings about the dog dissipated almost as quickly as her exhaled smoke.

CHAPTER 20

Sawyer's Crab was dimly lit, made even darker by an abundance of decorative fishing nets hanging from the rafters. Its floor-to-ceiling windows provided a panoramic view of the Pamlico Sound. Abby could see the Hatteras ferry receding in the distance, barely visible in the gathering dusk. To her left, at the dock where the *Jesse II* was tethered, lights flicked on. Naked bulbs strung between pilings, they swayed in the evening breeze, casting erratic shadows over the rippling dark water.

"Hope that business with the pony didn't ruin your evening," Steve said as they sipped their iced tea.

"It didn't. I was in a similar situation once, my ex-husband and I." She told Steve about the dog that ran out in front of them on the highway. "We asked an old farmer to call the state police and then went on our merry way."

The waitress brought their dinners—shrimp scampi for Abby, scallops for Steve, and a basket of hushpuppies. After making sure they had everything they needed, including plenty of butter and tartar sauce, she wished them an enjoyable meal.

"What's your ex do for a living?" Steve asked, passing Abby the hushpuppies and then taking two for himself.

"As little as possible unless he's changed. Last I heard, he'd joined an artist colony in the Catskills. This shrimp scampi is delicious."

Steve took the hint, at least as far as Abby's marriage was concerned. "My marriage didn't work out either," he said. "Marlene was from the mainland and couldn't handle the isolation. She finally decided to pack it in."

"You don't sound particularly sorry."

"I'm not and I'm sure Marlene isn't either. Nobody would ever accuse me of being good husband material."

Abby chuckled. "Somebody else told me that today."

"Joel?"

She shook her head. "Your name didn't come up when I talked to him."

"I wish it had. I'd like to know why he's acted so hostile toward me lately. Something I did or said must've really ticked him off."

Abby decided to seize the opportunity to learn more about Joel. "Your brother is an enigma. I mean his hostility toward you, plus the way he acted yesterday at the Inlet Inn. He seemed pretty laid back when I talked to him at the greenhouse. Which one is the real Joel?"

"If you'd asked me that a month ago, I'd say the laid-back version. Now I don't know what to think. He's probably uptight about his tomato business. I know I'd be worried sick if it was me sinking money in another greenhouse."

"Maybe Rhonda Tolbert's death had an effect on him," Abby said. "Mavis Gilbert told me about their affair."

Steve shook his head. "That's not what's bothering him now."

Abby decided any further probing would make Steve suspicious. She wanted to ask if he had noticed anything going on between Sheila Bostrum and Joel during the fishing trip, but to do so would mean revealing her real reason for being on the island. "Tell me about your kids," she said. "Based on your child support comment yesterday, I assume you've got at least one."

"I've got exactly one. Marlene moved out of state after she re-married, so I don't get to see Jenny very often. I'm hoping to get her to visit me this summer. Jenny wants to, but Marlene doesn't seem to think I have any rights, even though I've never missed a child support payment. What about you? Any kids?"

"A nine-year-old boy," Abby said and told Steve about Kevin.

As the meal wore on, conversation flowed easy between them, and they talked about many things, including the hurricane that hit the Outer Banks several years earlier and caused considerable damage.

"I don't mean the water actually rose above the houses," Steve said. "But it got inside a lot of 'em. Imagine looking around and everything you see, as far as you can see, is ocean. And you're not in a boat."

"No wonder your ex went back to the mainland. Is it true Nanticoke doesn't have a doctor?"

Steve nodded. "One of my responsibilities is to make sure people needing medical help get it as quick as possible. That's not always easy when the closest clinic is in Hatteras and the nearest hospital is in Bogue City."

"What do you do in bad weather?"

"Call in a coast guard helicopter if I have to, though sometimes the weather is too rough even for them. It's happened a few times, mainly with women going into labor. Usually we're able to take care of something like that ourselves if there aren't complications. We did have a stabbing during a bad storm a few years back. By the time we got the victim to Bogue City, he'd died from internal hemorrhaging."

"I thought you didn't have any crime out here."

"We don't have much. For one thing, there's no easy escape route. Unless a perp has a boat, his only way off the island is by ferry, and I can always call ahead and have deputies waiting at the terminals. That's not to say we don't have problems, but they're usually caused by outsiders who come here thinking they own the place."

Steve told her about a motorcycle gang that came to Nanticoke one summer and stayed at the campground north of town.

"The first night they didn't cause any trouble, but the next day they stole stuff in the village and pushed people around in the process. I deputized some of the toughest guys on the island, including Hector Creef, Juanita's husband, who's bigger than Earl Salter and strong as his backhoe. We went in and knocked heads and then carted the worst offenders off to the detention center at the coast guard station. Next morning I gave them the choice of taking the first ferry to the mainland or being prosecuted. They chose the ferry and we've never seen 'em since."

As soon as they finished eating, the waitress began clearing the table. "Be back in a jiffy with your dessert," she said, giving Steve a knowing look.

"There's a bar about a half mile from here," he said after the waitress had gone. "It's probably too country for your taste, but I figure we could stop in for a cold one after we walk off some of this meal."

"Fine with me, as long as my cold one can be non-alcoholic," Abby replied, hoping she wouldn't need to explain why she didn't drink alcohol. "Why'd the waitress look at you that way?"

"What way?"

"Like you share a secret."

Steve seemed puzzled. "Sorry, I didn't notice."

"We didn't order dessert. Did we?"

"Apparently it comes with the meal. Look, she's bringing it now." He nodded at the waitress, who was heading toward them with a large tray.

"Specially made for a special guest," she said, placing the tray, which had a sheet cake on it, in front of Abby. "We're all looking forward to reading your article."

The cake was elaborately decorated with dark chocolate and butter cream frostings to resemble the front page of a newspaper whose headlines read "Island Welcomes Writer." The perimeter was adorned with seashells, ships, whales, and anchors, all realistically rendered in various colors.

Abby stared at the cake in amazement. "I've never seen anything like this. It's a work of art."

"Juanita Creef made it," Steve told her. "She's famous for her cakes. Birthdays, anniversaries, you name it—Juanita is the person we go to when there's something special to celebrate. She made this one for me this morning and I drove it over after lunch. If you think it looks good, just wait 'til you taste it."

CHAPTER 21

Steve had warned Abby there was nothing scenic about the northern tip of the island, and he was right. The area had none of the southern part's charm. There was no village, just a few business establishments that had sprung up around the ferry dock—a gas station, a bait and tackle shop, and a storage facility for gasoline and diesel fuel. As they headed toward the beach on the ocean side of the island, they passed the Sand Dollar Motel—a cluster of multi-colored cabins that fanned out behind a small clapboard office like a raggedy-looking peacock's tail. Even the beach sand looked dirty, littered here and there with silt and driftwood.

"I hate to sound like a broken record but that was the best cake I've ever tasted," Abby said as they walked along the water's edge. "If Juanita started a catering business in Scarboro, she'd be rich in no time."

"Don't give her any ideas. Nanticoke wouldn't know what to do without Juanita Creef."

They had walked along the beach for about fifteen minutes when Steve took Abby's hand and led her to the top of a sand dune. He pointed toward a lighted cinderblock structure on the far side of the road.

"Behold the mecca of island night life," he said. "The

Salty Dawg." Still holding hands, they raced down the other side of the dune.

There were more pickup trucks than cars in the Salty Dawg's parking lot. Long before they reached the door, Abby could hear the rhythmic twang of country music. "Hope I won't be out of place with no boots and no drawl," she said.

"Any kind of footwear goes. You can fake the drawl. I'll introduce you as Tanya Tucker."

"If you don't behave yourself, I'll pretend I'm Tanya Harding."

They entered a long narrow room filled with the blue haze of cigarette smoke. In front of them was a jukebox around which several couples were gathered, most of them dancing. Many of the patrons noticed Steve right away and acknowledged him with a wave or a friendly greeting. A few walked over and shook his hand. After introducing them to Abby and making small talk for a while, he politely excused himself and led her to an empty booth along the wall.

A waitress wearing a sailor's cap appeared, and Abby made the woman's eyebrows lift by ordering ginger ale. When told Mountain Dew and Pepsi were the only non-alcoholic beverages available, she went with Pepsi. Steve ordered a draft beer.

Their drinks soon arrived, both in frosted glasses. As Abby picked up hers, the jukebox came alive with the opening lines of "Take This Job and Shove It."

"I've come close to saying that a few times," she said and took a sip of her drink, which was cold and palatable, sweeter than the caffeine-free colas she normally drank.

"Why didn't you?"

"I needed the job more than the satisfaction."

Steve asked how long she had worked at the *Gazette*, and she told him not quite two years. "Actually it's not so bad. I'd like it a lot better if I could get some challenging assignments."

"I don't see how they could get any more challenging than the one you've got now. If you make interesting reading out of Nanticoke in the wintertime, they ought to give you the Pulitzer."

Abby smiled, surprised that Steve had even heard of the Pulitzer Prize. "There's something I want to ask you," she said, not sure if she was looking for a reason to like this Outer Banks deputy better or not so much. "If that pony had been a human being, would you have seen things differently?"

"Well, sure. I wouldn't have shot a human being."

"That's not what I mean. What I'm getting at is…well, do you believe people have the right to die? I don't mean when there's a chance they'll get better. I'm talking about people who are suffering and have no chance of recovery."

Steve took a swallow of beer, then set the glass on the table and seemed to study it. "In other words, was I a Jack Kevorkian sympathizer? Is that what you're asking?"

"Close enough."

"He was too much of a showman to suit me, but I can't say I'm against what he did. As far as I'm concerned, if somebody wants to end his or her life, that's their business. And if they ask for a doctor's help, he shouldn't be penalized for providing it."

"That's amazing."

"What is?"

"That you'd see it that way."

"Well, how do you see it?"

"Exactly the same way." Abby went on to explain that her father had died of pancreatic cancer while she was in middle school. "He'd suffered horribly for months and wanted to end his life. Mom tried to find a doctor who'd help, but they all said they'd lose their licenses, or go to jail, if they did help. To me it's ridiculous that a society supposedly as enlightened as ours makes it a crime to do for a human being what you did for that pony."

"What's so amazing about us agreeing on that?" Steve asked, taking another sip of beer.

"I thought you'd be more of a—" She hesitated, not wanting to risk making him angry or hurting his feelings.

"Redneck?"

"Well…"

"We get the Internet out here, Abby. Newspapers and magazines too. Our TV reception might be a little fuzzy at times, but the news still gets through. I've probably got what you'd consider redneck ideas about a lot of things, but I try not to let others do my thinking for me. And I've found most islanders to be the same way. You could poll everybody in this bar and half of 'em would probably agree with you on assisted suicide. And those who don't can probably give some good reasons for disagreeing. Not everybody on Nanticoke is ignorant or stupid."

"Of course not," Abby said, not altogether displeased by Steve's rebuke. She raised her glass. "To the enlightened chief deputy of Nanticoke."

"I'm not sure that's a compliment, but I'll drink to it." He touched his glass to hers. "If you mention me in your feature, don't you dare refer to me as a liberal, Abby. We might have enlightened folks out here, but we've also got our share of knuckleheads that need dealing with when they get too rowdy. I don't want them thinking I'm soft. Hey, they finally put on something slow. Care to dance?"

The jukebox was playing the opening lines of "Help Me Make it Through the Night," Sammi Smith's version of a song Abby had never particularly liked but which now didn't seem lame at all.

She followed Steve to the dance area and nestled in

his arms, impressed by the gracefulness of his movements.

As they danced, she looked around at the other people in the tavern—the ones dancing nearby, those chatting at the bar and in the booths, the pool players at the far end of the room. In spite of the fact that she hadn't danced in years, basically detested country music, and hadn't played a game of pool in her life, she felt strangely at home, perfectly content to be spending time at this redneck bar with this semi-redneck deputy sheriff. Her real reason for being on the island seemed remote, hardly worth thinking about.

"Well, well, well," a female voice said. "If it isn't Deputy Dick himself looking all comfy cozy dancing cheek to cheek."

Turning, Abby saw a blonde in a low-cut dress standing a few feet away. Her eyes, which had the beginnings of crow's feet around them, smoldered with what could have been hurt or anger or both.

"How do you like the *Jesse II*, honey?" the woman slurred.

"It's a nice boat."

"Have you tried out that walnut bed below deck, or does the sex come later?"

Taken aback, Abby stared at the woman. "You're out of line with talk like that."

"Didn't mean to offend your sensibilities, hon. That bed's got quite a history. Legend has it Steve's great grandpappy won it in a poker game—from a slave trader no less. Then his granddad inherited it. I'm sure Steve'll tell you about him, if he hasn't already. He was the fisherman of the family. Quite a lover in his own right too. I understand he had a whole passel of kids, not all of 'em legitimate. Eventually the bed got passed down to lover boy here. To make a long story short, the damn thing squeaks so loud you'd think you were screwing in the back seat of a Model T Ford."

"You're drunk, Meg," Steve said. "And you're making a fool of yourself."

"Not the first time and probably won't be the last. Who's your new girlfriend?"

The song ended and people stopped dancing, many of them staring at the spectacle.

"I don't think that's any of your business. Where's Hank?"

"I do believe he's in the crapper."

"You better go back to the bar and wait for him."

Again, the jukebox came alive, this time with the lilting refrain of Rick Nelson's "Traveling Man."

"They're playing your song, Steve. Got a gal in every port, this deputy does. Probably two or three in some of the bigger ones."

Steve took hold of the woman's arm. "That's enough, Meg."

She pulled away, fixing him with a cold glare of contempt. "Don't you touch me again or I'll scream," she said in a low controlled tone. "You don't want that, do you? How would you explain it when Hank came running?" She turned to Abby. "Since lover boy lacks the couth to introduce us, I'll do the honors. My name's Margaret, but my friends and former lovers call me Meg. What's your handle, honey?"

"Jane Fonda."

The woman gave Abby a puzzled look. Then she shrugged. "Don't recall seeing you before. You from around here?"

"I live in Scarboro."

"Well, I'm sure our resident stud will show you a good time. Ask him about the night we went skinny dipping in Diamond Lake and Earl Salter was going to arrest us until he realized the guy in the water with a hard-on was Steve. Nice chatting with you, Jane, but I gotta run. Don't want hubby getting suspicious. Might start asking questions none of us could answer."

She turned and walked away, listing from side to side. Halfway to the bar, she broke into song, to the tune of "Cotton Fields," her voice loud enough to compete with Rick Nelson's:

> "Oh when those bed springs start squeakin'
> You can't do very much sleepin'
> In those old walnut beds back home…"

Steve took Abby's hand and led her back to their booth. For the first time since she met the man, he seemed at a loss for words.

CHAPTER 22

I was the one to call it quits," Steve told Abby as they made their way down Lake Street toward the Inlet Inn. "So I guess tonight was payback time." Aside from his voice, the only sound came from their footsteps and the distant barking of a dog. The air was crisp and smoke curled from chimneys. "Sorry you had to be there when it happened."

"I'm not," she said and meant it. The incident had been a much more effective warning than Mavis Gilbert's heavy-handed admonition. Though Abby was attracted to Steve Crothers, she really didn't know him. Meg's intrusion had underscored that fact. Watch out, it had said. Don't let this man charm you further than you're prepared to go.

"I'd like to see you again," Steve said as they climbed the inn's front steps. "Hope you haven't decided I'm not your cup of tea."

"I'd never think of you as tea. A shot of smooth whiskey maybe."

"Since you don't drink, should I take that as a rejection?"

"Not necessarily. What have you got in mind?"

"Dinner tomorrow night. This time I'll take my car.

We can eat in Hatteras, Buxton, or maybe one of the towns farther north. Avon has a theater. If something good is playing, we could take in a movie. Or we could go all the way to Nags Head. It's got night spots where you wouldn't need a drawl or boots to fit in."

The mention of Nags Head brought back bittersweet memories for Abby. She wondered what the area would be like after all these years, deciding she wasn't quite ready to find out. "Nag's Head is quite a ways away."

"We don't have to go that far. It's a date then?"

"Sure, why not?"

Steve kissed her on the cheek. "Thanks for being such a good sport about everything," he said and handed her the remainder of her cake.

"It was an interesting evening. Thanks again for the cake."

Once Abby was in her room, her thoughts kept going back and forth between her date with Steve and her investigation, which was nowhere near complete. Too keyed up for bed, she went over to the window and gazed at the moonlit grounds and then closed the curtains and plopped down in the easy chair.

Her thoughts finally settled on her investigation, which she had to admit really hadn't gotten very far, even with Don Horvath emerging as a possible suspect. She thought of Glen Turpin's request for a color picture of Sheila Bostrum—she didn't know what to make of that. There was something bizarre about a lot of what was going on, she reflected. Why had Joel and Terry put on that weird performance in the Inlet Inn dining room? Why were they planning to build a greenhouse that wouldn't get much sun? What kind of intrigue were they involved in with Sheriff Mountcastle and his deputy Duane? And was it more than just coincidence that Sheila Bostrum *and* Rhonda Tolbert had stayed at the Inlet Inn? All these questions remained unanswered. The more Abby thought about them, the more she wondered if she had made any progress at all.

At least Beth Harker had surfaced as someone who might provide some answers. Abby could kick herself for telling Joel she would wait until Sunday to contact Beth. That had really been dumb, tantamount to surrendering her most effective weapon, the element of surprise. Once Beth learned about the affair from Joel, who obviously would put the best possible spin on it, the chance of Beth's incriminating him—or possibly herself—would be slim.

Abby considered reneging on her word. It was folly to allow Joel Crothers, still very much a suspect, to dictate the terms of her investigation. Yet there was no real evidence against him and even less against Beth. The last thing Abby wanted was to break up a relationship, especially if both parties were innocent.

The next two days would be critical, she knew. Tomorrow she would concentrate on Don Horvath. Sunday she would drive to Murfreesboro to interview Beth. If nothing of substance came from either effort, then there was little chance she would ever find out what happened to Sheila.

After climbing into bed and switching off the light, Abby thought again of Steve Crothers. She might not be making much progress with her investigation, but she was sure having an interesting time. In spite of mounting evidence that Steve was a world-class womanizer, she looked forward to seeing him again. She even found herself wondering, as she drifted toward sleep, what would have happened if Meg hadn't been at the Salty Dawg. The way the evening was unfolding, she decided, she just might have learned firsthand what it was like to make love in an antique squeaky bed passed down from an old Casanova to a relative more than happy to carry on the family tradition.

❦

Abby woke with a start. Sitting up, she heard the wail of a siren followed by voices, people shouting something about a fire. She noticed a copper glow through the curtains, and groggy and disoriented, she got out of bed and stumbled over to the window. Pulling apart the curtains, she saw through the trees what looked like a huge orange cloth being whipped about by wind.

She threw on some clothes and went down to the lobby where several people had gathered. Everyone seemed to be talking at once.

"Are you sure we're safe?" a woman wearing a "Nanticoke is for Lovers" sweatshirt over her nightgown asked. "What if those trees catch fire? It could spread here."

"No way," a man in a bathrobe and slippers replied. "There's a lot of open space between us and those trees. A fire couldn't cross that."

"I'm going to pack our suitcase just to be on the safe side. Come get me if it heads this way. I don't want to end up a charred cinder."

"Isn't this exciting?" a woman in a low-cut nightgown asked the short swarthy-looking man beside her.

"Yeah, right up there with tornadoes and earthquakes. Let's go pack our things."

Mavis Gilbert, wearing jeans and a flannel shirt, entered the lobby. "Don't be alarmed," she said. "The fire is in the field at the bottom of the hill. It's too far from the trees to spread."

"Is it Joel's greenhouse?" Abby asked.

"Either that or his trailer."

Abby ran back to her room and got her coat. Deciding not to walk because of the uneven, slippery terrain and the marshy area at the bottom of the hill, she grabbed her keys and hurried to the parking lot. The night had grown darker, the moon all but hidden by a bank of clouds. According to the clock on the Corolla's dashboard, it was three forty-four.

As she drove through the village, she encountered more traffic than she had seen her entire stay on the island, all of it headed toward the fire. There was a minor traffic jam on the dirt road leading to Joel's property, and about a hundred yards from the field she decided to pull over and walk.

She soon realized the flames came from beyond the trailer, a huge writhing yellow hand that gripped what was left of the greenhouse.

"Stand back," one of the fire fighters yelled. "It's gonna collapse any second."

An old-fashioned hook and ladder truck was parked some thirty yards from the fire, and a large group of spectators had gathered nearby. Spotting Earl Salter and a distraught-looking Joel Crothers off to one side, Abby headed toward them just as a third person approached from the other side of the field, his face glistening with sweat.

"Lost him, damnit. Chased him all the way to the school before he give me the slip."

Realizing the man was Duane, the young deputy, Abby stopped and pretended to watch the fire, hoping to overhear the conversation.

"Was it Steve?" Earl asked in a low voice.

"Who else would it be? Glen's not even on the island."

"Let the feller talk, Joel. Tell us, Duane. Was it Steve?"

"I didn't see his face. But he was moving too fast for somebody as old as Mr. Turpin."

"Where were you when you first saw this person?" Earl asked.

"In the trailer, exactly where I should've been. I was waiting for him to start digging up her body. Never entered my mind he'd torch the damn greenhouse."

"It had to be Steve," Joel said. "When was the last time he didn't show up for a fire?"

The question seemed to puzzle the big man, and, for a moment, he stared at the flames as though hypnotized. "That don't necessarily prove nothin'. He could've had another fire needed puttin' out. Had a date with that reporter, didn't he? He's probably humpin' the bitch right now."

Abby's cheeks burned but only for a moment. "The bitch," she announced as she stepped forward, "happens to be right here."

The three men looked at her in surprise, Earl in embarrassed disbelief.

"No offense, ma'am. I didn't mean any disrespect."

"Forget it, lard ass. Whose body were you talking about?"

The men looked at each other, the light from the fire flickering on their confused faces.

"Was it Sheila Bostrum's?"

Still no one answered. A fireman yelled out a warning a few seconds before the rear portion of the greenhouse crashed to the ground, sending a shower of sparks into the air.

"More water over here."

"Why bother?" another fireman said. "It's like pissin' on a forest fire."

Abby focused her attention on the young deputy. "Tuesday afternoon I saw you and Terry talking to the sheriff. I heard enough of the conversation to know you're involved in a scheme that's got something to do with that

area where a second greenhouse is supposed to be built."
She turned to Joel. "And I've got a feeling your performance yesterday at the Inlet Inn was part of that scheme.
My guess is someone buried a body in the middle of that
area and you and/or Terry discovered it and reported it to
Mountcastle. His plan was to sucker Steve or Glen into
digging up that body. Correct me if I'm wrong."

Still no response from the three men.

"As Joel can attest, I know about Rhonda Tolbert and
Sheila Bostrum. They're the reason I'm here. The *Gazette*
sent me to investigate their murders."

"This isn't any of your business, lady," Duane finally
said, regaining a semblance of composure. "It's a police
matter. You'll get the details at the proper time."

"Hell, she already knows what's goin' on," Earl said.
"Might as well tell her the rest. Tell me too while you're at
it."

"We're not telling her anything," Duane replied then
turned to leave. "Sheriff Mountcastle will release the information when he gets good and ready."

"Where're you going?" Joel asked.

"To call the sheriff and see if he wants to make an
arrest on the evidence we've got."

CHAPTER 23

The Nanticoke jail had a single cell, a small rectangular room with a low ceiling and whitewashed cinderblock walls.

Steve Crothers lay on one of the two bunks, eyes closed, hands folded across his chest. The eastern sky, visible through the barred window, was flush with the promise of sunrise.

"That newspaper woman's here," Earl Salter called. "Wanna talk to her?"

Steve opened his eyes and pulled himself to a sitting position. "I'd rather talk to a lawyer."

"Mountcastle said you can make one call."

"There isn't an Outer Banks lawyer I'd hire to fill out the short form of my income tax. I'll wait until I get to Bogue City. What time is it?"

"Goin' on six. Want me to let the reporter in?"

"Yeah. Might as well give her something to write about."

The deputy unlocked the door and Abby stepped into the cell. The door clanked shut behind her.

"Give a holler when you're done," Earl said. The outer door sucked shut.

"Is this a sympathy visit?" Steve asked. "Or are you

here for an exclusive with Nanticoke's version of Jack the Ripper?"

Abby sat down on the end of the bunk. "I'm here because I'd like to know your side of the story," she said in a subdued voice.

"You actually think I've got one?"

"I don't know what to think, Steve. I'm not even sure why you've been arrested. Nobody around here will tell me anything."

"They think I killed Sheila Bostrum."

"I gathered that. But I don't know why you're supposed to have done it."

"To keep her quiet about the affair we'd been having."

The words took a moment to sink in. "You and Sheila...were lovers?"

"Afraid so."

"The summer she disappeared?"

"Yeah, that summer."

Abby took a deep breath, exhaling in a prolonged weary sigh. "You sure are a hard dog to keep under the porch, aren't you?"

Steve got up and went to the cell door. "Never pretended otherwise. I told you straight up I wouldn't make a good husband."

"So you did. There's something I probably should've told you too. My real reason for being on the island is to investigate Sheila's disappearance."

Steve showed no surprise. "I figured you were up to something other than that lame article about Nanticoke in winter. The *Gazette* couldn't be that hard up for material. Are you a cop?"

"No. I work for the *Gazette*. Why didn't you tell me you didn't believe my cover story?"

"I didn't want to scare you off. I liked you too much."

Abby looked at him, trying to figure out if he was trying to con her with flattery. She had absolutely no idea what the man was up to. "So you were the guy in Sheila's life that summer."

"I was definitely one of 'em. Whether I was the only one, I can't say. I didn't see her at all the last few weeks before she disappeared."

Groggy from so little sleep, Abby tried to make sense of what she was hearing. "Why would you need to keep Sheila quiet about the affair?"

"I was married at the time. My wife's maiden name was Mountcastle."

Abby stared at him in stunned silence.

"I know," Steve said, returning to the bunk. "Anybody with a brain should know better than to marry the boss's daughter."

"I don't understand. What's being Mountcastle's daughter got to do with this?"

"I'm sure he'll be happy to explain. More than likely he'll say I couldn't afford him finding out about Sheila."

"Why not?"

"He probably would have fired me."

"He didn't fire you when you got divorced, did he?"

"By then it was too late. I'd finished my probationary period. If he canned me then, it would have to be for a job-related cause. I've always been a good cop, Abby. There was no way Mountcastle could punish me—until now."

She had mixed feelings about what she was hearing. She wasn't exactly thrilled to know about the affair with Sheila or the fact that Steve really did have a motive for killing her, but she was encouraged by the seemingly straightforward way he responded to her questions. He didn't act like a man guilty of murder.

"I'd like to know about the affair," she said. "How'd it

start and what exactly went on between you two?"

Steve continued to gaze straight ahead, toward the window. "We met when I took Joel and some of his buddies on a fishing trip," he finally said. "He and Sheila were working at the same restaurant and—"

"I know about Captain Jack's. Tell me about the fishing trip."

"Four people went, including Joel. I took them out on a Saturday morning and brought them back late that afternoon. The two females went to the Inlet Inn to freshen up and get ready for a cookout on the beach. About four-thirty or so I was swabbing the *Jesse II*'s deck when I happened to look up and see Sheila standing on the dock. She made it clear she was mine for the taking. Like I told you, I was married at the time. Part of me wasn't happy with what I was about to do, but the other part…well, I guess it welcomed the opportunity."

"Did Joel know about this?"

"Not unless Sheila told him, which I doubt."

"Wasn't she more or less his girlfriend?"

Steve shook his head. "Joel already had a girlfriend. If he'd showed any interest in Sheila, I wouldn't have responded to her the way I did."

"Why didn't he take Beth Harker on the fishing trip instead of Sheila?"

"You'll have to ask him. My guess is he wasn't looking for a date to take along, just some fellow workers at the restaurant."

As far as Abby could tell, Steve wasn't acting any different from the way he always did. There was no urgency or fear in his voice, and he wasn't being evasive. If she had been administering a lie detector test, which in a way she was, he would have passed with flying colors. "Tell me more about you and Sheila," she said.

"I expected what we did to be a one-time thing and

assumed she felt the same way. I had no reason to think otherwise until she showed up a week or so later. I wasn't exactly disappointed to see her, but I knew what we were doing had to stop soon and I told her so. She didn't disagree. When we said goodbye the second time, she sounded like she meant it. But a couple weeks later there she was again, wanting to take up where we'd left off. This time I put my foot down. She got all bent out of shape. When I tried to explain that I was married and couldn't handle an on-going affair, she said I should've thought of that before we made love the first two times."

"So you kept seeing her?"

"For a while. She threatened to kill herself if I dumped her, which scared the hell out of me. But finally I got so fed up I told her I wasn't ever going to see her again, regardless of what she threatened. Turned out I never did."

"Do you think she killed herself?" Abby asked.

"At the time I thought she probably did. Now I don't, assuming that really was her body Joel and Terry found. It's pretty hard to commit suicide and bury yourself too."

"Yeah, I guess it is." Abby went to the window and gazed through the bars at the dimly lit street. The horizon was yellowish orange, minutes from sunrise. In the parking lot next to Graylock's Lair, a few seagulls were picking over last night's leavings. At least his account fits the facts, she decided. Sheila disappeared August third and, according to the Inlet Inn's register, she spent June twenty-fourth, July first, and July sixteenth on Nanticoke. "Why weren't you at the fire last night, Steve?"

"Never heard the alarm. I was so pissed off at Meg I couldn't sleep, so I made myself a stiff drink and the next thing I knew there was pounding on the door. It was Earl and that new deputy telling me I'm under arrest."

"Is that when you learned about Sheila's body?"

"Yeah. They must've found it while digging up fresh

dirt to put in the greenhouse. Apparently, Joel figured out about the affair and suspected I was the one who killed her. Instead of telling me about the body, he told Mountcastle."

Abby went back to the bunk and sat down. "As far as I'm concerned, Joel could've happened on Sheila's body because he knew exactly where to look. There are other possible suspects too, aside from Joel."

"Who?"

"Beth Harker for one."

Steve shook his head. "She wouldn't kill a mosquito if it had malaria and was getting ready to bite her. Who else have you got in mind?"

"Glen Turpin. Apparently Mountcastle suspected him as well."

"Earl told me about that. The drunk act Joel and Terry put on at the Inlet Inn was for Glen's benefit as well as mine."

"I figured as much. But why would Glen want Sheila dead?"

"After he and Mavis moved to Nanticoke, Mountcastle got a call from a police chief in some Virginia town asking to be notified if Glen ever moved again. Seems he'd been a person of interest in a murder there. The chief didn't want to lose track of him."

For the first time since entering the cell, Abby felt something other than gloom. "Who was the murder victim?"

"A student at the school where Glen was a teacher."

"Was the victim male or female?"

"Female."

"My God, Steve, aren't you beginning to see a pattern in all this?"

"Glen Turpin a serial killer? Stranger things have happened, I suppose. But Glen couldn't have set fire to

Joel's greenhouse. Earl said he wasn't on the island last night."

Abby's spirits soared. "Glen could have had it set. Or maybe somebody else set it for a reason totally unrelated to Sheila. Steve, I'm pretty sure Joel and Terry have been growing marijuana. Juanita said something that made me suspect it, and Terry pretty much confirmed it when he wouldn't show me that partitioned-off area at the back of the greenhouse. If they really are growing weed, a rival drug dealer could've set that fire to eliminate the competition."

Steve sat up straight on the bunk. "I'll mention that to my lawyer. Actually you'd make a pretty good defense counsel yourself, Abby, with all the suspects you've got lined up."

"There's one more—Sheila's stepfather. I've got a feeling they had a sexual relationship. I'll check it out when I get a chance, but right now Glen seems the likeliest suspect. My first night on Nanticoke I told him my real reason for being out here, and he's acted strange ever since. He even asked me for a color picture of Sheila."

"Why would he want that?"

"Who knows? It sounded fishy at the time and even more so now. Do you remember the name of the town in Virginia where Glen lived?"

Steve shook his head. "Mountcastle would have it on file."

"I'll ask him," Abby said and kissed Steve on the cheek.

Confident for the first time that her investigation was actually starting to get somewhere without a person named Crothers being the most likely suspect, she got up from the bunk and yelled for Earl to come open the cell door.

CHAPTER 24

Abby composed a brief article on her laptop computer, reporting that Sheila Bostrum's body had been discovered on Nanticoke Island and that Steve Crothers, the island's chief deputy, had been arrested for her murder. She transmitted the story to the *Gazette* and then, after plugging back in her room phone, called Charlene Greer's number. Getting her boss's voice mail, she left a message saying Steve might be innocent, in which case Sheila's murder was far from being solved.

"I'm hoping to talk to the sheriff this morning," she said. "I'll call after that to discuss what my next move should be."

The second ferry of the day left Diamond Lake with Abby aboard. She was able to cat nap in her car much of the way, and when she arrived on the mainland, she didn't feel as tired as she thought she would, considering how little sleep she'd had the previous night. Since it was Saturday, she was concerned Mountcastle wouldn't be in his office, but he was there. He even seemed happy to see her.

"I hope you understand I was in the process of setting a trap," he told her. "I was afraid if you knew what was going on, you might spoil the bait. I never really thought Glen Turpin killed Sheila, but I couldn't dismiss him altogether. Her body was found near the Inlet Inn, and the police chief in Wisteria, Virginia, had asked me to keep an eye on Glen because a student at the school where he taught had been murdered. The student was a boarder at Glen's house and was found dead on his front porch. I figured as long as we were setting a trap for Steve, we might as well let Glen sniff the bait too."

"Was it Joel who discovered Sheila's body?" Abby asked.

"Actually it was Terry Pitts but Joel was right there with him."

"That's a big field, Sheriff. Don't you find it strange they were digging where Sheila's body just happened to be buried?"

"That was explained to my satisfaction. You see, that's the least rocky part of the field. The dirt there is relatively easy to dig up *and* it makes the best soil for growing tomatoes. It also makes a good place to plant a body."

"Are you sure it was Sheila's body they found?"

"I am. The dental records match."

"What was the cause of her death?"

"I don't know yet. The body was too decomposed."

"Then how did anyone know it was Sheila?"

"Joel recognized her ring, which he remembered from when they worked together at Captain Jack's. Ever since Bostrum accused him of falling for Sheila, Joel had wondered if maybe Steve had been involved with her. When her body was discovered on Crothers property, Joel figured Steve killed her to shut her up—which is exactly what happened."

"I assume you had the body moved. How'd you manage that without Steve knowing?"

"We did it at night with the help of the coast guard."

Abby paused, giving the information a chance to sink

in. It occurred to her that Dorothy Horvath might learn of Sheila's death from the upcoming article in the *Gazette*. "Does Sheila's mother know about all this?" she asked.

"I told her first thing this morning. I didn't do it right away for the same reason I didn't tell you. I didn't want word getting out and messing up my chance to nail Steve." The sheriff reached for his pipe. "I haven't told Bostrum yet. I figured you might want to do the honors with him. Turned out he was right about a Crothers being responsible for Sheila's disappearance—just the wrong one."

"Sheriff, do you have to smoke that thing while I'm here?"

"Well, no, not if it bothers you." Mountcastle set the pipe back on his desk.

"I'm not so sure Steve is responsible," Abby said. "I know Glen was supposedly in Raleigh when Joel's greenhouse burned down, but he could've hired someone to set the fire. Or maybe he snuck back and set it himself."

"Duane said he saw Steve set that fire."

Abby shook her head. "Then he's changed his story. I heard him say he couldn't make a positive identification."

"And that's exactly what he'll say at the trial. He doesn't have to be a hundred percent sure. We've got the body and we can prove motive and opportunity. That ought to be enough to convince any reasonable jury."

"What exactly was the motive?" Abby asked, deciding to test the accuracy of Steve's perception.

Mountcastle didn't look happy with the question and hesitated before responding. "Steve was married to my daughter at the time," he said, his voice showing anger for the first time during the conversation. "If Marlene had found out about the affair, she would've left the son of a bitch in a heartbeat. And I'd have fired him just as fast."

"Was Steve's job that important to him?"

"I'll tell you how important it was. He never showed

the least bit of interest in my daughter until Everett Sawyer had his heart attack and put in for retirement. Steve was Everett's assistant then, and he wanted the job of chief deputy so bad he could taste it. All of a sudden, he's dating Marlene hot and heavy and before you know it they're married. Naturally, I gave him the job. Then as soon as his probationary period was up, he lost interest in Marlene and the marriage."

Since objectivity had never seemed to be Mountcastle's strong suit, Abby wondered if his account of what had happened between his daughter and Steve was accurate. "I was under the impression Marlene left the island because she couldn't stand the isolation."

"She'd have tolerated it if Steve had been a decent husband. He got what he wanted and then made her life miserable."

Abby started to mention Mountcastle's granddaughter and how much Steve loved her and then thought better of it. "Early this morning I had a long talk with Steve," she said. "He didn't act like a murderer. He was forthcoming about everything, including the affair with Sheila. He didn't have to admit that. If he'd denied having anything to do with her, I don't think you'd have much of a case. You probably wouldn't even be able to hold him very long."

"Wrong," Mountcastle said with obvious satisfaction. "We found a note on Sheila's body that proves beyond a shadow of a doubt she and Steve were lovers. The reason he was so forthcoming is he knew about that note."

"How could he?"

"Duane made the mistake of mentioning it to that lunkhead Earl Salter, and Earl told Steve after the arrest. I wanted to be the one to spring that on him. But it's not a big deal. The important thing is we've got undeniable evidence that Steve Crothers and Sheila Bostrum were lovers."

Abby felt a growing uneasiness in the pit of her stomach. "Tell me about the note," she said.

"It was in a little plastic coin purse Sheila had in her sweater pocket. The plastic is what kept it from deteriorating. I'm not going into the specifics of what it said because I don't want this case tried in the media."

"I've already told the *Gazette* about Sheila's body and the fact that Steve was arrested for her murder. That's all I intend to report unless I find evidence that Steve didn't do it. It might help if I knew what he said in that note."

"He didn't say anything. Sheila wrote the note. It's clear she'd have given it to Steve if he hadn't killed her first."

"What did it say?"

"It was a sappy kind of thing a young female would write. Obviously the affair had been going on for some time and Steve wanted out."

"I really would like to see the note, Sheriff," Abby said, her patience wearing thin.

Mountcastle shook his head. "I'm not going to take a chance it'll show up in the media before the trial."

"Then the only thing I can conclude is you're trying to hide something, especially since you've been less than candid with me in the past." Abby stood up. "I'll mention your lack of cooperation in my next article."

"Bitch," Mountcastle said under his breath then picked up his pipe and lit it.

"What's it going to be, Sheriff? I've got things to do."

Mountcastle sucked on the pipe and blew out smoke. "Is this conversation strictly off the record?"

"If you want it to be."

"If I show you the note, do you swear neither you nor your paper will mention it—at least not until after Steve is found guilty?"

"Or innocent. Yes, I swear."

The sheriff set the pipe in an ashtray and got up from his desk. "Wait here," he said and left the room. A minute later, he returned with a folded sheet of paper enclosed in a clear plastic sleeve. After carefully removing the paper, he unfolded it to reveal small, neat handwriting, the work of a blue ballpoint pen. "That's evidence, so be careful with it," he said, handing Abby the sheet of paper.

> *My darling Steve,*
>
> *You say you want me to go away and forget how good we are together, but I can't ever do that because I know deep in your heart you love me as much as I love you. I'm the one who can make you happy, not Marlene. You said you don't love her, so staying with her doesn't make any sense, not for you or her.*
>
> *I've never felt this way about anyone, Steve, and I can tell from the way you make love to me that you feel the same way. I can't just let you walk away. If ever there were two people who were made for each other, it's us. Please, please, please tell Marlene you don't love her anymore for both our sakes and hers too.*
>
> *Steve, I love you with all my heart, soul, and body, forever and ever.*
>
> *Sheila*

Abby handed the note back to Mountcastle. "Could somebody else have written that and planted it on the body?"

"The handwriting matches a sample of writing we know to be Sheila's."

"Steve would have to be a complete idiot to kill her but not destroy that note. It's the one piece of incriminating evidence linking the two of them."

"I can think of two logical explanations," the sheriff said, carefully refolding the note and replacing it in the plastic sleeve. "One, he didn't know the note was in Sheila's possession. Or two, he didn't think her body would ever be found."

"But if she was going to be meeting him, why write a note? She could've told him everything in person."

"Maybe she didn't know she'd be seeing him on that particular day. Or maybe she wrote it because it's harder for some people to say things in person than write 'em. Hell, Abby, I don't have to convince you of Steve's guilt. You won't be on the jury. Even if you were, I'd bet a month's salary that by the end of the trial you'd vote guilty just like the others."

Abby resisted an impulse to dump the pipe and ashtray in Mountcastle's lap as she got up from the chair. "Where exactly is Wisteria, Virginia?"

"About thirty miles west of Charlottesville. Will Ramsdell is the police chief. At least he was when he asked me to keep an eye on Glen."

Abby wrote the name on a piece of paper. "Thanks for the info," she said and turned to leave. "Even though I had to pry some of it out of you."

CHAPTER 25

Abby sat in her car near the sheriff's office and dialed the Horvaths' number on her cell phone, planning to hang up if Dorothy answered. After three rings, a man said a garbled hello.

"Don?"

"Yeah. Who's this?"

"If your wife can hear you, just pretend I'm a telemarketer and listen to what I'm saying. Wednesday night I talked to Dorothy about Sheila's disappearance, and now I want to talk to you. I'll meet you in twenty minutes at the marina across from the little strip mall of gift shops on Water Street. If you don't show up, I'll assume you're guilty, and I'll pass on what I know to the sheriff."

Before Horvath could respond, Abby clicked off her cell phone. Delighted with the way she handled the call, she cranked the ignition, pulled away from the curb, and headed for Port Austin. Nothing wrong with her thought processes now, she told herself. Her brain was humming like a set of well-oiled gears.

Twenty minutes later, she was standing at the edge of a long wooden pier, her back to the boat slips where many of the same pleasure crafts she had noticed Wednesday were tethered.

Small waves slapped rhythmically against their hulls and the nearby pilings.

There wasn't a person in sight and only two cars, both parked in front of the shop where Abby had bought gifts for her mother and Kevin. The longer she waited, the more her confidence waned. *He's not coming. He's calling my bluff and there's not a damn thing I can do about it.*

Minutes passed and finally a car pulled up to the curb. A man with a trim build, close-set eyes, and a receding hairline got out and headed in Abby's direction. He did not look happy.

"Don Horvath?" Abby called, making sure her handbag was unzipped, in case she needed quick access to her cell phone, then wondered what the hell she would do with it if he attacked her—throw it at him? What she really needed was her mother's pistol.

"What exactly am I supposed to be guilty of?"

"Sleeping with your stepdaughter for starters."

Horvath's jaw dropped. "Where'd you get that crazy notion?"

"Originally from Mary Bethune, who's in charge of Captain Jack's boarding house. The summer Sheila disappeared, Mary heard her talking on the phone in a romantic way to somebody named Don."

Horvath chuckled. "There's at least fifty guys around here named Don. I know some of 'em myself."

"According to one of Sheila's friends, the Don in question was you."

"What friend are you talking about?"

Don't say it. You don't want to put Angie in danger. "One Sheila always confided in about the men in her life," Abby said. "You were no exception."

"I don't believe you. Anybody had that kind of information, it would've come out during the investigation."

"Not necessarily." Abby paused, trying to think of a

reasonable explanation. "My source chose not to tell the sheriff."

"Oh yeah. Why?"

"The person decided to give you the benefit of the doubt...in case you might be innocent."

"I am innocent."

"Of Sheila's murder or of sleeping with her?"

"Haven't you heard? They found her body on Nanticoke. Her murderer is in custody."

"Her alleged murderer," Abby corrected. "Steve Crothers didn't kill Sheila."

"The sheriff sure thinks he did. You better go have a talk with him."

"I already have. If I talk to him again, it's going to be about you. I was hoping Dorothy wouldn't have to learn about any of this."

Horvath paused, his aura of confidence starting to fade. "You aren't going to tell her, are you?"

"No, but I will tell Sheriff Mountcastle. After he questions Sheila's friend, it's just a matter of time before he'll come knocking on your door."

The way Horvath glared at her made Abby's heart beat faster. If he attacked her, what could she do? Jump in the water and try to swim to safety? She wasn't a particularly good swimmer, so that was out. She could stand her ground and fight the guy, but Horvath was bigger and probably stronger. The only other alternative she saw was to run screaming toward the tethered boats hoping somebody would come to her rescue. *Damn it, Mom! Why didn't you lend me that pistol?*

To Abby's great relief, Horvath's anger seemed to subside. "Damn Sheila Bostrum," he muttered in frustration. "It's been five years and she's still tormenting me."

Abby's heart rate began to slow. "Want to tell me about it?" she asked, her confidence returning.

For a moment, Horvath was silent. "It was her doing," he finally said in a voice that sounded almost apologetic. "I never wanted it to happen. And I didn't do a thing to make it happen. I swear to God, not one single thing."

"What exactly did happen?"

"Sheila seduced me—that's what happened. You see, I work nights. Usually I don't go to bed until Dorothy leaves for her work in the morning, and I get up around three in the afternoon. One afternoon I woke up and found Sheila lying next to me in the bed. She was naked and she was doing things to me that I couldn't resist. I should've resisted—I know that—but at the time I just couldn't. It would have taken a saint under the circumstances."

"So you did have an affair with her."

"No, I did not. I had sex with her. I had sex with her one time and one time only. I've regretted it ever since."

Confident that Horvath's anger was no longer directed at her, Abby decided to try tightening the screws. "Normally when two people sleep together, that's the beginning of a relationship, not the end. I'm sure you and Sheila didn't just ignore each other."

"Well, I certainly ignored her. At least I tried to. She wouldn't take no for an answer. She said we were too good in bed not to continue our relationship. When I told her I wasn't going to have anything more to do with her, she laughed and said it was just a matter of time before she'd have her way with me again. Thank God, her job at the restaurant started a few days later, and she moved out of the house. But that didn't stop her from harassing me. She called me all the time, at home and at work. It was always the same, telling me what good lovers we were and how much she missed having my body next to hers. She said the filthiest things imaginable, like one of those phone-sex whores. I'd hang up as soon as I realized who it was, but then she started writing me letters and even coming to the house during the day and pounding on the door until I had no choice but to let her in. I didn't want her making a scene. I was afraid the neighbors would see us and word would get back to Dorothy. Once inside, she'd take off her clothes and parade around naked, coming as close to me as I'd let her, hoping I'd give in. I never did. As God is my witness, I never gave in to her but that one time."

He's like a fish on a line, Abby thought. Don't reel him in too fast or you might lose him. "How long did this go on?"

"Weeks. But it stopped long before she disappeared."

"How long?"

"Three weeks, maybe a month."

"All of a sudden or gradually?"

"All of a sudden. No more calls, no more letters, no more visits. My prayers were finally answered."

Abby felt on a roll. It seemed to her that she was both participant and observer, as though she were directing a movie in which she was also the star. Not only was she interrogating Horvath but watching herself perform. It was a phenomenal feeling, so wonderful it scared her. She wondered if she was getting manic or possibly already there.

"Any idea why she stopped contacting you?" she asked, trying to rein herself in, slow herself down, narrow her focus. She needed to put everything out of her mind except the task at hand, which was to question Horvath in such a way that she could determine whether or not he killed Sheila Bostrum. Nothing else mattered. If she really were getting manic, she'd deal with that later.

"Maybe she found some other poor slob to torment."

"A new lover?"

"Who knows? I really don't think Sheila wanted me as a lover. I think she wanted to punish me for marrying her mother. By putting me through hell—me, a

God-fearing Christian who believes adultery is a sin. I think she hoped my marriage would crumble under the stress. And if it didn't, at least she'd have made my life miserable, paid me back for taking Dorothy away from her father."

Abby didn't know whether to believe the man or not. "Her disappearance was convenient for you, wasn't it?"

"I can't deny that. I sweated blood because of that girl. For weeks, I prayed that God would lift my burden. Finally He did."

"Did you help Him along?" Abby expected a denial but hoped Horvath's response would be revealing nonetheless.

"No," he calmly replied. "The Lord doesn't need my help to accomplish His will. Sure I benefited by not having Sheila around any longer. But I didn't kill her. You'll have to look elsewhere if that's what you're after." Horvath paused. "What exactly are you after? Sheila's killer? Or do you intend to blackmail me, tell Dorothy about all this unless I pay for your silence?"

"How much would you pay?" Abby asked, hoping the man's response would provide a clue to his guilt or innocence.

"Not one single penny. But I'll tell you what I would do. The *Bible* teaches an eye for an eye, and if you so much as breathe a word of this to my wife, I'll hunt you down and make you sorry you ever did."

Abby wondered if the man was capable of making good on such a threat, deciding he probably was. "Did you threaten Sheila like that? Tell her you'd make her sorry if she didn't stop hounding you?"

"No, I did not. And I won't be blackmailed."

"I have no intention of blackmailing you. My interest is in whether or not you killed Sheila. And so far I'm not convinced that you didn't."

"Well, I can't do anything about that. I'd be lying if I said I wasn't happy to have her out of my life. But I didn't kill her. My conscience is clear about that. I just hope yours will be clear when it comes to Dorothy. She's suffered terribly, and she's suffering even more now that Sheila's body has been found." Horvath paused again, gazing in the direction of the tethered boats. "You know, I still find it hard to believe that girl was Dorothy's daughter. She had a lot going for her in the looks department, but she didn't have any character. She went through more boyfriends than you can shake a stick at, probably sleeping with all of 'em. She had no sense of morals, no concept of being faithful to a mate, or the body being God's temple. Young men were there to be used and thrown away and, as it turned out, so was I. What Sheila Bostrum did to me and what she was doing at least indirectly to her own mother—that was inexcusable. To my way of thinking, it was downright evil."

CHAPTER 26

As she watched Horvath drive away, Abby wondered if he had told the truth. Even if his relationship with Sheila had ended when he said it did, after their first sexual encounter, he still could have killed her. The man seemed capable of great rage and of inflicting even greater harm. She considered letting Mountcastle know what she had learned about Horvath but decided to wait and see what resulted from her Virginia trip. If it turned out that Glen Turpin killed Sheila, there would be no reason for the sheriff to have information that could jeopardize Dorothy's marriage.

Abby dialed Charlene Greer's number on her cell phone, once again getting her boss's voice mail. This time she clicked off without leaving a message and called her mother, who answered almost immediately. After learning that everything was fine at home, Abby explained that Sheila Bostrum's body had been found and the local deputy sheriff arrested for the murder.

"The guy you were planning to go out with last night?"

"Yeah, Mom, that guy. I did go out with him, and I think he's innocent. Right now, I'm heading for Wisteria, Virginia, to investigate a more likely suspect. I don't know how long it'll take me. I have to contact the police chief and follow up on any leads he might give me. Can you take care of Kevin a while longer?"

"Of course. But I'm worried about you, Abby. You don't sound like yourself. Are you all right?"

"What do you mean I don't sound like myself?"

"You sound all wound up. You're still taking your meds, aren't you?"

It suddenly occurred to Abby that she hadn't even thought about her medication since...when? Yesterday? "Of course. I'm just excited about the turn of events in this case."

"You've been under a lot of stress lately. That can trigger a manic episode, you know. Have you been getting enough sleep?"

"Everything's under control, Mom."

"I hope so. Take whatever time you need, Abby, but for God's sake be careful. I don't know what Kevin or I would do if something happened to you."

After ringing off with her mother, Abby took one of her lithium pills, making sure she drank plenty of water from the bottle she kept in her car. She tried Charlene Greer's number one more time, again getting her voice mail. Deciding that it didn't make sense to delay the Virginia trip any longer, especially since it could be hours before she actually spoke with Charlene, even longer if the woman happened to be taking Saturday off, Abby got out her atlas, picked out a route to Wisteria that looked suitable, and headed for Richmond. From there she would take Route 64 to Charlottesville. If she made good time, she should get to Wisteria well before dark.

As she drove, Abby reflected on what she had learned so far. Much of the evidence, she had to admit, pointed toward Steve.

The fact that he would have been fired had

Mountcastle found out about the affair with Sheila was definitely incriminating, as was the fact that Sheila's body had been discovered on Crothers's property. But there were other possible scenarios that could account for Sheila's death. The odds might not be in Steve's favor, but he hadn't been convicted yet.

She stopped for gas on the south side of Richmond and, while at the filling station, tried her boss's number again. This time Charlene answered. After congratulating her on the recently submitted story, she asked why Abby thought the wrong person was in custody.

Abby explained that the sheriff was too close to the case and had too much personally invested to consider anybody but Steve a serious suspect. "As far as I'm concerned, at least three other people could have killed Sheila. I'm on my way to Wisteria, Virginia, to investigate one of them."

"I think you should concentrate on what you've already submitted," Charlene said. "We've got the makings of a first-rate story here but you need to flesh it out. When was Sheila's body discovered and by whom? Why exactly did the sheriff think Steve Crothers and not someone else killed her? I assume you've already interviewed the sheriff."

"I talked to him this morning."

"Go see him again if you have to. What about Lloyd Bostrum? Have you interviewed him yet?"

"I tried before I went out to Nanticoke. He wouldn't talk to me."

"I imagine that will change once he realizes his daughter's body has been found and her killer arrested. Try talking to him again. I'm planning on this being our lead story tomorrow, Abby, and I envision several follow-up articles, including one on Bostrum. His reaction to what's happened should be interesting, especially since he asked the *Gazette* to get involved in the first place. Where exactly are you now?"

"The outskirts of Richmond."

Charlene sighed. "I wish you'd called before you left."

"I did. I kept getting your voice mail."

"Soon as you get to Wisteria then, I want you to sit down at your laptop and turn this story into something the *Gazette* can really be proud of. You'll do that, won't you, Abby?"

"I'll try. Can I have some extra time to finish the investigation?"

"I'm afraid not."

"You said I could have an extension if I needed one. I definitely do."

"I said you *probably* could have an extension. That was before I realized how shorthanded we'd be without Sid Beckwith. Work is piling up."

"I really do need more time," Abby pleaded. "Glen Turpin was a suspect in a young woman's murder in Wisteria. If he did kill her, there's a good chance he killed Sheila Bostrum and Rhonda Tolbert."

"I'll give you one extra day," Charlene said after a pause. "Be back in the office Tuesday morning."

"What if I have problems finding the people I need to talk to? Tomorrow is Sunday, which isn't the best time to conduct an investigation. The police chief might not be available, not to mention other people I'll need to interview. Plus, I'll need to go back to Bogue City to tie up loose ends there."

"I'm sorry but that's the best I can do. If I were you, I'd turn around and head back to Bogue City right now. Whether you do or not, keep in mind you'll need to submit an expanded version of your story no later than seven tonight. I've got a slot reserved on tomorrow's front page."

"But, Charlene—"

"See you bright and early Tuesday, Abby. If not before."

❧❧❧

A cold drizzle was falling when Abby reached the Blue Ridge Mountains some twenty miles west of Charlottesville. She whipped past an eighteen-wheeler struggling in low gear and a large RV that wasn't going much faster, glad she didn't have to follow either vehicle up the mountain, thereby wasting precious time. The higher she climbed, the thicker and darker the clouds became. Finally, they settled in around her like fog, forcing her to turn on her wipers and headlights and slow nearly to a crawl.

Near the mountain's crest, a sign announced the Blue Ridge Parkway and gave mileage to towns and cities along its route—Lydia, Luray, and Front Royal to the north, Buena Vista and Roanoke to the south. A motel and a nearby restaurant swung into view, followed by the parkway itself—a grass-covered embankment that emerged from an outcropping of rock to Abby's right, crossed Route 64 atop a stone viaduct, and abruptly disappeared into spumes of mist to her left. Since all she had eaten the entire day were peanut butter crackers and candy bars from the gas station in Richmond, she considered stopping. She decided to keep going, determined to save every minute she could.

By the time she was halfway down the mountain's western side, the rain had stopped. Five minutes later in the valley below, the sun was shining, as though the weather she just passed through existed in a separate time zone.

Once inside the Wisteria town limits, she stopped at the first motel she came to, the Shenandoah and, while registering, asked the desk clerk for directions to the police department.

Abby spent the next hour expanding her story, adding information she had learned from various people, including Sheriff Mountcastle, though, as promised, she left out any mention of a note found on Sheila's body. It was dark when she finally transmitted the story to the *Gazette*.

After freshening up a bit, she drove to the police station—an oblong brick building between a barber shop and a hardware store, both closed—just off the town's main street. Two officers were inside, a paunchy young man seated at a desk and a thinner, slightly older cop, mid-thirties perhaps, who was rummaging through an open filing cabinet on the far side of the room.

She told the younger officer that she was looking for Chief Ramsdell.

"Who?"

"Will Ramsdell. He used to be the police chief here. I'm hoping he still is."

"Harold Hawkins is the chief now, ma'am. He went home 'bout an hour ago. Is it something you need to talk to him about or will one of us Indians do?"

"It's Mr. Ramsdell I need to see. Any idea where I can find him?"

The young officer shook his head. "Sorry, I never met the man."

"I know Will," the other cop said. He closed the filing cabinet and came over to Abby. "What do you want to see him about?"

"Ten years ago he asked a North Carolina sheriff to keep an eye on Glen Turpin, who had just moved to the area. Apparently Glen had been a suspect in a murder here."

"Doesn't ring a bell."

"The victim was a student at the school where Glen taught and a boarder at his house."

The man nodded. "That sounds like the Lisa Strother case. You know something about her murder?"

Abby explained that she was investigating the murders of two young North Carolina women for the *Scarboro Gazette* and had reason to believe Glen might be connected to both. "I was hoping Mr. Ramsdell could fill me in on the details, in case there are similarities between Lisa's murder and the other two victims."

The officer scratched his head. "I had the impression there weren't any real suspects in Lisa's murder. But if Will said otherwise, that's good enough for me. He lives on the west side of town. I'll write down directions for you." He went to a nearby desk and began writing on a pad. "Will was a good cop. Tell him Marty said the place isn't the same without him."

"Did he retire?" Abby asked.

"Resigned." The officer tore off a sheet of paper and handed it to Abby. "He can give you the details—assuming he wants to talk about it."

CHAPTER 27

The last house on the street was a brick ranch tucked into a stand of straggly pines. The porch light was on, revealing a pickup truck in the driveway and a black and white cat nearby, crouched in a stalking position. As Abby approached, it scurried toward the colonial next door and disappeared behind a hedge. She rang the bell and, after a moment, a tall silver-haired man with a tanned, weathered face opened the door.

"Mr. Ramsdell?"

"I've been called worse."

Abby introduced herself, explaining that she worked for the newspaper in Scarboro, North Carolina, and asked if she could talk to him about a murder that took place in Wisteria several years earlier.

"You took longer than I thought. I figured you'd be here this afternoon."

"You were expecting me?"

"Leland Mountcastle called and said you were on your way. Said he'd arrested his former son-in-law for the murder you think Glen Turpin might have committed. You're probably wasting your time, Abby, but come on in and I'll tell you what I know."

As she entered the foyer, Abby smelled tomato sauce,

and it reminded her just how hungry she was. In the living room, she noticed a curio cabinet full of antique glassware—paperweights, art glass, depression glass, carnival glass, and cut glass—in nearly every imaginable shape and color. "I see you're a collector," she said, thinking even the Dromgooles would be impressed.

"Those pieces belonged to my wife. I was never much interested in glassware myself, but I couldn't bring myself to sell them. Mind if we talk in the kitchen? Otherwise, my spaghetti sauce is going to burn."

"It smells divine," Abby said and followed him into a combination kitchen-dining area with a sliding glass door that looked out onto a stone patio.

"Like something to drink—coffee, tea, orange juice, pop? I'd offer something stronger but I swore off the hard stuff."

"No thanks." The aroma of spaghetti sauce was much stronger as Abby sat down at a small wooden table next to the patio door. "Sorry I interrupted your dinner preparations."

"Normally I'd have eaten by now, but like I said, I expected you earlier, which is why I put off making this sauce as long as I did. Apparently, you think Lisa Strother's murder might be connected to another murder besides the one Mountcastle arrested his former son-in-law for. Tell me about the other victim."

"She was a young woman named Rhonda Tolbert," Abby said and went on to explain about Lloyd Bostrum's letter to the *Gazette* and his contention that Joel Crothers killed Rhonda as well as his daughter Sheila. "As far as I'm concerned, Joel is still a suspect in both murders, but after I found out Glen was a suspect in a young woman's murder here, I wondered if he might've killed all three. Sheila Bostrum and Rhonda Tolbert stayed at his inn on Nanticoke Island and Lisa Strother stayed at his house in

Wisteria. That's too much to be just a coincidence, if you ask me."

Ramsdell gave the sauce a stir. "To say Glen was a suspect in Lisa's murder is an overstatement. The truth is I didn't have a legitimate suspect. I asked Sheriff Mountcastle to keep an eye on him, in case something surfaced later on, but I never uncovered one shred of evidence against Glen or anybody else. They tell me every law officer has one crime that totally baffles him. Lisa's murder was mine. Have you had supper?"

"No, I haven't."

"Do you like spaghetti?"

"I love it."

"There's plenty here for the two of us."

Abby chuckled. "That remains to be seen. Your sauce smells so good I was considering inviting myself. Anything I can do to help?"

"You can fix the salad if you want to. Most of the ingredients are in the fridge. Tomatoes are in the pantry."

A few minutes later, Abby had washed and dried the lettuce and torn it into salad-sized pieces. By then Ramsdell had told her more about the Lisa Strother case, including the fact that the other boarder at Glen's house, also a student at the Blue Ridge Academy, thought Lisa had a crush on Glen. "Glen said it wasn't true but his denial made me suspicious. He acted nervous. In fact, he acted that way whenever I talked to him. He always seemed anxious and preoccupied, like a worried man with something to hide."

"That's exactly the way he's been with me," Abby said, thinking she might just prove Ramsdell wrong about this being a wasted trip. She began peeling a tomato. "You think something was going on between Glen and Lisa?"

"At the time I figured there might've been some hanky panky and Glen got scared people would find out, especially the higher-ups at the school. Just when I decided I was being overly suspicious, Glen and his sister moved back to North Carolina. Then I didn't know what to think."

"*Back* to North Carolina?"

"That's where they're from originally, a town called Caledonia."

"That's in my neck of the woods—well, almost. It's about forty-five minutes northwest of Scarboro."

"While I was investigating Lisa's murder, I asked the police chief in Caledonia to do a background check on the Turpins. I was hoping something would show up in Glen's past to justify my suspicion, but nothing did. In fact, the opposite happened. The report pretty much convinced me I'd been wrong about Glen—that, plus the fact that I never came up with any evidence."

Ramsdell gave the sauce a final stir, turned down the heat, and covered the pan with a lid. Then he got out a deeper pan, filled it with water, and set it on the stove.

"Who found Lisa's body?" Abby asked, slicing a tomato into wedges.

"Glen did, supposedly when he got home from the school library about ten-thirty that night. The coroner fixed the time of death about an hour earlier. Various people saw Glen at the library, but nobody could pin down precisely when he was there."

"Where exactly was the body found?"

"Under the front porch swing. According to Mavis, Lisa had been in her room most of the night studying for an exam and had apparently gone outside for a break. Judging from the bloodstains it was pretty obvious she was attacked while sitting in the swing. Mavis was watching TV on the opposite side of the house and didn't see or hear anything. Neither did the neighbors. It looked like somebody walked up to Lisa and, before she knew what was happening, slit her throat, which made me think she knew her assailant."

Abby finished slicing a pepper and began peeling an onion. "Did you ever consider the other boarder a suspect?"

"From all indications she and Lisa got along fine. Plus, the other girl was in the infirmary that night and couldn't have slipped out without being seen. I checked." Ramsdell finished buttering a loaf of Italian bread and placed it in the oven.

"Do you remember Mavis's daughter?" Abby asked, forcing herself to focus on her mission in spite of the delicious-smelling food nearby.

"I do. Pretty little girl. Does she still live with them?"

Abby nodded. "She's a big girl now. A young woman actually. Unfortunately, she's severely autistic. Could she have killed Lisa?"

"I don't see how. She was only seven or eight at the time."

Abby recalled the force with which Jelinda had pushed her away from the sandbox. Juanita Creef had even commented about the girl's exceptional strength. "You don't have to be big or strong to cut someone's throat."

"True, but I don't think Jelinda did it. There was no history of violence."

"What about Mavis?"

"Didn't have a motive."

"Maybe something really was going on between Glen and Lisa, and Mavis wanted it stopped."

The water had started to boil. Will opened a package of spaghetti and placed the contents in the pot.

"Quite a drastic way to stop it. Actually, that possibility did occur to me, which is why I asked the Caledonia police chief to include Mavis in his report. Turned out her record was as clean as Glen's, nothing at all to suggest she'd commit any kind of crime, let alone a murder."

"Do any of Lisa's relatives live around here?" Abby asked, thinking one of them might be able to provide some key information.

"Her parents live in Richmond. At least they did then. I talked to them a few times during the investigation, but neither could shed any light on the case. Lisa hadn't mentioned anything to them about Glen that sounded remotely incriminating. She did tell her mother she thought Mavis didn't particularly like her, but as far as I was concerned, that didn't make her a suspect. The other boarder told me Mavis wasn't very friendly to her either."

ભભભ

While eating her second helping of spaghetti, Abby asked what Will did for a living now that he was no longer a police officer.

"I'm a jack of all trades," he told her. "I do electrical work, some carpentry, plumbing if I have to."

"Why'd you give up being a cop?"

"After my wife died, I started doing things a cop shouldn't do. Like getting drunk for days at a time. I wasn't fit for the job anymore and after a while the mayor relieved me of it. I have no complaints. I was given every opportunity to straighten myself out but I wasn't up to the task."

"You seem pretty straightened out now."

"It's taken a while, but I'm getting there."

"Marty told me you were a good cop. He said to tell you the place isn't the same without you."

Will smiled. "Marty came to my rescue more than once those first couple of months after Martha died. I don't see a ring on your finger. Are you single or divorced or somewhere in between?"

"Divorced."

"Any kids?"

"A nine-year-old boy. Right now he's staying with my mom."

"I've got something in the basement I bet he'd like. I'll show it to you after supper. More bread?"

"Please. It's delicious."

Will passed her the Italian bread and took a slice for himself. Then he told her he wasn't happy with the way he handled the Lisa Strother case and wished he had done things differently. "For one thing, I shouldn't have been so heavy-handed in the way I investigated Glen. He probably didn't have any choice but to leave town. The official word at the school is he resigned, but I doubt that was the case. After the murder, they probably considered him a liability, especially with me poking around asking embarrassing questions. I should've been more discreet."

After they finished eating, Abby asked if it would be possible to see the report the Caledonia police compiled on Glen and Mavis.

"I don't see why not, assuming it hasn't been lost or misplaced. I'll check on it first thing in the morning."

"Would the police department have a picture of Lisa Strother?"

"Should have several. Why?"

"Yesterday Glen asked me for a picture of Sheila Bostrum. It was such a strange request I'm wondering if there's some physical similarity between her and Rhonda Tolbert."

"And if there is, you think it might be shared by Lisa Strother?"

"I know it sounds far-fetched."

Will shrugged. "Maybe not. The problem is you might not be able to tell much from the photographs we took of Lisa. Murder victims normally don't look like they did when they were alive. The Blue Ridge Academy might be a better approach. Maybe they have a yearbook with Lisa's picture in it. If not, they might have a picture of her in their files somewhere. The trick is to get those arrogant eggheads to cooperate. Unless you're a parent of one of their students or somebody thinking of sending a kid there, they generally won't give you the time of day. I'll see what I can come up with tomorrow and get back to you. How about some desert, Abby? There's pecan pie and vanilla ice cream."

"Sounds tempting. But if I eat anything else, I'm afraid you'll have to bring in a crane just to hoist me out of this chair."

"A little pie and ice cream won't hurt you. If we need a crane, I know just where to rent one."

CHAPTER 28

The buzzing noise startled Abby. It sounded farther away than her alarm clock should, the pitch lower, more of a drone than the whine she was used to hearing. She reached out anyway, not realizing she wasn't in her own bed until she felt neither clock nor bedside table. It took several more seconds for her to realize that she was in a motel almost two hundred miles from home.

She got out of bed, located the clock on the chest of drawers, and switched off the alarm. Opening the curtains, she noticed ice crystals on her car's windshield. The sky was a cloudless blue, the sun just beginning to crest the mountain in the distance. She wondered if Will was up and considered giving him a call. Better wait, she told herself. You don't want to impose too much on the man's good nature.

Abby had enjoyed her evening with Will Ramsdell. Not only had he filled her in on the Lisa Strother murder case, but he had provided a pleasant interlude, a chance to relax after four days of hectic and—Yes, Mom—stressful activity. She had learned that his wife had died of ovarian cancer and that his son had gotten into drugs his senior year of high school and was currently in a half-way house in Charlottesville. She had told him about her dead father and brother and that she was a recovering drug addict herself, and later on she felt comfortable enough in his presence to share the fact that she was bipolar. The only awkward moment had come when she got ready to leave. Sensing that he wanted to kiss her, she casually turned away before he could make his move.

After checking her cell phone for voice mail, she took a shower and then went to breakfast at a nearby restaurant that had been converted from an old streetcar. When she returned to her room, the phone was ringing.

"Ramsdell's Investigation Agency," said the voice at the other end of the line. "Where there's a Will there's a way. Have you had breakfast yet?"

"Just got back from Sullivan's Diner. You sure sound frisky this morning."

"That's because I have in my possession a copy of the Caledonia police report on Glen Turpin and Mavis Gilbert."

"You work fast, Will."

"I gave Marty a call first thing this morning and he got it for me. The bad news is Lisa's pictures are missing."

"Any chance the local newspaper would have one?"

"There isn't a local paper. It went out of business years ago."

"What about the library?"

"Closed on Sunday. The only other possibility is the Blue Ridge Academy. I still haven't figured out the best way to approach them, especially since most of the staff won't be there today. We'll discuss it when I pick you up. How soon can you be ready?"

"I'm ready now."

"See you in ten minutes. What's your room number?"

"One-twenty-seven. I'll be the bloated woman standing in the doorway pretending to be Nellie Bly."

ഇരുഇ

Driving through downtown Wisteria, Will told Abby she would probably have more success if she tackled the Blue Ridge Academy by herself. "At least that should be plan A. When I investigated Lisa's murder, I was persona non grata there. I doubt they'll feel any different now." He pointed toward a gently sloping hill in the distance with buildings neatly arranged in a semi-circle near the top. "That's it up there. Let's hope whoever's on duty will be reasonable about things."

As Will pulled up in front of the ivy-covered administration building, several pigeons exited the cupola. They flapped out over the neatly manicured grounds, circled, and one by one returned to the cupola.

"Good luck," he said as Abby opened the passenger door of his truck. "You're going to need it."

She quickly discovered that he was right. The only office in the administration building that wasn't locked belonged to the dean. Since no one was at the reception area, Abby went to the doorway leading to the inner office where a middle-aged woman with long black hair sat behind a mahogany desk surrounded by matching bookcases.

"Dean Taylor?"

Looking up, the woman regarded Abby above the wire frames of her reading glasses. "Yes?"

"Sorry to bother you but I don't know where else to turn. I'm looking for a picture of a former student who was here ten years ago. Her name is Lisa Strother."

"And who might you be?"

Abby introduced herself and explained that she worked for the *Scarboro Gazette*. She had considered giving a phony reason for wanting the picture, but neither she nor Will had been able to come up with an explanation that sounded remotely as plausible as the real one. "I'm investigating the murders of two young North Carolina women," she said. "I'm wondering if they might've been killed by the same person who killed Lisa."

The dean removed her glasses and placed them carefully on the desk. "You think Lisa's picture will help you make such a determination? How so?"

"I'm checking to see if there are physical similarities between the victims beside their age."

"You must have a suspect in mind. Exactly who is this person?"

"I'd rather not mention any names. The person I have in mind could very well be innocent."

"You think Glen Turpin killed them, don't you?"

The question took Abby by surprise. "He had ties to all three victims," she said after a pause.

"What kind of ties did he have to the North Carolina victims?"

Abby explained that Glen operated an inn on the barrier island Nanticoke and that the two victims in question had stayed there.

"One was found buried on property adjacent to the inn, and the other did her practice teaching on the island and stayed at the inn while she was there."

The dean brought her hands together and steepled her fingers. "I'm afraid I can't help you. We don't ordinarily keep pictures of our students in their files. Even if we did, a file from that long ago wouldn't be available now."

"I was thinking more in terms of a yearbook picture. Wouldn't the school have copies of old yearbooks?"

"It's doubtful we'd have them from that long ago. Our library has barely enough room for the books our students need on a regular basis. It's closed this morning anyway."

"Someone here must have access to old yearbooks. It's very important that I see a picture of Lisa."

"Listen, Ms. Burlew. I'm a busy woman. I don't ordinarily spend Sundays in my office unless I have important work to do. I told you the yearbook you're looking for isn't available. I'm not going to waste my time trying to track it down."

Keep your cool, Abby told herself. Maybe she'll listen to reason. "I appreciate the fact that you're busy, Dean Taylor. I wouldn't bother you if I weren't working on a case involving three murdered women. There could be a serial killer on the loose."

The woman dismissed Abby's argument with a flick of her wrist. "If you think Glen killed anyone, you're sorely mistaken. I knew him personally and he isn't capable of murder. His reputation and the reputation of this school were dragged through the mud ten years ago. I have no intention of helping you do it again."

"If the school was so sure of his innocence, why did it force him to leave?" Abby asked, her voice beginning to show her frustration.

"What choice did we have? No parent would send a daughter here thinking there might be a murderer on the staff."

"That's what this is all about, isn't it? You're more interested in avoiding bad publicity than seeing a killer brought to justice."

Leaning forward in her chair, the woman picked up her reading glasses and put them back on. "Have a good day, Ms. Burlew. And please be so kind as to close the door behind you."

℘℘℘

Will was reading the Caledonia police report when Abby returned to his truck. "You were right. Being helpful isn't what this school is all about."

"Who'd you talk to?"

"The dean. She threw me out of her office."

"Guess it's time to try plan B." Will handed Abby the

sheets of paper. "I was hoping it wouldn't come to this, but maybe what this school needs is a little police intervention. While I'm in there, you might check out that report to see if I missed anything."

Ten minutes later, a smiling Will Ramsdell emerged from the administration building and strode purposefully toward his truck.

"You got it?" Abby asked as he opened the door.

"Next best thing. The school librarian is going to meet us at the library. She's been instructed to hunt up the yearbooks covering the years Lisa was a student here."

Abby looked at him in amazement. "How'd you manage that?"

"I told the dean that Wisteria's current police chief was leaving soon and I'd been offered my old job back. I said if the school didn't cooperate, my first official act would be to reopen the Lisa Strother murder case. I made it clear that this time there would be full media coverage." Will smiled. "It wasn't a total fabrication, Abby. Marty told me my replacement just interviewed for the chief's job in Lynchburg. Let's head over to the library before it occurs to Ms. Taylor to call the police station or the mayor to see if I was bluffing."

CHAPTER 29

Don't get your hopes up too high," Will told Abby over the rim of his coffee cup. "Photographs don't always tell the truth about a person. Lisa might have looked different from her picture. So could the Tolbert girl."

They were having lunch at the Skyline, the restaurant Abby had passed the previous afternoon near the mountain top. She had already checked out of the Shenandoah Motel and was planning to leave for North Carolina immediately following the meal.

"Pictures don't lie about beauty marks," she said, still elated over what she had found out from Lisa Strother's yearbook photograph. "I know Rhonda had one and I'm pretty sure it was near the corner of her mouth, just like Lisa's. Now if they just have the same color hair."

"A lot of young redheads must have beauty marks."

"How many roomed at Glen Turpin's house or stayed at the Inlet Inn? I just hope the *Gazette* has a picture of Sheila Bostrum. Wouldn't it be something if all three turned out to look alike?"

"If they do, you better pick up the nearest phone and call Sheriff Mountcastle. It'll mean there's a serial killer on the loose."

Abby had always known her assignment carried the potential for danger. Until her encounter with Don Horvath, however, the danger seemed more abstract than real, something that couldn't actually happen to her. But when Horvath stood between her and safety at the Port Austin marina, he was more than an abstraction. Had he wanted to, he could have killed her. The same situation could occur again, and this time she might not be so lucky.

"When you investigated Lisa's murder, what did you learn about her?" she asked. "I mean, was she kind of wild?"

"She wasn't a prude by any means. She'd had her share of dates, and it was obvious from talking to various people that she wasn't a virgin."

"Who did she date?"

"Two seniors from the local high school plus a freshman at the University of Virginia. And, yes, I checked them out. None had a history of violence, and their relationships with Lisa didn't seem all that serious."

"It's amazing how much alike those girls were, Will. Your description of Lisa fits Rhonda Tolbert and Sheila Bostrum to a T. All were young, pretty, and promiscuous. That coupled with their physical resemblance is quite a coincidence, wouldn't you say?"

"I would, but whether it's more than a coincidence remains to be seen. Hell, Abby, half the young women out there today fit that description." Will chuckled. "I was born forty years too soon. I see your point, though. Their similarities might have made them targets for the same killer."

"Is there anything else about Glen Turpin you haven't told me? What about the women in his life? Did he go out with anyone in Wisteria?"

"As a matter of fact, he did—the music teacher at the Blue Ridge Academy. They dated for several years. I didn't get the impression they were in love, though they were obviously fond of each other. She left for another job about a year before Lisa was murdered. I have no idea where she is now."

"Did Glen go out with anybody after she left?"

"Not as far as I could tell."

"Was the music teacher a lot younger than Glen?"

"Actually they were about the same age."

Abby sighed. "Another theory down the drain. What about Mavis? I suppose her reputation in the community was as sterling as Mother Theresa's."

"Beyond reproach. A lot of her time was devoted to taking care of her daughter and keeping house for Glen and their boarders. She did all the appropriate things. Supported her church. Attended school functions. She even taught a course in beginning bridge at the YMCA where Glen taught an advanced class."

"What about her ex-husband? Did you learn anything about him?"

"Only what the police report said about them getting divorced. They were living in Caledonia at the time."

"Did Mavis go out with anybody when she lived in Wisteria?"

"Not that I'm aware of. Like I said, she was pretty much a homebody."

"She sure doesn't fit the profile of a serial killer, does she?"

"That doesn't mean she isn't one. The point is, you shouldn't go around trying to pin down who the killer is, Abby. That's Mountcastle's job. Just tell him what you've found out and let him take it from there."

She took a sip of coffee and gazed through the picture window adjacent to their table. Visibility seemed limitless, the view stretching for miles across a valley of rolling farmland to the foothills beyond. A set of railroad tracks stitched together the fields, and a two-lane highway swung down from the north, paralleling the tracks for a while before drifting away toward woodlands to the south. A river meandered through the scene, crossing under a railroad trestle that reminded Abby of a bridge on Will's train layout.

He had showed it to her after supper last night, a huge basement arrangement with fifteen engines and over a hundred pieces of rolling stock, not to mention stations, water towers, bridges, and most every kind of accessory—a milk platform, a log loader, an operating sawmill, a magnetic crane, several floodlight towers. There was also finely detailed, hand-made scenery and landscaping—hills, roads, embankments, tunnels, even a pond with a boat in the middle containing a figure of a boy holding a fishing pole.

Will had run some of the trains for Abby, and then he had let her run the one of her choice, six matching streamlined C&O passenger cars headed by a large steamer he called a yellow belly Hudson. When she told him how much Kevin would enjoy seeing the layout, Will extended an open invitation to the two of them. Later over coffee when Abby happened to mention that Kevin planned to try out for Little League baseball in the spring but was worried he might not make a team, Will told her that was another reason to bring the boy for a visit. Then he had gone back down in the basement, returning a moment later with a suitcase full of baseballs. "I used to pitch these to my son," he said. "Ben was a darn good high school baseball player, and I taught him everything he knows. Well, almost anyway. I'd enjoy working with Kevin, assuming I could tear him away from the trains long enough for some hitting and fielding." Then he had given her two of the baseballs to take home to Kevin.

"It's strange how all the evidence points to Glen,"

Abby said. "And yet everybody I talk to thinks he's a decent, upstanding man. The principal of Nanticoke's elementary school holds him in high regard. The dean of the Blue Ridge Academy knew him personally and said he's incapable of murder. Even I find it hard to picture him killing anyone."

"There are plenty of instances where people were amazed when they found out someone they were close to was a murderer," Will reminded her. "Some of the nicest, most respectable people have a dark side. Glen could be one of 'em."

"Point taken. It's got to be him, don't you think?"

Will shrugged. "Looks that way. But you never know about cases like this. They have a tendency to work out different from the way people think. You've done a fine job of investigating, Abby, but you don't have enough evidence to point a finger at anybody in particular."

"I know. That's why my next stop will be Caledonia. I have to go within a few miles of there anyway, and I'd like to talk to somebody who actually knew Glen and Mavis. That police report isn't exactly an in-depth study. I'd love to talk to the Turpin's old housekeeper. She probably knows more about that family than anybody else does. Hopefully she's still around."

"Have you got a map that shows Virginia and North Carolina?"

"There's an atlas in my car."

"I'll show you the quickest way to Caledonia. Better yet, how about letting me drive you? Or we could take both our vehicles, whichever you prefer. I'll have us there in no time."

Abby shook her head. "Thanks anyway, Will."

"I don't think you understand just how dangerous this assignment is, Abby. Whoever committed those murders isn't going to sit back and wait for you to gather evidence that'll send him to death row. Who besides Mountcastle and Steve Crothers knows you're here?"

"Nobody except my boss at the paper and my mother. Kevin, of course."

"Others could find out you've been snooping around. Dean Taylor might still be in touch with Glen and could call him. Promise me one thing, Abby. If you do come up with evidence pointing to Glen or Mavis—or anybody else, for that matter—tell Mountcastle what you know and let him handle it. That's what he's paid to do."

"I doubt he'd take me seriously. The only murder he's really interested in is Sheila Bostrum's, and he's convinced he's locked up the guilty party."

"All the more reason for me to come with you. Mountcastle would probably listen to me. I promise to stay out of your way."

"I can't, Will. I really need to do this by myself."

"What'll you do if the killer comes after you—bat your pretty eye lashes at him?"

The question gave Abby pause, and she wished she had used a similar argument when trying to borrow her mom's pistol. "Stop being an old mother hen, Will. I'll be fine. If things look like they might get out of control, I'll ask for help."

"I just hope you don't wait until it's too late. At least give me a call and let me know what you find out in Caledonia." He took out his wallet and withdrew a business card. "That's got my home phone number on it," he said, handing it to Abby. "I haven't gotten around to getting a cell phone yet. Where can I reach you in case I remember something I should've told you?"

He handed her a second card, and she wrote her cell phone and home phone numbers on the back. "My cell phone doesn't work everywhere, so if I can't be reached on it and I'm not at home, I might be at my mom's."

"Better give me her number too just in case."

In the parking lot, Will pointed out in Abby's atlas the best way to get to Interstate 95, which would take her within a few miles of Caledonia. Then, standing next to the Corolla's open window, he apologized for trying to kiss her the previous night. "Hope I didn't give you the wrong impression. I mean the reason I wanted to kiss you, well, it wasn't because…What I mean is you're special, Abby. I wanted to kiss you because…because…Hell, whatever it was, it's not because I'm an old letch trying to get you in the sack."

She smiled. "You're a good man who's just starting to get over a terrible loss, Will. I appreciate everything you've done for me. You've been great."

"Good luck and be careful," he told her then turned toward his truck.

"Wait," Abby said, stopping him in mid stride. "You forgot something." She took his arm, pulled him down, and kissed him lightly on the lips. "Thanks again," she said and started the car's motor.

CHAPTER 30

As she drove through the Virginia countryside, Abby thought of Will with fondness, hoping she hadn't given him the wrong impression with her goodbye kiss. She suspected he had something of a crush on her—due, no doubt, to her coming along at a vulnerable time in his life. Obviously, he was a man who had been in deep mourning and was just now beginning to emerge from it, ready perhaps to have a go at living again. Anyway, the kiss didn't matter, she reasoned, because she most likely would never see him again, though the idea of bringing Kevin to Wisteria for a day was appealing. He'd get such a kick out of the train layout, and he and Will could put that suitcase full of baseballs to good use. The idea of Will and Kevin enjoying each other's company made her think of her own father and how much she regretted that Kevin had never gotten to know him. Low key and good natured, they were very much alike and would have had wonderful times together.

It was true, Will would be good for Kevin in the absence of a real grandfather, but try as she might, Abby couldn't imagine herself becoming romantically involved with him.

Steve, on the other hand, was a different story. She

wondered how he was holding up in the Bogue City jail. Most likely Mountcastle was delighted to have him there and was making his life as difficult as possible. Because of the failed marriage with his daughter, the sheriff was so prejudiced against Steve that there was no way he would pursue other suspects unless forced to do so by evidence so strong it couldn't be ignored.

Abby was disappointed she hadn't been able to do more to prove Steve's innocence. As helpful as Will had been, her Wisteria trip hadn't been the success she had hoped. About the only thing of value she had really learned was that Lisa Strother had a birthmark similar to Rhonda Tolbert's near her lip. She hadn't found any actual evidence to implicate Glen or Mavis. In fact, the opposite had occurred. Their reputations were so stellar no reasonable person would seriously consider either of them a murder suspect.

Knowing her allotted time for gathering evidence was about to end, Abby felt a growing sense of urgency. She still thought it too much of a coincidence that all three murder victims had a connection with Glen and Mavis. Caledonia, therefore, would be crucial. If she didn't discover anything there, she probably wouldn't get any closer to proving Glen's or Mavis's guilt, and Steve's fate would most likely be sealed.

౿ఌ౿ఌ

There wasn't much to distinguish Caledonia from other sleepy North Carolina farm towns. It had a high school, several churches, some large old homes, three blocks of stores, a small strip mall, a John Deere dealership, and little else. Abby had been through it several times but never had a reason to stop. She filled her tank with gas and asked directions to the police station, which turned out to be just around the corner next to a feed store.

The officer inside, a young man not much older than Abby, was talking to an elderly black man who was complaining about a parking ticket he had found on his car.

"It's Sunday, Chief. We never had to feed no meter on Sunday."

"That ordnance went into effect two months ago, Arthur," the policeman replied in a courteous manner. "There were signs around town pointing that out. The notification was also published in the *Scarboro Gazette*."

"Well, I never noticed the signs and I don't get no *Gazette*."

Abby sat down on a bench near the door and waited while the two men discussed the matter. The situation was resolved with the policeman tearing up the ticket and the black man agreeing to pay the meters on future Sundays.

Abby approached the cop and introduced herself, telling him she worked for the *Gazette* and was doing research on the Turpins, an old Caledonia family. "I was wondering if you know anything about them."

"Afraid not. I haven't lived in the area very long. What kind of research are you doing?"

Abby told him that ten years ago the Caledonia Police Department did a background report on two of the Turpins for the police chief in Wisteria, Virginia. She read the report this morning, she said, and was hoping she could talk to someone about it. When the cop gave her a quizzical look, she explained that she had been in Wisteria earlier in the day and the police chief in question had showed it to her.

"Why did he want a report on the Turpins?"

"He thought one of them might've committed a crime in Wisteria, and he wanted to know if there was anything in their background to confirm the suspicion."

"What kind of crime are we talking about?"

"Murder," Abby said with reluctance. If word got out that the Turpins were being investigated for murder, whatever good reputation the family still enjoyed in the Caledonia area could be damaged and a lawsuit might result.

The officer picked up a copy of the *Gazette* from the adjacent desk and glanced at the front page. "I thought your name sounded familiar. How many murders are you investigating, Abby?"

"I'm not sure Sheila Bostrum's is solved," she told him. Not knowing what else she could do under the circumstances, she explained how she happened to read the background report on Glen and Mavis, and why she thought Glen might have killed Sheila Bostrum. "That report is kind of sketchy. I was hoping you or somebody here could elaborate on it."

"The chief back then died last year, and I was brought in from the outside to take his place. Only one of my officers goes back that far. I'll give him a call. If Bob remembers something about the Turpins, I'll let you talk to him."

After checking the computer on one of the desks, the young chief picked up the phone and punched in a number. "This is Warren Phelps, Mrs. Grimes. I'd like to speak to your husband. Don't worry, I'm not going to ask him to come in." A moment later Phelps began a conversation which Abby could tell almost immediately wasn't going to provide much useful information.

"I guess you could tell I pretty much struck out," he said after switching off the phone. "Bob remembers a report being done on the Turpins but he wasn't involved in it. He said Chief Davis handled it personally, probably for political reasons since Judge Turpin was alive then and had clout. Bob didn't know Glen or Mavis and he doesn't know anybody you could talk to about them other than possibly the judge's sister. He's not sure she's still alive, but if she is, she's in a nursing home over in Odessa. He doesn't remember her name. She was married at one time, so her last name wouldn't be Turpin."

"Maybe Nettie Bragg would know. She was the Turpins' housekeeper. I hope she's alive and still lives around here."

"Well, let's check that out." Phelps returned to the desk and rummaged through a phone book. "You're in luck. There's a Jeannette Bragg at 386 Decker Street. That's across the railroad tracks on the west side of town. If I wasn't the only guy in the office, I'd take you there. But it should be easy enough to find."

☙☙☙

The small clapboard house had a lone tree in the front yard, a gnarled, leafless oak with a sweep of branches that overhung both the sagging porch and a portion of the un-paved street. Attached to the trunk was a sign: *BEWARE OF DOG. HE'LL GRAB YOU.*

"Does Nettie Bragg live here?" Abby asked the young black who answered the doorbell. Wearing baggy jeans and a Charlotte Hornets' sweatshirt, he looked to be in his early teens.

"Who wants to know?"

"My name is Abby Burlew. I'm a reporter for the *Scarboro Gazette*."

"I'll get my mom."

A moment later, a tall black woman appeared in the doorway. "Mama's out of town," she said, regarding Abby with mild suspicion. "Is there something I can help you with?"

"I wanted to ask about a family your mother used to work for," Abby said after introducing herself. "The Turpins."

"There aren't any Turpins around here anymore," the woman replied, curiosity replacing the suspicion on her face. "They're all dead or moved away. What do you want to know?"

"Whatever I can find out about Glen and his sister Mavis."

"I don't mean to be rude but why exactly are you interested in them?"

Abby hesitated, not wanting to make the mistake of saying too much. "There's a remote possibility one of them committed a crime."

"Glen or Mavis? What kind of crime?"

"It's a long story. May I come in?"

The woman pushed open the door and held it while Abby entered the small living room. "I'm Melva Johnson, Nettie's daughter," she said. "That's my son Michael. Mama's visiting her sister in Smithfield. We're keeping an eye on the place."

A plump cocker spaniel rushed up and began nuzzling Abby's feet, wagging its nub of a tail.

"Part of the job involves feeding that rascal. Stop being a nuisance, Max. Don't worry, he won't bite."

Abby patted the dog, who began jumping up on her slacks and licking her hand. "Is this the ferocious beast that sign out front warned about?"

Melva chuckled. "The answer to that is *yes* and *no*. Mama put that sign up years ago before she even had a dog."

"Can't hardly say she's got one now," her son offered.

"You don't argue with success, Michael. Mama's one of the few people around here never had a break in. Take Max in the kitchen and keep him occupied so Abby and I can talk."

"Aw, Mom, let me stay. This sounds interesting."

"I'll tell you about it later. Now you and Max va-moose."

With a sigh, the boy headed toward the door at the far end of the room. "Come on, fleabag," he said, not un-kindly, and slapped the side of his leg. The dog scampered after him, both disappearing through the doorway.

"Have a seat and tell me what you think one of the Turpins did," the black woman said, sitting down on one end of a small upholstered sofa.

Abby sat down at the other end of the sofa. "I'm not sure they did anything. Since they might be innocent, I'd rather not say anything that could tarnish their good name." Or bring a lawsuit.

Though she looked disappointed, Melva nodded. "How'd you know Mama worked for the Turpins?"

"Her name came up when I stopped at the police sta-tion downtown," Abby said, not wanting to have to ex-plain about the police report. "About the only thing I was able to learn is that Judge Turpin's sister is in a nursing home in Odessa, assuming she's still alive."

"I forgot about Mrs. Sledge. She must be a hundred years old by now."

"I understand your mother helped raise the Turpin children after the judge's wife died."

"That she did. Judge Turpin would've been lost without Mama. So would his children."

Encouraged by the woman's knowledge of the Turpins and her apparent willingness to share it, Abby asked how well Melva knew Glen and Mavis.

"Well enough to know they aren't criminals. Mama used to take me with her to their house when I was little. Glen didn't have a mean bone in his body. Mavis wasn't as friendly, but she certainly had good character. Neither of 'em ever got in any trouble that I know of. Now if you'd told me their younger sister was a suspect of some kind, I wouldn't have batted an eye. That gal was a firecracker."

"I didn't know they had a sister," Abby said.

"Emily was the youngest. She was wild and irresponsible, just the opposite of Glen and Mavis. If there was trouble to get into, she'd find it. And if there wasn't any available, she'd invent some just so she'd have something to do."

Abby wondered if Emily might have been bipolar. "What sort of trouble are we talking about, Melva?"

"Everything from skipping school to getting pregnant. Emily had at least one abortion that I know of, and that was while she was a junior in high school. She was also involved in a car accident that killed two people. A farmer and his wife were stopped at a railroad crossing and along comes this car full of drunk teenagers and plows into the back of their truck. Pushed it right out in front of a train. Emily wasn't the driver but it came out at the trial she supplied the booze. She'd swiped it from her father's cupboard."

"Where is she now?"

"God only knows. She left Caledonia right after high school. My guess is she ended up in New York City or maybe on the west coast. She liked to be where the action is. Wherever she figured the most excitement would be, that's where she would've headed."

Interesting, Abby thought, but irrelevant to what I'm here to find out. She shifted her position on the sofa, her body stiff and a bit sore from all the driving she had done. "Was there anything unusual about Glen or Mavis, any strange behavior or character trait?"

Melva shook her head. "Nothing that I know of. Mama might remember something but I doubt it. Like I said, they were both real upstanding young folks. Never did anything to make me think they'd end up committing a crime."

Abby nodded, disappointed that Melva's view of Glen and Mavis was consistent with what she had learned from others. "I'd really like to talk to your mother, in case she's got a different take. Do you expect her back soon?"

"She plans on leaving Aunt Thelma's right after supper, so she should get here around nine, nine-thirty at the latest."

When Abby asked if it would be all right if she came back then, Melva nodded. "As long as you don't stay long. Mama'll probably be tired from the trip."

"I'll keep it as brief as I can. In the meantime, I'll see if I can talk to Mrs. Sledge. Do you know her first name?"

"Narcissa. I wouldn't count on learning much. Last I heard, she didn't have many marbles left. And that was a few years ago."

CHAPTER 31

Seven miles of farmland separated Caledonia from Odessa, a drive that took Abby almost an hour because of a flat tire she got midway between towns. She pulled over on the widest portion of shoulder she could find and changed the tire herself, thankful she had paid reasonably close attention the time her ex-husband changed one. As she was tightening the final lug nut, a farmer in a pickup truck stopped and made a big production about not driving over fifty miles an hour until she got that "silly-looking doughnut" replaced by a full-sized tire.

She had no trouble finding Maplegrove Retirement Center, a complex of stucco buildings set back from the highway on the outskirts of Odessa. The building that housed the nursing home looked modern and efficient, including the sliding glass door which opened automatically when Abby approached then quietly glided shut behind her. The receptionist, an impeccably dressed middle-aged woman, greeted her with the obligatory smile.

"Would it be possible for me to see Narcissa Sledge?"

"Are you a relative?"

"I'm a friend of her niece and nephew," Abby replied, relieved that Mrs. Sledge was apparently still alive. "They asked me to look in on her if I was ever in the area."

"Well, that's quite a coincidence," the receptionist said. "Mr. Turpin was just here."

Abby felt a surge of apprehension. "How long ago?" she asked, trying to appear calm. The last thing she wanted was for Glen to know she was checking up on him.

"He left about one-thirty. I showed him the article in the *Gazette* about that girl's body being found on Nanticoke. It really seemed to upset him." The woman handed Abby a sheet of paper. "If you'll sign the register, I'll have an aide take you to Mrs. Sledge's room."

Abby signed about ten signatures below Glen Turpin's name, using a fictitious name in case he happened to return. She had to wait only a moment before an aide appeared, a friendly young woman with a pretty face but hips too large for the rest of her body. She led Abby down a hallway past rooms where elderly people lay on their beds or sat in chairs, some watching television, others staring into space. Near the end of the hall, they overtook an old woman shuffling along in bedroom slippers and an ancient-looking man inching along behind her with the help of a walker. The aide spoke to both by name, but only the man responded, giving them a toothless smile.

"Here we are," the aide said and ushered Abby into a room where a tiny bird of a woman sat gazing out the window. She had a humped back and skin that resembled crinkled parchment stretched to the tearing point by the bones underneath.

"This is your lucky day, Mrs. Sledge. You've got another visitor."

The old woman's head slowly turned. "Another visitor?" she said in a low gravelly voice. "I haven't had a visitor in a coon's age."

"Where do you think those flowers came from?" The aide nodded at the table where a vase of roses stood between a worn leather-bound Bible and a trio of black-and-white photographs set in connected brass frames.

Realization slowly spread across the wrinkled face. "Glen *was* here today. And he brought roses, my favorite flower."

"Nothing wrong with your memory now," the aide said in a good-natured way. "You just have to warm it up a little, like I do my Chevy on a cold morning. This is Alice Martin, Mrs. Sledge. She's a friend of Glen's. I'll leave you two to talk."

"Alice?" the old woman muttered as the aide left the room. "I had a dear friend named Alice. Alice Stainback. You're much too young to be her. I don't believe we've met, have we?"

"We haven't," Abby said, sitting down opposite the old woman in a utilitarian metal and vinyl chair. "I spent a few days at the Inlet Inn recently. Glen and Mavis asked me to stop by when I got a chance."

Mrs. Sledge looked confused. "That's nice. The three of you stayed at an inn?"

"Glen and Mavis live there and run the place. It's on Nanticoke Island."

The confusion seemed to deepen. "I thought they lived in Virginia...a nice town called...oh, what's the name of that town anyway? All I can think of is arbutus."

"Wisteria. They did live there, but they moved to Nanticoke a few years ago."

The old coals were finally stoked and there was a flicker of recognition. "Of course. How could I forget Glen telling me about Nanticoke? They renovated an old run-down monstrosity—didn't they?—a house once owned by a sea captain. I always wanted to visit the Outer Banks, but Joe and I had a little cottage at Blowing Rockand, took our vacations there. The view from our screened-in porch would take your breath away—valleys and peaks and way, way over yonder through the mist an old man lying on his back, hands folded on his chest."

"Grandfather Mountain," Abby said, the old woman's description bringing back a host of bittersweet memories. "I went to Blowing Rock for my honeymoon."

"You did?"

"We couldn't see the mountain from our motel, but we got a good view of it from the golf course across the highway."

Abby remembered the walk she and Mark took the last night of their honeymoon. It was dusk and Grandfather Mountain resembled a long gray cloud on the horizon. Lightning bugs flickered all around, tree frogs and crickets cranked out their rhythmic chatter, and the scent of honeysuckle hung in the air like perfume. As they crossed one of the fairways, the sprinklers came on, startling them into whoops of laughter. They decided to embrace the spray, skipping hand in hand right through it. When they got back to their room, they smoked a joint and then made love on the floor and again in the shower.

"Don't know how I could forget Glen coming to see me," the old woman was saying. "My brain reminds me of an old tabby cat I once had. His name was Henry. He spent most of the time sleeping, but when he finally did get up, he'd race around the house making a nuisance of himself, especially if there was a chill in the air. I can see Glen clear as a bell now. He sat right where you're sitting. He didn't act like himself, though. He seemed tired and preoccupied, maybe even a little sad. That's not like Glen. That's not like him at all."

"He's probably just worn out from all the driving and bridge playing he's been doing lately," Abby suggested, hoping to alleviate the old woman's concerns.

Confusion clouded her face. "Bridge? I didn't know Walter played bridge. When did he take up that game?"

"We were talking about your nephew Glen," Abby said gently.

"Oh. Of course. You'll have to excuse me. Henry took a snooze again. It's hard to keep him awake and on his feet for very long. What were we saying about Glen anyway?"

"You'd just mentioned how tired he looked when he was here earlier. I'd like to know more about Glen, Mrs. Sledge. And Mavis too. Did you know them very well?"

"Indeed I did," the old woman said, her face relaxing into comfortable recollection. "We lived in the same house for…let me see. It was at least three years with Glen, a lot longer with Mavis. Probably six years considering the time she spent there after she and her husband separated. You see, after my husband died, Walter invited me to move in with him." Her glance shifted to the photographs on the table. "My husband was a pharmacist, you know. That's him on the left. I took that picture the day he left to fight the Nazis."

Looking closer, Abby saw a proud-looking young man in an army uniform, feet wide apart, hands behind his back. "Quite a handsome soldier," she said. "That's him in the middle picture too, isn't it?"

"Oh, yes. It was taken on our wedding day. That's Walter on the right. A person couldn't ask for a finer brother."

Abby thought of her own brother, and she had to will herself to focus on the picture of a white-haired man in judge's robes. Although the man projected the self-assurance of someone who has succeeded in life and knows it, there was more than a hint of gentleness in his face.

"Walter took his judgeship quite seriously," the old woman said. "He never lost sight of the fact that all human beings have frailties and deserve a fair shake."

"Glen didn't want to follow in his footsteps?" Abby

asked, trying to ease Mrs. Sledge back to the subject of her nephew.

"Regarding the law, you mean? Heavens no. Glen wasn't cut out for the law, and he was smart enough to know it."

"Why wasn't he cut out for the law?"

"Much too sensitive. A lawyer has to defend people that are often less than savory, and a judge must pronounce a harsh sentence when circumstances warrant. I don't think Glen could have done either, at least not on a regular basis."

"He sounds interesting," Abby said, hoping to learn something that suggested Glen had a dark side. "Tell me more about him, Mrs. Sledge."

"More about Glen?"

"And Mavis too. They both seem like fascinating people."

"What exactly do you want to know about them?"

"Whatever you remember that made them unique. Start with Glen, if you don't mind. He seems so mild-mannered. Didn't he ever get angry about anything?"

"Angry? What a strange question?"

"I was just using that as an example," Abby said, wishing she could come up with a subtle but effective way to probe the old woman's memory. "Actually I'd be interested in hearing anything you remember about Glen and Mavis. Anything at all."

Mrs. Sledge shrugged. "Well, I'll do my best. Both were excellent students, always getting straight A's or close to it. They took after their father when it came to academics. Walter was second in his class at Georgetown, you know. How he could have remained on the bench and still managed to raise three children is beyond me. I always hoped he'd find another suitable mate and get married again, but it wasn't to be. Of course, he had Nettie to help him. And after my Joe died, I helped out as best I could, though the children were almost grown by then."

Abby tried to steer her back to Glen and Mavis, but mainly she just listened, periodically asking what she hoped was an appropriate question. As long as she could keep the old woman talking about the Turpin family, she told herself, the more chance she had of learning something about Glen or Mavis that might suggest one of them was capable of murder.

After about a half hour, however, Abby began to think her efforts would prove futile. The only thing she had learned so far that hadn't been covered in the police report was the fact that Mavis's husband, a high school math teacher, had committed suicide shortly after he and Mavis divorced.

"How did Paul kill himself?" she asked, on the off chance something sinister might emerge.

"He shot himself I believe. Yes, that's what happened. Horrible thing. I can't imagine pointing a gun at my head and actually being able to pull the trigger. Can you?"

"Not really. Where was Paul at the time of his death?"

"He'd moved out of state...to West Virginia I think it was. Mavis didn't attend the funeral. She had great contempt for the man, though I've never understood why. She and Paul seemed to get along fine while they were married."

"Why'd they split up?"

"I don't really know. One minute they seemed like a happy couple, and the next Mavis was back living with her father. I've got a feeling it had to do with little Jelinda. The strain of having a severely retarded daughter might have been too much for them."

After a while, Abby decided she had learned all she could from Narcissa Sledge and got up to leave. Trying not to show her disappointment, she thanked the old woman for sharing her remembrances. Then she took hold of her right hand and gently squeezed the bony fingers.

"Come back and see me when you can," Mrs. Sledge told her. "An old woman like me can't have too many visitors."

Only when Abby turned toward the door did she notice the small framed photograph on top of the chest of drawers. Her heart racing, she went over for a better look.

"That girl with the birthmark near her mouth—who is she, Mrs. Sledge?"

"Oh, that's my niece. Emily was Walter and Lucile's youngest child."

"She's very pretty," Abby said, hardly able to contain her excitement. "Beautiful hair. I can't tell what color it is."

"Red," the old woman replied. "I don't know where in the world she got it. Nobody else in our family ever had hair that color. It was as red as a summer sunset kissing the brow of Grandfather Mountain."

CHAPTER 32

"Good evening, Holmes," the young woman said as she hurried toward the table where Abby was working on her second cup of iced tea. "Your ever-faithful Watson has arrived."

"Sorry to do this to you, Becky. I owe you big time."

"I'm glad you called when you did. Another five minutes and I'd have been out the door."

"Did you get the pictures?"

"The *Gazette* doesn't have a picture of Sheila Bostrum. At least I couldn't find one. You might check when the regular crew comes in tomorrow." Becky withdrew an envelope from her pocketbook. "Here's the article on Rhonda Tolbert."

Abby removed the contents, a two-column story with the headline "East Carolina University Student Found Murdered." Between the headline and the article was a photograph of the victim, an attractive-looking young woman with a small beauty mark near the right corner of her mouth.

"I knew it! There it is. But damn it, you can't tell a thing about her hair. It could be any color."

"It's red," Becky said with more than a little smugness.

"How do you know?"

"I called the sheriff's office in Greenville."

"I'm surprised they'd give out that kind of information."

"I pretended to be the Bogue City sheriff's secretary.
Good thing I didn't have to answer any questions."

"You really did that?"

"Hey, when you call in Becky Stroup, you get the
best. I've read my Conan Doyle and Agatha Christie, and
I'm a Sue Grafton nut. What time do we interview the
housekeeper?"

"We?"

"You don't think I broke a date with Charles just to be
your gofer, do you? I want to be in on the action, at least
whatever's going down tonight."

"Actually, I'm glad for the company. I wasn't looking
forward to going back to Nettie Bragg's neighborhood all
by myself." The yearbook Abby had borrowed from the
Blue Ridge Academy was on the table near her coffee cup.
She opened it to the last two pages of the section reserved
for seniors and pointed at a student. "That's Lisa Strother,
the girl who boarded at Glen Turpin's house in Virginia.
Her body was found on his front porch."

Becky put Rhonda Tolbert's picture next to Lisa's and
compared the two. "They don't really look alike, do they?
There are similarities, though—the hair color, the beauty
mark. They're both nice looking."

Abby nodded. "What if I told you I saw a picture of
Glen Turpin's younger sister and she's not only nice
looking but a redhead with a beauty mark near one corner
of her mouth?"

"You're kidding. Was she murdered too?"

"I don't know. But there's got to be a connection.
Emily left Wisteria right after high school and never returned. If she's alive, I'd sure like to talk to her."

"I think you should talk to the Bogue City sheriff. He

needs to know what you've learned."

Abby closed the yearbook. "I don't trust him enough to turn over any information just yet. He's extremely biased against his former son-in-law, the deputy he arrested for Sheila's murder."

"Speaking of whom, congratulations on your front-page article. Very impressive."

"Thanks. But my heart wasn't in it. I think Steve is innocent."

A waitress came and took their orders. While they waited for their meals, Abby told Becky about Steve, including their date Friday night.

"Seems to me you might be a bit biased yourself," Becky said. "If it turns out this hunk of a deputy really is innocent, any chance he could be Mr. Right and you'll end up sewing fish nets on Nanticoke for a living?"

Abby shook her head. "Absolutely out of the question. The island is nice but I wouldn't want to live there." After a moment, she added, "Though once or twice lately I have found myself wondering if there's a newspaper in the area that could use a feature writer who can double in a pinch as a reporter."

೧৩೧৩

An hour later, they were sitting in Abby's Corolla, which was parked in front of Nettie Bragg's house.

Although the porch light was on, darkness prevailed beyond the steps, undiluted by the streetlight in the next block. Except for a portion of trunk and a few lower branches, even the oak tree in the front yard was invisible.

"There's something I think I should tell you," Becky said after a while. "It's about Charlene."

"What about her?"

"Her attitude toward you."

"She doesn't think I'm ready to fill Sid Beckwith's shoes, huh? What a surprise."

"She thinks you're headstrong and scatterbrained. At least those are the words she used while talking to our illustrious editor-in-chief. It was right after you called saying you were on your way to Virginia. I hate to say it, Abby, but I think Charlene might be looking for a reason to fire you."

"That possibility has occurred to me. How'd you happen to hear the conversation?"

"I was taking my break in the snack bar when they came in for coffee. Apparently they didn't notice me...or didn't care if I was there."

Abby nodded vaguely. "Do you think she's right, Becky? About me, I mean."

"Well, sometimes you do seem kind of revved up and say the first thing that pops in your head. Don't take me wrong, Abby. I like you just the way you are."

"I'm trying, Becky. Believe me, I'm trying."

"I know you are, girl. Just don't give the bitch any ammunition she can use against you." Becky paused. "I wish Nettie Bragg would show up. It's getting cold and I'm starting to feel like a sitting duck."

"You're the one who insisted on being in on the action, remember?"

"I wanted to be part of the investigation, not a prospective victim for whoever might be roaming the streets at this hour. What time is it anyway?"

"Almost nine-thirty. You know, there's one thing that still bothers me about all this, Becky. Why would Glen want a color photograph of Sheila Bostrum? If he killed her, he'd know exactly what she looked like."

"Maybe he figured if he comes under suspicion, the fact that he requested her picture would make him look innocent. Or maybe he wants it as a trophy. Psychos get their kicks in strange ways. Uh oh, here comes a car. I hope that's Nettie and not a bunch of black dudes wanting to know what we're doing in their hood this time of night."

The vehicle turned into the narrow driveway, pulled up near the porch, and stopped. The lights went out and the door on the driver's side slowly swung open.

Abby opened her door. "Mrs. Bragg?" she called as she exited the Corolla.

"Are you from the *Gazette*?"

"Yes, ma'am. I talked to your daughter this afternoon."

"Melva said somebody might be here. But she didn't say anything about there being two of you."

"This is my friend Becky who works with me at the paper. She brought me an article I needed to see."

"All right, come on in. I'll do what I can to help."

Abby, with Becky following a few steps behind, accompanied Nettie Bragg into the house. The cocker spaniel greeted the black woman with excited yaps.

"Hey, Max, you silly old rascal." Nettie patted the dog's head and tugged at his ears. "You miss me?" She was heavier than her daughter and not quite as tall. Although her face was lined with creases, there was still a youthful look about her, especially her eyes. She turned to Abby. "Apparently you think one of the Turpins is a criminal. What kind of crime they supposed to have committed?"

"I don't know yet if they're guilty of anything," Abby said, not wanting to reveal any more than she had to about her suspicions. "I'm just looking into the possibility."

"The possibility of what?"

The look on Nettie's face told Abby she wouldn't get far unless she showed her cards. "That one of them might be a murderer."

"That's nonsense, far as I'm concerned. But have a

seat and we'll talk about it." Nettie indicated the upholstered sofa.

"I know it sounds incredible," Abby said after she and
Becky sat down. "But the victims are all connected with
Glen and Mavis in ways that can't be ignored. One stayed
at their home in Virginia and was found murdered on the
front porch. The other two stayed at their inn on Nanticoke
Island. At least two had red hair and a mole or beauty mark
near their mouths. I'm not sure if the third victim had
similar features, but I'd bet my next paycheck on it."

"Sounds like coincidence to me," Nettie said, easing
herself into the rocking chair across from the sofa. The dog
jumped in her lap and began nuzzling her hand.

"This afternoon I drove over to Odessa and had a long
visit with Narcissa Sledge," Abby said. "I found out that
Emily Turpin also has red hair and a beauty mark next to
her mouth. In my opinion, that's at least one too many
similarities to be coincidence."

The black woman's face took on a distant look. "I'd
forgotten about that little mole," she said, her eyes
re-focusing on Abby. "But what's Emily got to do with
any of this?"

"I was hoping you could tell me."

"I'm sure I can't," Nettie said, stroking the dog's head
in a preoccupied way. "I'm sure I can't."

"Did something happen that turned Glen or Mavis or
possibly both of them against Emily?"

Nettie shook her head. "Nothing I'm aware of."

"Your daughter told me that Emily was reckless and
irresponsible. Could that have caused bad feelings?"

"I'm sure they didn't like some of the things Emily
did, but they didn't hate her."

"How about Emily's abortion or the fact that she
contributed to two people's deaths? Were either of those
things particularly disturbing to Glen or Mavis?"

"They bothered Judge Turpin a lot more. Glen and Mavis were young then and had their own lives to lead. I don't think they were affected very much by what their sister did."

Becky leaned forward on the sofa. "Abby told me that Emily's mother died during childbirth. Could Glen or Mavis have blamed their sister for that?"

"Not a chance. Nobody in that family blamed Emily for what happened to Miss Lucile."

"I wish I could talk to Emily about all this," Abby said. "Any idea how I might contact her?"

"Last I knew about that girl's whereabouts was the year she finished high school. She couldn't get out of town fast enough."

"Where did she go?"

Nettie shrugged. "I'm not sure she even knew herself until she got there, wherever it was. As far as I know, she didn't keep in touch with anybody from Caledonia, including Glen and Mavis. She didn't even come back for their father's funeral."

"There must've been a problem," Becky offered. "A teenager doesn't leave home with no forwarding address unless something's terribly wrong."

Nettie nodded in reluctant agreement. "When Emily was in her early teens, a lot of friction developed between her and Judge Turpin. As good a man as he was, he didn't know much about raising a daughter, and he really didn't have the time or patience. A lot of Emily's upbringing fell on my shoulders and on Mrs. Sledge's after she moved in, and we just weren't up to the task. Judge Turpin used to get furious when Emily didn't act the way he wanted, neglecting her schoolwork or getting home at ungodly hours. . After she was involved in those train-crossing deaths, the judge started taking after her with his razor strap. That didn't work either. Emily just rebelled even more. Then at the first opportunity she up and left."

"Are you sure she actually did leave?" Abby asked. "Could somebody have killed her and pretended she left?"

"No, she took the bus. I didn't actually see her get on it, but I helped pack her things. Glen drove her to the bus station. I saw them leave the house with him carrying her suitcases."

"You're sure that's where he took her?"

"There weren't any bad feelings between him and Emily, never. Glen Turpin was a gentle man and a loving brother. No way he'd ever harm his sister, let alone kill her."

Abby nodded, thoughts of her own brother creeping back into her consciousness. "What about Mavis?" she asked, willing herself to focus on the here and now. "Were there any bad vibes between her and Emily?"

"Not that I'm aware of—at least not while Emily was living in Caledonia."

"Something happened later on?" The dog was licking Nettie's face, and she gently but firmly set him on the floor. "Don't bother me now, Max," she said and returned her attention to Abby. "About a year after Emily left Caledonia, Mavis did do something that made me wonder."

Abby felt a stirring of the same anticipation and excitement she experienced after noticing Emily's picture in Narcissa Sledge's room. "What, Nettie?"

"Well, after Mavis and her husband separated, she and her daughter moved back in with Judge Turpin. Mavis hadn't been there a day before she set to destroying every trace of Emily's presence—pictures, old clothes, books, toys Emily played with as a child. I remember she found this old teddy bear of Emily's and ripped it to pieces, and all the while tears were streaming down her cheeks."

"Why would Mavis do that?" Abby asked, her question addressed as much to herself as to Nettie Bragg.

"I don't rightly know. At the time I figured it didn't have anything to do with Emily but was just Mavis's way of letting out her frustrations over little Jelinda's brain damage or the loss of her husband or maybe a combination of the two. I still think that's why she did it. But I'd be lying if I said it didn't look, for all the world, like that anger and frustration was directed at Emily."

CHAPTER 33

A bby felt her shoulder being shaken, gently at first, as though someone was reluctant to disturb her. Too enmeshed in her dream to respond, she had just made an impassioned closing argument to a jury of twelve women. The jurors, all of them ex-lovers of Steve Crothers, responded with raucous laughter, especially Meg, the foreman. The prosecuting attorney, Leland Mountcastle, quickly joined in, as did the spectators. The judge, Mavis Gilbert, allowed the laughter to swell to a crescendo before rapping her gavel and demanding order. The courtroom fell silent.

"Ladies of the jury," Mavis said. "You've heard the evidence against this flagrant womanizer, and you've listened patiently to the defense mounted by his misguided attorney. The time has come for a verdict. What say you? Is Steve Crothers guilty or innocent?"

"Guilty!" the jury shouted in unison. "Guilty!"

The spectators, led by a grinning Don Horvath, began to chant: "Guilty as charged…guilty as charged…"

The shaking increased. "Abby, for God's sake, wake up."

She opened her eyes, slowly focusing on the anxious face of her mother. For a moment, before reality began to take hold, she had no idea where she was. "What time is it, Mom?"

"Almost nine. Don't worry, I took Kevin to school."

"I didn't want to sleep this late. I have to talk to Charlene Greer and call Sheriff Mountcastle. And I've got to get that damn tire fixed. Why didn't you wake me earlier like I asked?"

"Last night you looked more tired than I've ever seen you, Abby. I'd have let you sleep even longer, but there's something in the paper I think you should see."

"What?"

"A Nanticoke man committed suicide yesterday. He left a note saying he killed three young women."

Abby sat bolt upright, the image of Steve Crothers hanging from a makeshift noose in the Bogue City jail flooding into her consciousness. Then the full import of what her mother said registered in her mind.

"*Three* young women?"

"It's on the second page. The article didn't get the play yours did. I almost missed it."

Taking the paper from her mother, Abby began reading. "My God," she said when she saw the dead man's name. "I can't believe this. I thought it was somebody else. This is crazy." Hurriedly she scanned the rest of the article. "Mom, I need to get back to Nanticoke right away. This investigation is far from over."

"What's this all about, Abby? I've got a feeling you're in over your head, something really dangerous."

Abby decided to make another pitch for borrowing her mother's pistol. "You're right about the danger, Mom. I really could use your pistol. Actually, I could've used it when I was questioning a guy in Port Austin. If he'd attacked me like I thought he might, I'd have been toast. You'd have read about my death instead of Glen Turpin's."

For a long moment, Lillian stared at her daughter. "Have you been taking your meds, Abby?" she finally asked.

"I resent that, Mom."

"I didn't mean it that way. I'd just like to know."

"Yeah, I've been taking my meds."

"Will you take your lithium and then eat some breakfast before you go?"

"The lithium, sure. I don't have time for breakfast."

"Yes, you do. Don't worry about your tire. You can take my car. I'll drive yours until you get back. In the meantime I'll get your tire repaired."

ᴄ⊃ᴄ⊃

An hour later, Abby knocked on Charlene Greer's partially open door and stepped into her office. The woman looked up from her computer and gave Abby a cold glare of contempt.

"I can explain everything."

"What's to explain?" Charlene pointed to a copy of the *Gazette* on her desk, open to the second page. "It's all right there."

"There's more to it than that. A lot more."

"Of course there is, and you weren't available to report on it. This has to be a journalistic first, Abby. A newspaper assigns a story and stations the reporter at the scene of events. The story breaks—I mean it really breaks, big time. When does the paper learn about it? When the story comes off the damn wire service."

"I've been investigating ever since you gave me this assignment, Charlene. First in Bogue City and on Nanticoke then in Virginia and finally yesterday in Caledonia and Odessa. For your information, Glen Turpin didn't kill anybody, including himself."

"Then the bullet lodged in his brain and the suicide note found next to his body must be figments of Sheriff Mountcastle's imagination."

"I didn't say that. But suicide notes can be forged. Glen's sister must have written this one after she shot him."

"His sister? Why would she kill him?"

"She probably got scared I'd break the case, which I was about to do. Or maybe Glen was going to report her to the police. I know he suspected something from the way he'd been acting. When he learned that Sheila Bostrum's body had been found near the Inlet Inn, he probably realized once and for all that Mavis not only killed Sheila but Rhonda Tolbert and Lisa Strother as well."

Charlene rolled her eyes. "Who's Lisa Strother?"

"Another young woman who reminded Mavis of her sister. There's a strong resemblance between Emily as a teenager and two of the three girls who were murdered. The third victim—"

"Whoa!" Charlene held up a hand. "You're telling me Mavis Gilbert is a serial killer because she hates her sister?"

"That's exactly what I'm telling you. I don't know what caused that hatred but I intend to find out."

Charlene chuckled. "Abby, if three murders occurred every time someone disliked a sibling, this country would have a population half the size of the Canary Islands."

"I'm not talking about dislike," Abby said, trying to control her anger. "After Mavis left her husband and moved back in with her father, she started destroying everything in the house that ever belonged to Emily. That suggests pathological hatred."

Charlene didn't respond immediately, apparently taking what Abby had just said with a certain amount of seriousness. "Assuming she did have such hatred, why not just kill Emily instead of bothering with substitutes?"

"Maybe she did. But if she didn't, it's because she didn't know where to find her. Emily left Caledonia right after high school. Nobody has heard from her since."

"What about the third victim? You said only two resembled Emily."

"The third one is Sheila Bostrum. I'm hoping the *Gazette* has a picture of her somewhere. If it doesn't, I'll find out from Steve what she looked like when I get to Nanticoke."

Charlene shook her head. "You're not going back to Nanticoke, Abby. There's nothing more to be gained by your presence there."

"But I've found out who the real murderer is. It's just a matter of time before I can prove it."

"I don't think you've found out anything but a few interesting tidbits." Charlene held up the newspaper. "The real story is right here. We had a chance to break it with an in-depth, front-page blockbuster, not this generic piece of crap we were forced to print. The *Gazette* had a wonderful opportunity and you blew it."

You bitch, Abby wanted to say. You're really enjoying this, aren't you? "I did what any good reporter would've done. I tried to find out the truth. I went where the evidence led."

"Be that as it may, I want you at your desk and working on an article about Glen Turpin that we can use in tomorrow's paper. The fact that you've already done research on him and his victims will give us an advantage over other papers. The *Gazette* might not have broken the second phase of this story, but we can still do the best job of fleshing it out."

"I'm telling you Glen didn't commit those murders."

"And I'm convinced he did. Now go to your desk and work on that article. Keep Mavis Gilbert out of it. If you need to mention her, don't you dare say anything even remotely suggesting she killed anybody. I'd hate for you to add a lawsuit to the problems you've already caused the *Gazette*. Understood?"

"Yes," Abby said. She turned and left her boss's office and headed straight for the parking lot.

CHAPTER 34

As Abby was driving through Bogue City on her way to Cedar Point, her mother was on the phone with a potential customer who had called Coldiron Energy with a question. His furnace needed replacing and he wanted to know whether he'd be better off sticking with fuel oil or converting to propane. Since Coldiron sold both types of fuel, Lillian had explained the advantages and disadvantages of each and then said it was pretty much a wash. "It costs more to heat with propane," she told him, "but you'll spend less on furnace maintenance."

"Then it sounds like I'm damned if I do and damned if I don't."

"I know exactly how you feel," she replied in a weary tone. "Probably a lot more so."

"You got the same problem?"

"Hasn't got anything to do with furnaces. Whatever you decide, keep Coldiron in mind. Our prices are always competitive. Most instances you'll find we're actually the lowest."

As she hung up the phone, Lillian wished the choice she faced a few hours earlier had been as simple as the caller's. The guy didn't know how lucky he was. His dilemma could be resolved by tossing a coin. Heads it's fuel

oil, tails it's propane. Depending on a few market varia-
bles, he might lose a few bucks, but that's all he'd risk. No
one's life would be at stake. Nobody's daughter might die
as a result.

All morning long Lillian had worried that she had
made a terrible blunder lending Abby her pistol. Con-
ceivably, it could save Abby's life, but it also could directly or indirectly be the cause of her death. Talk about
being damned if you do and damned if you don't.

As the office manager for Coldiron Energy, Lillian
had other duties besides answering the phone, but so far
today, she hadn't been able to focus on any of them. She
had tried looking on the bright side. Abby had made great
strides over the past two years. She had stopped doing
drugs. She hadn't had a manic episode in...how long?
Nearly a year. Her recent bout with depression had been
short lived, corrected by an adjustment in her medication.

It's not like she's out of her head or being irresponsible, Lillian thought. Nobody is going to take the pistol
away from her and shoot her with it. And she's certainly
not going to shoot herself, accidentally or otherwise. Is
she?

Lillian knew there was always a chance that someone
with bipolar disorder could cycle into mania, depression,
or a combination of the two, even if she was taking her
medication exactly as prescribed. Any number of things,
including stress, a change in daily routine, or too little
sleep, could trigger an episode. Last night Abby had
looked like a zombie. Clearly, she hadn't been getting
enough sleep.

During a lull between calls, Lillian thought of her
dead husband, deciding there was no way he would have
supported her decision. She could hear him now. '*What
were you thinking? You don't give a person with bipolar
disorder easy access to a firearm, regardless of how well*

*she's been doing lately. The likelihood she'll need it to
defend herself is miniscule compared to the chance of the
gun itself causing a problem. You messed up big time, Lil.'*

᠊ᠣᠧᠣ

Seagulls swooped and climbed in the gathering dusk
as the final ferry of the day motored across Diamond Lake
toward the terminal. Abby waved to Steve when she saw
him waiting on the dock, feeling a rush of exhilaration
when he broke into a smile and waved back. A moment
later, the ferry, its propellers reversed and churning water,
nestled against the rubber tires that padded its stall. A
deckhand began removing wheel chocks from beneath the
cars while another swung the boarding ramp into place and
lifted the barrier gate.

At her first opportunity after exiting the ferry, Abby
pulled over to the road's sandy shoulder and got out of the
car.

"I almost didn't recognize you," Steve said, hurrying
toward her. He hugged her and then kissed her on the lips,
a kiss Abby fully participated in. "Why the different car?"

"Mine had a flat, so I borrowed my mother's. How's it
feel being a free man?"

"Terrific. I was beginning to wonder if I'd ever know
the feeling again."

"Did you get your deputy's job back?"

"I did. Mountcastle wasn't happy about it, but that's
his problem. How're things going with you, Abby?"

She brushed a lock of wind-blown hair away from her
face. "Not so good. My boss raked me over the coals for
not being here when Glen supposedly committed suicide.
She'll probably enjoy firing me even more. I'm supposed
to be at my desk right now working on a story about Glen
for tomorrow's paper."

"You said *supposedly* in connection with his suicide. Why?"

"I'll explain later. Right now, I need to ask you something. What color was Sheila Bostrum's hair?"

Steve gave her a quizzical look. "What difference does that make?"

"Just tell me. It's important."

"She was a brunette."

"Are you sure it wasn't red?"

"Positive. Her hair was a half shade lighter than yours."

"What about a birthmark or a mole? Did she have one somewhere around her mouth?"

"No. What's the big deal about hair color and birthmarks?"

Abby tried to hide her disappointment, but without much success. "If Sheila had been a redhead with a birthmark near her mouth, things would've been a lot simpler."

"How about clueing me in on what you're talking about."

"It's a long story, Steve. I'd like to unwind a little before I tell it."

He nodded. "Sure. We can go to my place if that's okay."

"Anywhere but the Inlet Inn."

A few minutes later, Abby stood in a sparsely furnished living room gazing at a painting that hung on the wall behind a worn leather sofa, a seascape done in muted greens, blues, yellow, and gold.

The only other furniture in the room was a La-Z-Boy recliner, a wooden coffee table, a roll-top desk, and a small portable TV.

"Nice painting. Where'd you get it?"

"The Dromgooles' shop. Marlene took the good stuff

and I wanted something nice in here. Get you something to drink—coffee, pop, water?"

"Some cold water would be nice."

A moment later, Steve brought two glasses of ice water from the kitchen and sat down with Abby on the sofa. "To your vindication at the *Gazette*," he said, touching his glass to hers.

"It'll take a miracle just to save my job."

"That job is safer than you realize. Tell me why you said *supposedly* in connection with Glen's suicide."

"I don't think he committed suicide, Steve. I think Mavis killed him. And I'm pretty sure she killed Sheila Bostrum and Rhonda Tolbert too, plus that girl the Virginia police chief thought Glen might've killed."

Steve's face registered only mild surprise. "What brought you to that conclusion?"

During the next few minutes, Abby told him what she had learned about Mavis Gilbert's hatred of her sister and the physical similarities shared by Emily Turpin, Lisa Strother, and Rhonda Tolbert. Steve listened quietly, occasionally taking a sip of water. When Abby had finished, he went over to the desk, opened a drawer, and took out an envelope.

"Read this. By the way, Glen's suicide note was typed. Anyone could've written it."

The front of the envelope specified in neatly-lettered script "To be opened only in the event of my death." Underneath was Glen Turpin's signature. Her heart racing, Abby withdrew the folded handwritten letter, unfolded it, and began to read.

Dear Jo,
I hope you never have to read this because it will mean I'm placing a terrible burden on your shoulders. Please forgive me. There's no one else

I trust enough to be custodian of this information.

The second paragraph was one sentence long and it gave Abby a start: "I think it's possible, maybe even probable, that Mavis is a murderer."

The next few paragraphs explained the reasons for Glen's suspicion. They were basically the same ones Abby had unearthed: Mavis's hatred of her sister and Emily's similarity to Lisa Strother and Rhonda Tolbert. *Both were pretty and promiscuous, and both resembled Emily physically with their red hair and beauty spots*, the letter said. It then gave the reason for Mavis's hatred, an affair Emily had with Mavis's husband Paul, a teacher at Caledonia High School.

When Jelinda was two years old, Mavis took a night class at East Carolina, the letter continued. *Paul stayed with Jelinda on those nights, but they were rarely alone. Emily was a high school senior that year, and I know for a fact that she and Paul became lovers.*

Bingo, Abby thought. The smoking gun we need. Before the letter ended, however, Glen briefly argued in Mavis's favor.

I don't know for certain that my sister killed anyone. This whole thing could be a series of circumstances completely unrelated, except in my own suspicious mind. I know Mavis didn't have to settle for substitutes, at least not at first. She found out about the affair long before Emily left Caledonia. She even told our father about it. There was an especially nasty scene during which he forbid Emily ever to set foot in our house again, though eventually he relented and allowed her to stay until she finished high school.

Glen concluded the letter by saying the only decision he wanted Josephine to make was whether or not to turn the letter over to the police.

If I should die a natural death, it would probably be better if you held onto it—unless, of course, there's another suspicious murder. Never, under any circumstances, confront Mavis yourself. If she is a killer, she probably wouldn't hesitate killing you.

Delighted to have found the proof she needed, Abby handed the letter back to Steve. "How'd you get this?"

"Jo Devereaux gave it to me this morning. After reading it, she came to the same conclusion you did, that Mavis killed Glen to keep him quiet and make it look like he murdered those girls. I asked her not to say anything about this. Before making an arrest, I want to be sure I've got enough evidence to make the charges stick."

"I don't see what else you could possibly need. I can corroborate everything in that letter."

"It might seem like an open and shut case to you, Abby, but a good lawyer can make a shambles of evidence like this. I've seen it happen. He'll point out Mavis's spotless record and her reputation in the community as a fine, upstanding woman and devoted mother with no sign of mental illness. He'll say it's ridiculous to think a woman like that would go around killing people who remind her of her sister, even if the sister did have an affair with her husband. Then he'll stress the fact that Mavis had every opportunity to kill Emily. If she didn't bother killing the real McCoy when she had the chance, why kill substitutes years later?"

Abby shook her head. "That doesn't seem like much of a defense to me. Some people's hatred takes a while to fester and grow. Apparently by the time Mavis's reached pathological proportions, Emily wasn't around."

"If her hatred was that strong, wouldn't she have found a way to track Emily down? And what about the fact that Sheila and Emily don't look alike?"

"There are other similarities besides the red hair and birthmarks. All three victims were about the same age, attractive, and promiscuous."

"So are a lot of girls between seventeen and twenty-one. And don't forget the suicide note."

"Which you said was typed. What about Glen's letter? A person doesn't suggest his sister murdered three people and then turn around and commit suicide because he actually killed those people himself."

Steve put the letter back in the desk and returned to the sofa. "A good lawyer could reconcile that apparent contradiction," he said, picking up his glass from the coffee table. "He could say Glen wrote it as an insurance policy in case he came under suspicion. What better way to make himself look innocent than point to a letter he wrote years earlier saying somebody else committed the crimes?"

"Then why commit suicide?"

"Once Sheila's body was found, he must have figured it was all over, no matter what his defense. He probably thought it was just a matter of time before I'd be exonerated and the finger of suspicion would point at him. Or, who knows, maybe his conscience got the better of him and he didn't want me taking the rap for something he did."

Although Abby could see the logic in Steve's reasoning, she was disconcerted by the intense way he seemed to be defending Mavis. "You sound like you think Glen really is guilty."

Steve shook his head. "I'm ninety-nine percent sure he didn't kill anybody. I'm just anticipating what Mavis's defense will be if she's brought to trial on the evidence we've got. What I don't want happening is a jury turning her loose because they think there's reasonable doubt."

"So what are you saying—you're not going to arrest her?"

"I'd just like to wait until we've got something a little more air tight."

"Seems to me the only thing we lack is a signed confession."

"Which is exactly what I hope to get. Or at least the equivalent of one. I've given this a lot of thought, Abby, and I've got a plan. If it works, we'll have an open and shut case. Mavis will be brought to justice and you'll have an exclusive that will make your boss at the *Gazette* eat crow for the main course and humble pie for desert."

Abby snorted and reached for her glass. "I'd like that. Exactly what have you got in mind?"

"I'll tell you later. Right now, let's get supper started. How does porterhouse steak sound?"

"Good," Abby said, though she was too keyed up about Glen's letter to be interested in food. "Anything I can do to help?"

"Just come out to the kitchen and keep me company. I'll explain my plan after I get the steak going."

୧৲৩

Amazed at how much thought Steve had put into his plan, Abby felt it had a reasonable chance of succeeding. Her biggest concern was that she might not be able to play her part in a convincing manner.

"Don't worry about that," Steve told her as they sat down to eat. "The big challenge is getting your hair the right color. You'll have to dye it or find a red wig. Good thing you drove your mother's car. If Mavis sees it, she won't have any reason to connect it with you."

The steak turned out to be tender and tasty, and, after the meal, Abby felt revived enough to go with Steve for a walk on the beach. When they returned to his house, he fixed a pot of decaffeinated coffee and they watched a program on TV.

"It's getting late," he said when the program ended. "You're more than welcome to spend the night here, Abby. Or you can rent a cabin at the Sand Dollar tonight instead of tomorrow. Your choice. If you'd rather stay here, I'll sleep on the couch and you can have my bed."

"I wouldn't want to put you to any trouble."

"Of course, there's a third option."

"I sleep in your bed and you get a room at the Inlet Inn?"

"That's not exactly what I had in mind."

"What exactly do you have in mind, Steve? Sometimes we mainland gals need things spelled out."

"You're putting me on the spot, Abby."

"Spit it out, deputy. You don't seem like the shy type to me."

"Well, if you must know, we could both sleep in my bed."

"Hmmm," Abby said, as though the idea hadn't occurred to her but now she was giving it some thought. "You don't think we'll be so tired come morning that Mavis will have an unfair advantage?"

"She won't stand a chance," Steve said, taking Abby's hand and pulling her close. "She's as good as convicted."

CHAPTER 35

Opening her eyes, Abby found sunlight streaming into the room and Steve propped up on an elbow looking at her.

"Good morning. Have I told you how beautiful and sexy you are?"

"Only about ten times," she said, laughing.

"That's not nearly enough. Come here so I can tell you again." He pulled her over on top of him, kissed her, and slid his hands under her nightgown and over her breasts.

"Deputy, you are bad."

"That's not what you said last night. If I remember correctly, you told me how good I was."

"You mean when those bed springs were squeakin' and we weren't doin' very much sleepin'?"

"Yeah," he said and pulled her nightgown up over her head. "In that bad ole deputy's bed back home."

❧❧❧

An hour later, they sat at the kitchen table eating toast, scrambled eggs, and sausage, which they had fixed together after showering and dressing.

"I think I'll go with a wig," Abby said. "I really don't want my hair dyed red. I'm not sure red dye would work anyway over my brown hair."

"A wig could be hard to come by, especially a red one."

"I'll give Angie Dake a call after we get to the Sand Dollar. She might be able to give me a lead."

Steve looked puzzled. "Where have I heard that name before?"

"The fishing trip, remember? She's the one whose panties you didn't get into."

"Oh yeah. Where'd you run into her?"

"She works at a beauty shop in Buxton. I questioned her last week when Joel was still my number-one suspect. If I can find the right wig on the Outer Banks, why couldn't we use a deckhand on the Hatteras ferry to deliver the note?"

"By the time he got back from delivering it, the ferry would be long gone and so would his job."

"Duh," Abby said and slapped her head with the heel of her hand. "The mainland ferry it is."

"Another thing—two ferries cover that route. When one leaves Nanticoke, the other is leaving Cedar Point. Make sure you don't take the same one both ways. If you do, the deckhands will probably recognize you, wig or not."

Abby finished the last of her coffee. "You've got this all figured out, haven't you? What if I can't persuade a deckhand to deliver the note?"

"If worse comes to worst, I'll get Earl to do it. Mavis might get suspicious, which is why I hope you can work your charms on one of the deckhands. There are two on each ferry. If one turns you down, try the other."

"Want me to pick up a tape recorder while I'm on the mainland?"

"You've got enough to do just finding the right wig." Steve glanced at his watch. "We better get a move on."

"What if Mavis asks the desk clerk about my hair color, and it's the same clerk who checks me in? Remember, I won't have the wig until I get back from the mainland."

"That's a chance we'll have to take. If she asks anybody what you look like, it'll probably be the deckhand who delivers the note. You can't register after you get back from the mainland because I need access to the cabin while you're gone. Plus there's a remote possibility the Sand Dollar won't have a vacancy later in the day. We don't want to go through all this preparation for nothing."

Abby nodded, hoping Steve's ability to trap a killer turned out to be as good as his ability to make love. Even almost as good will work, she told herself with a shiver of contentment as she got up from the table.

᠄᠅᠄

A half hour later, Steve waited near the ferry dock while Abby rented a cabin at the Sand Dollar Motel. She asked the clerk, a fat man with a pencil-thin mustache and greasy-looking black hair, for a cabin with as much privacy as possible.

"You can have the one farthest from the office," he told her. "Feel free to do whatever you want with whoever you want. Just don't make a lot of noise doing it. One thing we don't tolerate at the Sand Dollar is excessive noise."

"I'll try not to scream during my multiple orgasms," she said, enjoying the look on his face as she took the key and walked away.

A few minutes later, Steve knocked lightly at her cabin door. While he examined the rough-hewn interior, she went to the wall phone in the kitchenette and dialed the number of Mane Street Salon. When Angie Dake came on the line, Abby identified herself and asked if a store in the Bogue City area sold wigs.

"Hawthorne's did the last I knew, but it's been a long time since I was there. It's on Fifth Street in Bogue City. Farber's Boutique in Port Austin sells wigs too, if I remember right. Why would you want one, Abby? Your own hair looks great."

"Oh, it's not for me. A friend of mine is vacationing down here and she's anxious to try one."

"I'm surprised you're still in the area. Why'd that Turpin creep kill Sheila anyway? The paper wasn't real clear about that."

"Actually, I'm not convinced Glen killed anybody," Abby said, immediately noticing Steve holding up his hand and shaking his head.

"You're not? Why?"

"Just an off-the-wall feeling. No evidence to back it up. Thanks for the info, Angie. Hope to run into you again sometime."

Abby hung up and began thumbing through the phone book looking for Farber's Boutique.

"I wish you hadn't said that about Glen," Steve told her.

"What difference does it make? Angie doesn't know Mavis Gilbert. She certainly doesn't know Mavis is a murder suspect."

"What if Mavis goes over there to have her hair done and the beauty shop is all abuzz with what you said? Loose lips sink ships. I'd hate for ours to get torpedoed by our own carelessness."

Abby nodded. "I'll be more careful from now on. Any problem if I call the shops Angie recommended?"

"Go ahead. Whatever time you can save looking around for a wig will be to the good."

ೞೞೞ

Once the Cedar Point ferry was underway, Abby pushed the front seat of her mother's car as far back as it would go, stretched out her legs, and tried to relax. She wondered if she had taken her morning dose of lithium. Deciding she hadn't, she reminded herself to do so when she got to the mainland then realized the pill container was in her suitcase at the Sand Dollar. Take one as soon as you get back, she told herself. Do *not* forget.

Steve soon occupied her thoughts, and she wondered how long their relationship would last now that she had slept with him. Last night had been great, no question about it. Steve was an accomplished lover, and she had to admit she did feel the exhilaration of someone newly infatuated.

Based on what she knew of Steve's past, however, Abby doubted their relationship would last. She wasn't even sure she wanted it to. They really didn't have a lot in common. He was clearly wedded to Nanticoke and would never leave, and she couldn't see herself becoming a permanent resident.

Just let happen whatever will happen. Don't expect too much, and you won't be disappointed. If it turns out he's interested in more than a short-term relationship, then you can let that happen too. If you decide that's what you want.

Only for a brief moment did she try to envision herself and Steve as a married couple. Forget that nonsense, she told herself. One ex-husband is definitely enough.

CHAPTER 36

Abby found Farber's Boutique in Port Austin with little difficulty. Glancing at her watch as she got out of her mother's car, she saw it was eleven-fifteen, more than two hours before the next ferry would leave for Nanticoke, plenty of time, she reasoned, to get the wig and have a leisurely lunch before returning to Cedar Point.

The prospect of another round of sweet and sour chicken at the Golden Dragon made her mouth water.

"I called earlier to see if you had a red wig," she told the clerk who came to wait on her. "You said you'd hold it for me."

The clerk's face clouded with concern. "I hate to tell you this but after you hung up I discovered the red wig I thought we had was missing. One of the other clerks must have sold it. I'm very sorry."

Abby felt a knot of dread in the pit of her stomach. "Not nearly as sorry as I am. I came all the way from Nanticoke for that wig. Are you sure you don't have a red one?"

"I looked all over the store. Couldn't you make do with something other than red? We've got a variety of colors."

"I need red, damn it. Is there another store around here that sells wigs?"

"I think Hawthorne's in Bogue City does. If you'd like me to call and make sure, I will."

"I'll make the call. Just get me the number."

The clerk looked up the number in the phone book and Abby dialed it on her cell phone. The person who answered told her Hawthorne's did, in fact, sell wigs but had no red ones in stock.

"Are you sure? I'm desperate for one."

The woman said she was sure and suggested Abby try Farber's Boutique in Port Austin.

"That's where I am now."

"Then I'm afraid you're out of luck. As far as I know, we're the only two stores in the area that carry wigs. If you absolutely have to have a red one, you might consider getting a blond one and dying it red."

"It's possible to do that?"

The woman said she had never tried it but didn't see why it wouldn't work.

"Show me your blond wigs," Abby told the Farber's clerk after clicking off her cell phone. "And please hurry. If I buy one, I'll need to use your phone book again. Hopefully there's a beauty parlor around here that can get me in for a quick dye job."

ⱥⱥⱥ

Forty minutes later, Abby was standing in line at the local K-Mart anxiously looking at her watch. "I hate to be rude," she told the cashier who was chatting with a customer. "But I'm in a huge hurry."

Although both women gave her nasty looks, the cashier did speed up. A moment later Abby put the items she was purchasing on the counter: a box of hair coloring, a packet of hair clips, a styling brush, and a small trav-el-size hair dryer.

"I need to check that package," the cashier told her.

Abby opened the Farber's bag, revealing a blond wig.

"Let me guess," the woman said. "There's a mas-querade party and you're going as Little Red Riding Hood."

"You're not far off. Please hurry."

The cashier rang up the purchases and put them in a bag.

"Is there a bathroom I can use?" Abby asked after handing the woman two twenty-dollar bills.

"Right over there." The cashier nodded toward a cor-ridor just beyond the customer service desk. "It's all the way back on the left."

∽∾∽

A few minutes later, Abby, wearing plastic gloves, stood in front of a small sink and squeezed a tube of color cream into a bottle of what the directions called a devel-oper. She vigorously shook the bottle for about a minute and then began squeezing the liquid onto the wig, working it in with her hands, glad she had helped color her moth-er's hair and was familiar with the process.

An overweight woman, with a hardened face that might have been pretty at one time, waddled into the bathroom and gave Abby a disapproving look before disappearing into a stall. A few minutes later, she flushed the toilet and emerged. "That stuff smells worse than my shit," she said as she washed her hands in the adjacent sink. "What're you doing anyway and why here in a public bathroom?"

"It's a long story and you don't have time to hear it," Abby said and continued to squeeze out hair coloring and work it into the wig. The woman dried her hands and left. Two minutes later a security guard walked in, a slender young woman whose dark gray uniform looked a half size too large.

"What's going on?" she asked.

"I'm trying to dye this darn thing," Abby told her, squeezing another dollop of solution onto the wig.

"Well, you can't do it here."

"I need to get it done right away, and this is the only place available. None of the beauty shops in the area has an opening until late this afternoon."

"That's not my problem. You'll have to take the wig somewhere else. Like maybe your home. Look at the mess you're making."

"I'm a long way from home, and I don't have anywhere else to take it. Give me a few more minutes, and I'll be out of your...hair."

"Very funny. You're getting out of here now, lady. Stop what you're doing or I'll call the police."

"I am the police," Abby said, after a brief pause. "I'm an FBI agent working a sting. My job is to impersonate a red-headed woman, and because of a sudden change in my chief's plans I need to be ready in less than an hour. The success of the sting depends on it."

The woman looked incredulous. "Do you have some identification?"

"It's in my handbag."

"I'd like to see it please."

"I can't get it for you right now because my hands are a mess. If you really need to see it, you'll have to get it yourself. But be real careful. There's a pistol in that handbag and it's got a hair trigger."

The security guard went over to Abby's handbag and peered inside. "Is the identification in your wallet?"

"Yes." Abby continued working the liquid into the wig.

The woman gingerly removed Abby's wallet and began examining its contents. "I don't see anything that says you're with the FBI. According to this, you work for the *Scarboro Gazette*."

"That's the woman I'm impersonating. If I really did work for the *Gazette*, you think I'd be in a bathroom in the Bogue City K-Mart busting my butt to dye a wig?"

"I don't know what to think, lady. I'm going to let the sheriff sort it out. If your story isn't legit, you're in big trouble."

"Do what you have to," Abby said, thinking the last person she wanted to explain herself to right now was Leland Mountcastle. "But you better check the sporting goods area first. I saw a guy over there stuffing golf balls into his coat pocket."

The woman left and Abby continued working the hair coloring into the wig as fast as she could. When she finished, she placed the wig and conditioner into the boutique bag, which she in turn put into the bag containing the hair dryer and the styling brush. After removing the gloves and washing her hands, she picked up the K-Mart bag with one hand and her handbag with the other and hurried from the store.

ꮯꮥꮯꮥ

Ten minutes later, she was at a Sunoco station on the outskirts of Port Austin pumping gas into the tank of her mother's car. Because of time constraints, she shut off the pump long before the tank would have been full.

"May I use your bathroom?" she asked the attendant after handing him twenty-five dollars. "You can keep the change."

"Thanks. It's around the side. I'll get the key."

Abby ran to the car, got the K-Mart bag, and hurried to the bathroom. Once inside, she locked the door and turned on the water, swishing it around in an attempt to clean the sink. Then she began rinsing the wig.

"Yes!" she said a moment later when she saw the resulting color was pretty much what had been shown on the package. After rinsing out the excess dye, she applied the conditioner that had come in the hair-coloring kit, rinsed it out after a couple minutes, and patted the wig as dry as she could with paper towels from the wall dispenser. Then she pinned back her own hair in a bun, fit the wig on top of her head, and plugged in the dryer. Although the electrical outlet was on the opposite wall, the bathroom was so small she was able to see herself in the mirror above the sink as she began drying and styling the wig. She liked what she saw.

A few minutes later, there was a flurry of knocking which Abby barely heard above the noise from the dryer. She turned it off.

"What's going on in there?" the attendant asked. "It sounds like you're using a blow dryer."

"That's exactly what I'm doing. My hair is all wet and I'm drying it. I'll be out in a minute."

"Hurry up, will you? Another customer needs to use the bathroom."

Glancing at her watch, Abby saw that she had exactly thirty-seven minutes before the next ferry was scheduled to leave for Nanticoke. "She'll just have to wait. She doesn't need it nearly as much as I do."

CHAPTER 37

A woman with fiery red hair and a beauty mark near the right corner of her mouth rolled down her car window and beckoned to a deckhand standing near the railing, a paunchy middle-aged man who had just withdrawn a pack of cigarettes from his shirt pocket.

"Excuse me. I have a favor to ask."

The man put a cigarette in his mouth and the pack back in his pocket. After zipping up his jacket, he struck a match and bent toward his cupped hands, eventually producing smoke. Straightening up, he took a drag of the cigarette and tossed the match overboard. He glanced at the woman, took another drag, and slowly headed toward her car.

"What is it, ma'am?"

"I need someone to deliver a note when we get to Nanticoke. I'll pay you for your trouble."

The man sucked on the cigarette, blew away smoke. "Who you want it delivered to?"

"Mavis Gilbert. She runs the Inlet Inn."

The man gave her a quizzical look. "This got somethin' to do with her dead brother?"

The woman's face took on a distant, melancholy look. "Glen was my brother too."

"You're Mavis's sister?"

The woman nodded. "I read about Glen in yesterday's paper."

"You want a note delivered to your own sister?"

"It's a long story and I'd rather not go into it now. I'll tell you this much. Many years ago, Mavis and I had a big falling out. I don't know if her feelings toward me have changed over time but I doubt it. This note will let her know I'm on the island and where I'll be staying. I don't want to catch her by surprise at the funeral and cause a scene. Will you deliver it for me?"

The man took a final drag of his cigarette and flipped it into the water. "Yes, ma'am. Be glad to."

"Can you do it right after we dock?"

He nodded. "We got a few minutes before we start loading."

"I want the note given directly to Mavis, no one else."

"I'll make sure she gets it."

The woman handed the man an envelope, which he put in his jacket pocket. Then she held out a twenty-dollar bill.

"No need for that. I'm sorry about your brother." The man turned and ambled across the deck, disappearing around a corner of the bulkhead.

Moments later land appeared, a dark speck on the horizon that grew to a smudge, elongated, and gradually turned the color of copper. Objects materialized: the lighthouse, the coast guard station, a stretch of sandy beach, a few houses, the Diamond Lake inlet. The wind increased, whipping waves into whitecaps.

Near the rear of the ferry, an old man with a patch over one eye got out of an ancient Pontiac sedan with a badly dented fender. His appearance matched the car's in decrepitude. Tall and unshaven, he wore a wrinkled Boston Red Sox baseball cap, a faded flannel shirt, bib overalls, and a pair of running shoes that had seen better days. After closing the car's door and stretching his upper body one way and then the other, he limped over to the vehicle in front of his, a pickup truck with a rifle rack behind the seat. He tapped on the window.

"I'm down on my luck, friend," he told the driver, a burly man with close-cropped hair and a partial beard that covered his upper lip and the front portion of his jaw. "Could you spare a little somethin' to help tide me over 'til my next job? I been lookin' hard for work, but a one-eyed man with a bum leg ain't exactly in demand these days."

"I'm not your friend and I don't give money to strangers," the bearded man said and rolled up his window.

Touching the brim of his cap, the old man limped to the next car, a Ford Focus with an elderly couple inside. This time he went into a more elaborate spiel, telling the car's occupants that he had lost his eye in a hunting accident and that his bad leg had resulted from a fall.

"Ya see, I was helpin' my son put on a new roof and all of a sudden I took a step backwards and down I went, splat, right on the dang patio. Don't know how it could've happened. We were almost done and I hadn't come close to takin' one awkward step."

Eventually getting two dollars for his efforts, he tipped his cap and moved on to the next car, tapping as before on the glass. The redheaded woman rolled down the window a few inches.

"If you don't want your cover blown, just pretend I'm giving you a hard-luck story," the man said in a low voice. "When we finish talking, you might give me a couple bucks to make it look good."

Abby stared in amazement. "Will? Is that you?"

"It ain't Walter Brennan."

"What are you doing dressed like that? And what are you doing here?"

"Up until now, trying to keep an eye on you without you knowing it. I must say you looked a lot better as a brunette."

"I'm not wearing this to look good. Where'd you get that old clunker?"

"Borrowed it from a friend. It drives a lot better than it looks. How come you've made yourself up to look like a floozy, Abby?"

"That's my business. Why the hell are you following me?"

"After I read about Glen Turpin in Sunday's paper, I tried to call you. That suicide note sounded suspicious to me, and I thought it might to you too. When you didn't answer, I called your mother. She and I both thought you might need some help, so I decided to keep an eye on you. When I realized what you were up to, I figured we'd better have a talk."

"Just what am I up to, Will?" Abby asked, her anger rising.

"Posing as a Lisa Strother look-alike, probably to entice Mavis Gilbert or whoever killed those girls to make you their next victim. Great idea, Abby. If you're still alive when the weekend rolls around, we can play some Russian roulette for relaxation."

"I'm not in any danger."

"Is that what your friend the deputy told you?"

"What we're doing is none of your business. I resent your spying on me, Will. I told you I didn't want you along and I meant it."

"I don't blame you for being mad. But, for God's sake, don't go through with this ridiculous and dangerous scheme."

"It's a good plan and I am going through with it."

"Then tell me the details so I can try to make sure you don't get killed."

"I don't want a nursemaid. I thought I made that clear. You're meddling where you're not wanted...or needed."

Will pulled down the brim of his cap so the sun wouldn't be in his eyes. "Why are you being so stubborn about this, Abby? What the hell are you trying to prove?"

For a moment, the only sounds were the dull drumming of the ferry's motor and the screeching of gulls overhead. "That I can handle a difficult assignment without some man following me around like a puppy dog," she said. "Now go away and stop bothering me. If you don't, I'll have you arrested. I mean it, Will. If you don't stay on this ferry and go back to the mainland, I'll have Steve lock you up for harassment. Now get in that piece of crap you're driving and leave me the hell alone." She started to roll up the window then stopped and reached for her purse. "Here's a dollar for your lame poverty act. It's ninety-five cents more than you deserve."

ↄↄ℄ↄ

From her vantage point in the post office parking lot, Abby watched the deckhand march down Lake Street, his movements stiff and official looking, as though he were a courier delivering an important document. He passed the post office and the tiny barbershop before crossing to the far side of the street. A moment later, he disappeared down the Inlet Inn driveway.

As Abby waited for the man to reappear, she kept watch for Will Ramsdell, hoping she had convinced him to leave the island. Her anger had subsided and she regretted treating him so harshly since he obviously cared for her. But a milder response, she knew, would only have encouraged him to keep following her, thereby jeopardizing Steve's plan.

The deckhand soon reappeared, hustling along as before, glancing at his watch as he reached Lake Street and headed toward the ferry slip. Abby let him get almost a block away before she started her mother's car and followed, catching up to him near the church. She pulled over to the curb and lightly tooted the horn.

The man hurried over to her car. "Mission accomplished," he said.

"You gave the note directly to Mavis?"

He nodded. "I watched her read it. For a while there I thought she was gonna faint."

"What did she say?"

"She wanted to know when and where I'd seen you and what you look like. I didn't get the impression she's looking forward to meeting up with you."

Abby felt like giving a whoop of joy. "Thank you very much. I really appreciate this. Please let me pay you for your trouble."

The deckhand waved away the money. "Hope things work out between you two, but I wouldn't count on it." He turned and headed for the ferry.

As she watched the man recede from view, Abby thought of Sid Beckwith. "Bet you wouldn't have done a bit better than me," she muttered. "Hell, you probably wouldn't have done as well."

CHAPTER 38

After parking in front of her cabin at the Sand Dollar Motel, Abby noticed that the curtains were drawn—strange since she distinctly remembered leaving them open. She decided Steve must have closed them. But where was his car? With a growing sense of unease, she crossed the small wooden porch and tried the door. Finding it unlocked, she opened it and stepped inside. When she flipped on the light switch near the door, nothing happened.

"Steve?"

There was no answer. In the semidarkness, she noticed someone sitting in the recliner on the far side of the room.

"Steve, is that you?"

The table lamp flicked on. "You got the wrong cabin, lady. This one's taken."

Abby gave a snort and closed the door. "It's that good, huh?"

"I wouldn't have recognized you."

"Where's your car?"

"I didn't want Mavis seeing it, so I had Earl drop me off." Steve got up from the chair. "Did she get the note?"

"She did. She even asked the deckhand what I looked like."

"Round one has definitely gone to us." Steve put his arms around her and gave her a hug. "Did you have any trouble?"

"Did I ever. Farber's didn't have a red wig after all. Neither did any other store in the Bogue City area. I'm actually wearing a blond one I dyed red myself. How'd you turn on the lamp from that chair?"

"Hooked up a switch between two extension cords. Even with a full moon, it won't be as light in here as when you opened that door. Mavis won't be able to tell if it's Emily Turpin, Flo Nightingale, or Jane Fonda sitting there. Look what else I rigged up." Steve went over to the bookcase near the front door, leaned down, and extracted a tape recorder from the bottom shelf. "Voice activated," he said, holding it up for Abby to see. "All we have to do is turn it on."

"I'm surprised you found one on the island."

"I had to go to Buxton to get it. Come see what I got us for supper."

Abby followed him into the kitchenette, immediately noticing a pistol lying on the small Formica table.

"What's that for?"

"Your protection. You probably won't need it, but I'd rather be safe than sorry. Pick it up and get the feel of it. Don't worry, the safety is on."

Abby started to tell him she didn't need another pistol, but her mother's was so small and toy-like in comparison she decided she'd probably be better off with this one. "It's heavy."

"Don't hesitate to use it. Just click off the safety, point at your target, and pull the trigger. It has a recoil, so keep your hand steady." After showing Abby how to operate the safety catch, Steve took the pistol and set it on the table next to the recliner. "Check out what's in the fridge," he said as he returned to the kitchenette. "Then we'll go over our plan again. I want us to know exactly what we're doing when Mavis gets here."

"If she gets here," Abby said and opened the refrigerator door. "I've got a feeling she won't show up."

のくの

Shortly after dark, Abby made sandwiches from the cold cuts Steve had bought in Hatteras. They kept their voices low as they ate, in case Mavis happened to arrive earlier than expected.

"I told Earl to keep an eye on the Inlet Inn and call if he sees her leave," Steve said. "But it's always possible she'll slip out the back. That's what I'd do if I were her—wait until Jelinda goes to sleep and then ride one of their bicycles out here. Both have one. Mavis could claim she never left the inn."

"Don't you think this is a little far to ride a bike?" Abby asked.

"Not if you're as robust as Mavis Gilbert. She has to be strong to drag Sheila's body down that hill and dig a grave."

"It must've been her that set fire to Joel's greenhouse. I wonder why Duane thought he was chasing a man."

"Probably never occurred to him a woman was involved. Besides, Mavis is as big as a lot of men."

After supper Abby made a pot of coffee. They discussed their plan a final time, going over ways Mavis might deviate from what they hoped would be her course of action.

"Remember the pistol," Steve told her. "Mavis might have one…or at least a knife. If she attacks you without warning, I might not be quick enough to stop her."

Abby washed the dishes and then sat with Steve on the sofa, the two of them talking quietly as they listened for noises that might indicate someone approaching the cabin. They heard only the usual sounds, the periodic blast of a ferry's horn, the drone of an occasional vehicle on the adjacent road, the distant barking of a dog.

"Have you seen Joel since you got out of jail?" Abby asked after pouring their second round of coffee.

"Talked to him this morning. He feels bad about the whole thing. Ever since Lloyd Bostrum accused him of killing Sheila, he thought I was the one who did it."

"Why?"

"Something she said about being all tangled up with somebody named Crothers. Naturally, Bostrum thought she meant Joel. Joel figured it had to be me, which, of course, it was. But instead of talking to me about it, he let it fester. That's why he's been so hostile toward me lately."

When it grew dark, they talked less and in even quieter tones. As the evening wore on, Abby felt more and more on edge, and not just because of the coffee. She began to have major doubts about the effectiveness of their plan.

"What if Mavis remembers Emily's handwriting? She'll know somebody else wrote that note."

"Nothing we can do about that. If she figures out what we're up to, we haven't lost anything. We'll turn over the evidence we've got to the county prosecutor and hope for the best."

At eight forty-five, the telephone rang, jangling Abby's nerves so badly she wondered if she would be able to talk. Taking several deep breaths in an attempt to calm herself, she went into the kitchenette.

"It might be Earl," Steve called. "But don't forget the hanky just in case."

She picked up the receiver and placed a handkerchief over the mouthpiece. "Hello," she said in a low, tentative voice.

There was no response from the other end of the line. "Hello? Who's this?"

The only sound was faint breathing.

"Mavis, is that you?"

There was an abrupt click followed by a dial tone. Abby hung up the phone, her heart pounding. "All I could hear was breathing. It had to be Mavis. Maybe I shouldn't have acted like I expected her to call."

"No, that was okay. The desk clerk might be able to tell you something about the caller."

After dialing the office and speaking briefly with the man who had registered her, Abby told Steve that the caller had been a woman. "She asked for my cabin number." Remembering what she said about not yelling during orgasms, she realized how foolish she had been to call attention to herself that way. "I hope she didn't ask him what color hair I've got."

"Don't worry about that. Even if she did, the guy probably wouldn't remember." Steve put his arm around her. "My guess is she'll be here within the hour."

"That's not exactly a comforting thought. I don't know what scares me more, the thought of her showing up—or not showing up."

Steve went over to one of the overhead kitchen cabinets and took down an unopened pint of bourbon. "I brought this in case you needed something to calm your nerves."

"No thanks," Abby said, though she was sorely tempted. "If she does show up, I want to be in complete possession of my faculties."

"A little bourbon won't hurt you."

She waved away the bottle. "I'm not worried about

myself so much as our plan. I'm beginning to think it's got more holes than a colander."

"It's the best one we could come up with under the circumstances," Steve said, putting the bottle back in the cabinet. He took Abby's hand, led her to the sofa, and sat down beside her. "I still think it'll work."

Again, the telephone rang. Abby almost knocked over the coffee table getting up to answer it.

"Take it easy, Ab. And don't forget the hanky."

This time the caller was Earl Salter, who asked to speak to Steve. Abby handed over the phone and waited.

"What is it?" Steve asked in a low voice. He listened for a moment then said thanks and hung up the phone. "She's on her way. Earl saw her head north on a bicycle."

"My God, it's really happening. Does Earl know about our plan?"

"He knows we're up to something. I don't trust his judgment enough to tell him the details."

"Is he going to wait nearby in case something goes wrong?"

"Not a chance. I don't want that big lummox any-where near this cabin. He'd burst in at exactly the wrong moment and ruin everything. I'm afraid it's just you and me, kid. And it's going down soon."

CHAPTER 39

An hour passed with no sign of Mavis Gilbert. As the night wore on, Abby became increasingly anxious, expecting any moment to hear a flurry of knocking or a window shattering or some indication that the woman was attempting to gain entry to the cabin. Abby adjusted and re-adjusted her wig so many times she felt as though she had a nervous tic.

"What the hell is she waiting for? It's almost eleven."

"Maybe it's time we turned out the lights," Steve said and got up from the sofa.

"Want me to take my position?"

"Not yet."

Steve switched off the lights, starting with the lamp near the front door, which was controlled by the switch he had rigged up earlier in the day. Abby could barely see him as he returned from the bedroom area and sat down beside her on the sofa. "Do you think she'll try to break in?" she asked.

"If she does, that's as good as a confession, especially if she has a weapon."

"What if she sets the cabin on fire?"

"Actually, that wouldn't be a bad idea. But she'd be taking a chance you'd survive. I think she'll want to make sure you're dead."

"What a comforting thought. I don't know how you can be so calm with her out there and us not knowing what she's going to do."

Steve reached for Abby's hand. "We're ready for whatever she tries."

As her eyes adjusted to the dark, Abby began to feel less apprehensive, more confident their plan actually might work. She felt almost content to be sitting next to Steve, holding his hand in the near darkness.

"Hear that?" he whispered, breaking the spell.

"I heard a car go past a minute ago. Nothing since then."

"She's on the porch."

Abby listened carefully but could only identify the usual night sounds. Then she heard it, the faint but unmistakable creaking of a board. Panic gripped her.

"Now we take our positions," Steve said, releasing her hand. "Don't worry, Ab. You'll do just fine."

Galvanized by fear and adrenaline, she got up from the sofa and made her way to the recliner. Feeling along the table as she sat down, she picked up the pistol. She released the safety and put the pistol in her lap, covering it with her sweater. She noticed Steve near the front door, saw him quietly unlock it after bending down to switch on the tape recorder. A moment later, she watched his shadowy form glide across the room and disappear into the kitchenette.

As she waited in the semi darkness, Abby thought of the time she and Matt were in the family room watching TV, waiting for Michael Myers to jump out from behind the sofa and attack Laurie Strode. It had been a deliciously scary feeling. There was nothing exhilarating about the way she felt now, nothing remotely pleasurable.

There was a series of knocks, not unexpected and not particularly loud, but they made Abby gasp. She took several deep breaths. "Come in," she said in as controlled a voice as she could muster. "The door's unlocked."

There was no response. A vehicle with a leaky muffler roared away from the dock area. The noise increased, rattling the cabin's windows before it gradually subsided and blended with the night. Slowly the door swung open, revealing the outline of a large woman silhouetted against the moonlight.

"Emily, are you there?"

"Yes," Abby replied, barely able to contain her anxiety.

"Turn on the light. I can't see a thing."

"Not until we've had a chance to talk."

Another vehicle went past, this one not nearly as loud as the first.

"Why should sisters who haven't seen each other in ages talk in the dark?"

Abby hesitated, searching for an appropriate response. "First we need to confess," she said. "Then we can see each other's faces." God, she thought. I hope that doesn't sound as lame to her as it does to me.

"Confess? What are you talking about?"

"We need to acknowledge the terrible things we've done to each other."

"I haven't done anything to you."

"Maybe not directly. What about those young women who reminded you of me?"

"Young women? You're talking crazy, Sister. The years must have addled your brain."

"Glen told me about them, Mavis. You might as well own up to what you did."

The woman's silence lasted long enough to make Abby wonder if she would respond at all.

"Just what is it our recently deceased brother accused me of doing?" Mavis finally asked in a sarcastic tone.

"He—he said you murdered them."

"And just who am I supposed to have murdered?"

"Lisa Strother for one. Rhonda Tolbert for another."

"Why on earth would I do that?"

Abby hesitated, trying to find an appropriate combination of words. "It was your way of getting back at me for breaking up your marriage."

Mavis laughed. "Nice try, dear. The truth is you're a better bridge player than an impersonator. And your bridge game is, well, let's be charitable and call it barely adequate. It is Abby Burlew sitting there pretending to be my long lost sister, isn't it?"

Overwhelmed with disappointment, Abby sat mute. Remembering the pistol, she slid the middle finger of her right hand into the trigger guard.

"Doing a feature about the island in winter never quite rang true. Then shortly after your arrival, Glen got all bent out of shape. You had to be the cause of that. What's the matter, Abby, cat got your tongue?"

Deciding there was nothing else she could do at this point, nothing she could say, Abby switched on the lamp.

"Ah, there you are. You don't look much like Emily, even with that wig and fake beauty mark. And for your information, Emily ruined more than my marriage. She would know full well why I want revenge."

"Why?" Abby asked, surprised at the amount of control still left in her voice. "Why do you hate her so much?"

Mavis glanced around the cabin, as if making sure the two of them were alone. "Emily ruined my daughter's life," she said in a low voice, all trace of sarcasm now gone. "The bitch you're impersonating caused Jelinda's brain damage."

The revelation stunned Abby into momentary silence. "How?" she finally asked.

Mavis took a deep breath, let it out, then took another.

"When Jelinda was a toddler, I signed up for evening classes at East Carolina, not realizing I was providing my husband and my slut of a sister the perfect opportunity for an affair. It was all very convenient. I'd be gone a few hours and Jelinda would be asleep in her crib. Or so they thought."

A breeze moved the cabin's door forward, causing a creaking sound, and then a gust slammed it shut, giving Abby a start. Mavis seemed oblivious to the noise.

"One evening Jelinda kept getting out of her crib and opening the door on them, interrupting their fornicating. The third time it happened, Emily grabbed her and shook her like a rag doll."

Mavis took another deep breath, slowly exhaling in a long audible sigh.

"When I got home that night, Jelinda was awake and irritable, not at all herself. Up until then she'd been the sweetest, most affectionate little girl you could imagine. The next day she acted sluggish and wouldn't eat. Her pediatrician thought she had a virus and told me not to worry, but soon I noticed other abnormalities. Jelinda wouldn't make eye contact. She'd stopped saying 'Mama' and 'Dada' and the other simple words she'd learned. She also engaged in bizarre activities, things she'd never done before like flapping her hands and playing with her spittle. Her doctor finally referred me to a neurologist. One of the things he asked after diagnosing Jelinda as autistic was whether she'd had any falls lately or been shaken."

Again Mavis paused, her face showing more anger now, though her grief was still obvious. A gull shrieked in the distance, clear and resonant on the night air.

"Eventually my husband's conscience got the better of him, and he told me what had happened, but by then Emily had long since left Caledonia. I couldn't locate her. If Glen knew where she was, he wasn't telling."

For a moment, Abby felt sympathy for Mavis Gilbert, felt she was as much victim as victimizer. Then she remembered that at least three innocent people were dead because of the woman's need for revenge, and a fourth, Mavis's own brother, had died because of her desire to escape detection.

"So you settled for substitutes, three young women who reminded you of Emily."

"Two," Mavis corrected. "Contrary to Glen's belief, I didn't kill Sheila Bostrum. I didn't even know the girl. Apparently she spent some time at the inn, but I have no recollection of her."

"But you did kill Lisa Strother and Rhonda Tolbert?"

"They were reckless little trollops who flaunted their promiscuity. They got what they deserved."

Abby waited a moment, hoping Steve had heard enough. "What did Lisa do that was so promiscuous?" she asked, curiosity having replaced some of her fear.

"On two separate occasions I saw her slip past my bedroom on her way to Glen's. I overheard her seduction attempts. The second time she had the nerve to parade naked into his room. Glen didn't give in to her that night, but who knows when his resolve would have ended? When he didn't remove her from our home, I did."

Just one more question, Abby told herself. *One more incriminating response and Steve will have heard enough.* "And Glen—you killed him too, didn't you?"

"When he learned the Bostrum girl's body had been found near the inn, he was sure I'd killed her. Nothing I said could convince him otherwise. He was going to report me to the authorities."

"You really didn't kill Sheila?" Abby asked, deciding Steve's continued absence meant he wanted her to dot all the I's and cross all the T's.

"No."

"But Glen's suicide note said there were three victims."

"That's because I wanted to put the entire matter to rest, including any suspicion regarding the Bostrum girl. I didn't want to kill Glen, but he left me no choice. I couldn't risk going to prison. Jelinda needs me. Now, of course, there's you to contend with."

I was right, Abby thought as Mavis withdrew a utility knife from her pocket and pushed open the blade. Don Horvath killed Sheila. "Stay where you are. I've got a pistol."

"I was wondering how you planned to deal with me."

Abby got up from the chair. "Come on out, Steve," she said, glancing in the direction of the kitchenette. "It's over."

Mavis looked to her left and then started forward. "It'll take more than a good imagination to stop me."

"We've got all the evidence we'll ever need and then some, Steve." Abby pointed the pistol at Mavis. "I'll shoot if I have to."

The woman raised the knife. "You don't have the nerve."

Abby squeezed the trigger and there was a soft metallic click. Horrified, she tried again with the same result. Frantically she pulled the trigger three more times and still the pistol wouldn't fire. The knife cut into her right shoulder, barely missing her neck.

"Steve!" she screamed. "Help me!"

Mavis slashed at her again, the blade sending a hot flash of pain through Abby's left arm, which she had raised to protect her neck and face.

She swung the pistol, but Mavis stepped back, taking a glancing blow on the arm.

Abby managed to avoid the next slash of the knife but not the one after that, feeling a burning sensation on her left side, as though a hot iron had seared her skin.

"Steve!"

Again, Mavis raised the knife. Abby drew back the pistol, holding it by the barrel, determined to hit the woman and keep hitting her until one of them collapsed. Just as she started to swing the pistol, there was a noise that resembled a car backfiring.

Mavis looked stunned. Slowly she turned around, as though to see who or what had caused the sound. There was a second blast and she crumpled to the floor.

Abby made her way to the sofa and sat down. Her arms and shoulders were bloody, and she felt dizzy and had trouble focusing her eyes. She noticed Steve squatting next to the bookcase.

"Why'd you wait so long?" she asked in a voice not much louder than a whisper.

Steve glanced at her and then turned his attention back to the recorder. When he finally stood up, Abby saw that he was wearing gloves.

"Oh, my God!" she said, overwhelmed by the realization. "It was you. You killed Sheila."

"I was hoping you'd never have to know. If Mavis hadn't made such a big deal about not killing her, everything would have worked out. I'd have shot her the moment she made a move toward you."

"Why'd you do it, Steve? Why'd you have to kill Sheila?"

"She was going to tell Marlene everything if I stopped seeing her. I couldn't let that happen." He went over and took the knife from Mavis's hand. "The sad thing is you and I probably had a future."

"Yeah...until the next sexy broad came along." Abby fumbled around in her handbag searching for metal.

"There wouldn't have been another one," Steve said, moving toward her. "You probably won't believe me,

Abby, but I really did care for you. I wish it hadn't come to this."

Afraid she wouldn't be able to squeeze the trigger more than once, she let him get closer, her eyes focusing on the utility knife in his hand. When he was about three feet away, almost close enough to touch, Abby pulled out her mother's pistol, aimed at Steve's torso, and fired.

Even though she was sure she had wounded him, he continued coming toward her with the knife. She tried to fire a second time but was so weak her arm collapsed and the pistol clattered to the floor. Slowly and relentlessly the knife kept moving toward her.

"You bastard," she whispered, overcome by dizziness and on the verge of losing consciousness. "You sick bastard."

CHAPTER 40

A little girl crouched in her family's back yard, hoping to get close enough to a robin to sprinkle salt on its tail. "I'm going to get you," she whispered.

The bird cocked its head and looked at her then went on searching for a worm.

The girl inched forward, careful not to make a sudden move. She positioned the shaker directly above the tail feathers, hesitated a moment, then flipped it over. Down rained the salt. But the robin was too quick and flew to another part of the yard.

There was a dark coil lying in the grass. An old bicycle tire, the girl thought until the coil began to move. An arrow-shaped head slid toward her, a forked tongue flicking in and out of a scaly gray mouth. The girl gasped and quickly stood up, but the snake's head lifted with her. Its yellow lidless eyes fixed on her eyes, riveting her to the spot. There was a sharp rattling sound, the clatter of dry corn stalks in a cold November wind.

The snake's mouth opened, revealing fangs like bent nails. Its head swayed back, hovered, and then shot forward. The girl screamed—

"It's all right, honey. You're safe now."

Abby kept screaming until she felt a gentle hand stroking her forehead. Opening her eyes, she saw a woman in a white uniform, a nurse.

"You were just having a bad dream. No wonder, after all you've been through."

She looked at the woman, who was middle-aged and had a round, pleasant face. "Where am I?"

"Bogue City Hospital. They brought you in around four this morning."

"What time is it now?"

"Almost noon." The nurse adjusted a tube connected to a bottle of intravenous fluid. "You'd lost a lot of blood."

"What happened? How'd I get here?"

"I'm sure the sheriff will tell you all about it. He's spent a good part of the morning in the waiting room."

"My mother and son were here, weren't they? Or did I dream that too?"

"They left about a half hour ago. You were pretty much out of it, so they went to find a motel."

Glancing around, Abby noticed a bouquet of flowers on the chest of drawers.

"That's from your boss at the *Gazette*," the nurse said. "She called earlier. Want me to read the note?"

"I suppose."

"'Congratulations on a job well done. All of us at the *Gazette* are proud of you and wish you a speedy recovery.'"

Abby rolled her eyes then grimaced because of the pain. "I need to know what happened. Can I talk to the sheriff?"

"I'll see if he's still here." The nurse moved toward the door.

"There's something I need to tell you," Abby called after her. "I'm bipolar. I'm on lithium but I haven't taken any since…I'm not sure when."

"What's your dosage?"

Abby told her and the nurse said she would check with the doctor on duty. "Don't try to get up. You've got enough stitches in you to make a dress."

A moment later, Mountcastle appeared. Looking quite pleased with himself, he went over and stood next to Abby's bed. "You had a close call, young lady. Lucky for you Will Ramsdell was there."

"Will? I thought he went back to the mainland."

"That's what he wanted you to think. He followed you and rented the cabin next to yours."

"I didn't see his car."

"He parked it near the ferry dock. Problem was he dozed off after your lights went out. The shots that killed Mavis woke him up. When he heard a third shot—the one you must have fired—he came running."

"Is Steve dead?"

"Unfortunately, no. The doctor said the bullet barely missed his heart. The good news is the best he can hope for is life in prison." The sheriff glanced at his watch. "I'd like to get a couple things straight for the record, Abby. You thought Mavis Gilbert killed all three of those girls, including the one in Virginia?"

"That's right."

"And you and Steve set a trap to get her to incriminate herself on tape?"

"Seemed like a good idea at the time. Apparently, it was Steve's way of diverting suspicion from himself."

"The Devereaux woman told me about Glen's letter incriminating Mavis. The trick was to make Mavis look guilty of all three murders but not let her go to trial where, naturally, she'd deny killing Sheila. Am I making sense so far?"

Abby nodded, wincing as her neck and shoulders throbbed with pain. "Did you listen to the tape?"

"Yeah. Mavis said she killed the Strother girl and Rhonda Tolbert but denied killing Sheila. That's why Steve tried to kill you. I assume he'd have destroyed the tape or at least erased the part about Sheila."

"He even gave me a pistol that wouldn't fire. If it was to his advantage to have Mavis kill me, he could stay hidden until she finished me off. Then he could kill her, put bullets back in the pistol he gave me, and claim I didn't have the nerve to pull the trigger. Even if I hadn't tried to fire that pistol, my fingerprints were all over it. Steve had seen to that. But I did try to fire it. When I started hitting Mavis with the butt, I guess he couldn't risk my knocking her out. That would've made it hard to convince people he tried to come to my rescue."

Mountcastle nodded. "Apparently, he hoped she'd confess to being a murderer without saying who she did or didn't kill. Then when she made a threatening move toward you, he'd kill her. Everybody would think he'd done it to protect you. Is that the way you see it?"

"Exactly."

"You'll need to testify to all this at the trial."

"I wouldn't miss it for the world." Abby was about to ask if Lloyd Bostrum had been told the latest about Steve when the door opened and the nurse re-entered the room.

"Time's up, Sheriff. The patient needs to rest."

"Guess I've got about all I need for now. You take it easy, Abby. We'll talk again when you're feeling better."

The nurse checked Abby's blood pressure and took her temperature. "What's your psychiatrist's name?" she asked. "Your doctor wants to check with him before prescribing any lithium."

"Dorene Milsap. Her office is in Scarboro."

The nurse jotted down the information. Then she gave Abby a shot. "This will help you get back to sleep. That's what you need most now, sleep."

After the nurse left, Abby closed her eyes and drifted into a relaxed wooziness, not unlike the way she used to feel when smoking pot.

"About ready for another spaghetti dinner?"

The voice pulled her back from the edge of sleep. Opening her eyes, she saw Will standing near the bed.

"Hi," she said in a weak voice.

"Hi, yourself. How do you feel?"

"Like one of your baseballs after the stitching process. Thanks for being there when I needed you."

"Actually, you took care of things yourself. All I did was call the coast guard, which fortunately had a helicopter available. You're not supposed to have any visitors other than your mother and Kevin, but I figured if Mountcastle could see you, so could I."

"Sorry I was so nasty, Will."

"You're forgiven. By the way, I invited Kevin up to see my layout and take some batting practice. Your mom said she'll bring him. Speaking of Lillian, there are some antique shops in this area. While you're recuperating, we thought we'd check out a few of 'em."

Abby smiled, glad that Will and her mother seemed to be hitting it off. "That shot the nurse gave me—it's making me real—woozy."

"Don't fight it. Sweet dreams, Abby. You did good. Real good. You should be proud of yourself."

"For what?" she said, closing her eyes. "I almost got myself killed."

It wasn't long before she drifted to sleep. She dreamed she was playing high school basketball against the Kinston Lady Tigers, the conference's perennial powerhouse. Her whole family was there—her mother, father, and Matt. She had just made a basket and all three were cheering, especially Matt whose voice carried above all others in the gymnasium. Abby glanced up to see if she could catch his eye. He stood and gave her the thumbs-up sign. A moment later, after stealing the ball and racing to the other end of the court for a layup, she glanced up again, but this time the only familiar face she saw was that of her mother. There was no sign of Matt or her father, and suddenly she realized why. Neither one could have been at the game: by the time she was a sophomore and tried out for the girls' basketball team, both were dead.

Abby woke up depressed, as she always did after having this recurring dream. Sometimes her depression would last for days, but today would be different. When she opened her eyes, she saw her mother and Kevin standing next to the bed. She reached out a hand toward them and was able to smile.

About the Author

John W. Daniel grew up in North Carolina and sets most of his fiction there. He has a BA from North Carolina State University and an MA from Wake Forest University. He has taught English at Fishburne Military School in Waynesboro, Virginia (where he also coached the baseball team); the College of the Albemarle in Elizabeth City, North Carolina; and the State University of New York Agricultural and Technical College at Alfred, New York. He also has worked as a contract specialist and an industrial specialist at the US Army Tank, Automotive, and Armaments Command (TACOM) in Warren, Michigan. Now retired, at least from gainful employment, he lives with his wife Sharon and their cat Fonzie in the hills north of Elmira, New York. He especially enjoys O-scale model railroading; reading; gardening; and, on days when the course isn't getting the better of him, golfing.